# BEAUTIFUL *Deep*

LARGE PRINT EDITION

Published by Velvet Pen Books
United States of America

www.jordynwhitebooks.com

ISBN 978-1-945261-41-1

Printed in the USA

Cover Design: Sarah Eirew
Cover Photography: Lindee Robinson
Photography

## Books by Jordyn White
## Available in Large Print:

### Firework Girls Series

Forbidden Heat
Midnight Heat
Eternal Heat
Nuclear Heat
Holiday Heat

### Beautiful Rivers Series

Beautiful Mine
Beautiful Fall
Beautiful Dark
Beautiful Deep

### Hearts on Fire Series

Heart of Glass

# Beautiful Deep

# Chapter 1

## Emma

"Normally I would never consider hiring someone without speaking with their former employer," Alice says. "But Rose has been with us a long time and I trust her judgment. Her recommendation got you in the door."

Rose barely knows me. She's a casual friend of my roommates, and was kind enough to go on a limb for me when she heard about my situation.

"I appreciate you giving me the chance," I say.

"Well, I haven't offered you the job yet."

Right.

We're sitting in a small office on the ground floor of the famous Rivers Paradise Resort. The walls are concrete blocks painted light gray and covered in posters about food safety and employee rights. I'm in a hard metal chair, and the banquet manager, Alice, is in the tilt-back swivel chair behind the desk. The door is closed, but we're just off the kitchen of one of the restaurants here, so the muffled sounds of a dozen employees prepping for the lunch rush punctuates the air.

I'm wearing the only black slacks I own that don't have some sort of food stain on them, and a crisp white, button-down shirt with sleeves that cuff at the wrist. I wanted to show her I can look the part. My hands are in my lap, perfectly still. I'm not one to fidget when I'm nervous, but my palms are moist enough that if she offers to shake my hand at the end of this, I'll have to wipe them on my pants first.

Alice looks at the application that's sitting on her desk.

"Rose tells me there was some sort of situation at…" Her finger lands lightly on a spot halfway down the paper. "Powerhouse Personal Chef. She says you have a good reason for not wanting us to contact them."

"Yes."

"Would you like to tell me about it?"

"I'm sorry. I can't."

Alice purses her lips, as if she expected that I'd bring her into my confidence about what happened at my last job. Not a chance.

"It's nothing that would affect my performance here," I hurry to say. "I'm sure I would do a great job for you. I'm familiar with the logistics of preparing for large groups. Even though most of what we did at Powerhouse was for individuals, we catered events as well. I can do food preparation, service, cleanup. Anything you need."

Honest to god, anything.

Alice leans back and laces her fingers over her stomach. She seems a no-nonsense sort of person. She has tidy, short brown hair and unpainted fingernails cut to the quick. When she led me to this office, she had the swift, purposeful steps of someone who's used to people following her orders. "How long have you known Rose? You've only been in Swan Pointe a month, correct?"

Well, shit. I can't have her questioning the legitimacy of this recommendation, otherwise I may as well thank her for the interview and leave right now. But I'm so desperate for this job, I think I'd beg if it came to that. This is the closest I've come to finding work since everything happened almost a month ago. I can't live off the kindness of friends forever. I need money. I need this.

"Yes, I met her when I moved here, but she's known my friend Aaron since he moved here nine months ago, and he vouched for me. He and I've been friends a long time. Several years."

Back when I was living a completely different life. When I was a completely different person.

This answer seems to satisfy her, thank God. "About your reasons for leaving your last job, there are some questions I need to ask you."

"Okay." I subtly rub my hands on my thighs, trying to get rid of the moisture on my palms that's driving me crazy, then make them sit still again.

"Was there theft involved?"

I straighten slightly. "What? No. Nothing like that."

"Were you ever under the influence at work?"

"No."

"Ever fail a drug test?"

"No. I don't use."

"Did you have issues with tardiness or attendance?"

She seems intent on going down a list of possible infractions. I'm hoping she doesn't guess what happened, because I'm not admitting to anything, but I don't want to lie to her either.

"No."

"Poor performance?"

"No. My performance reviews were always positive. I was actually promoted ten months after I started there. I knew my job and I'm a hard worker."

She purses her lips slightly, narrowing her eyes and tilting her head a bit as she considers me. "Do you have trouble following the orders of your superiors?"

Only when they tell me to get on my back or get out the door. "No."

"There were no insubordination issues?"

The skin on the back of my neck tingles unpleasantly. How many more boss-related questions does she have? Because she's sniffing a little too close to the target for my pleasure. "No. I don't have a problem with authority."

She exhales sharply through her nose and looks at the ceiling, searching for other reasons she can guess at, apparently.

"Did you violate company Internet policies?"

"No." I scoot to the edge of my seat and lean forward. "Look, I really need this job. What happened at Powerhouse was..." A train wreck. A disaster. The dumbest fucking thing I've ever done in my entire life, and I blame myself as much as my asshole boss. "...A misunderstanding. It won't come back to haunt you here. I promise."

She puts one elbow on the arm of the chair and props her chin on her thumb, rubbing one finger slowly over her mouth as she considers me.

Oh please let her hire me. Over the past year I've discovered I have more grit than I ever thought, but I don't think I could hack it as a homeless person.

"I know banquet work isn't exactly the same as personal chef services, but I'm a quick learner. If you give me a chance, I promise I won't let you down."

Holding my eyes firmly, she puts her elbows on the desk and leans in slightly. "I'm going to hold you to that."

I'm waiting at the end of the employee side of the underground parking garage when I hear the roaring of Pierce's motorcycle. A minute later he comes into view and I start walking toward him. He's a broad-shouldered guy, and with his black tee and "kiss my ass" expression, he looks the part of a tough-as-nails biker. You'd never know he's a professional artist with a rooftop garden full of flowers he and his boyfriend tend together.

"That was fast." He brings the motorcycle to a stop. "I take it things went well?"

I'm grinning. "I got the job."

He smiles. "We knew you'd find something sooner or later."

I appreciate the optimism that he and Aaron have had over the past month. They've had more faith in me than I've had in myself at times, that's for sure.

"Hopefully I'll be able to get out of your hair soon." They've been good about letting me crash on their couch ever since they rescued me from L.A. a month ago, but it has to be driving them crazy. It's driving me crazy, anyway.

"Eh, you're fine." His standard answer.

"Thanks for the ride." I grab the helmet from the back and put it on.

"No problem. I needed a break anyway. My painting is pissing me off." When Pierce isn't busy stressing about the upcoming art show at the Swan Pointe Civic Center, he's swearing at his current work in progress. His paintings always turn out great, but the wailing and gnashing of teeth seems to be part of his process.

I climb on and hang onto his thick waist, then we make a tight U-turn and exit the parking garage. The Rivers Paradise Resort is situated on a bluff overlooking the Pacific Ocean, and is one of the dominating industries in this little tourist town. It's one of the best places in Swan Pointe to work for, or so I'm told.

I would've taken anything. Literally anything. But this is actually a pretty decent job, in an area that at least interests me.

It's something. More than something. Hell, they even offer health insurance.

As we drive through the manicured grounds of this central California luxury haven, I look at the vast, sparkling expanse of water to my right and feel hopeful for the first time in a long time that I might actually be able to put my life back together.

I just have to keep my head down, do my job, and not sleep with the boss. Shouldn't be too hard.

# Chapter 2

## Rayce

My younger brother Connor and I are on the main floor of the Swan Pointe Civic Center's yearly Art Invitational, headed for the wine bar. Drinks first, art second. That's our motto when we come to things like this together.

Once in line, I do a quick scan of the room, making a mental note of the people I'll need to network with while I'm here. The large, open space is lined with art panels, has several floating displays in the center, and of course tables of food. Every room has its own spread of hors d'oeuvres and desserts, not to mention a bar with local wines and brews.

This event is one of our favorites. It's one of the biggest art shows in California, takes up all three floors of the center, and draws artists nationwide. I almost always find something interesting to buy. We used to come here with our parents, back when they were still alive.

It's been a while since Connor and I have done something just the two of us. Now that he's married, and my younger sister Lizzy is engaged, the three of us don't do a lot without significant others these days. But Connor's wife had a friend's bachelorette party to attend tonight, so he and I came together.

I was relieved not to need a date. While there are plenty woman I could've asked, there wasn't anyone I was interested in sharing this particular evening with. Of course, there are always people wanting to rub shoulders at these events, and it doesn't hurt to have a date on your arm in situations like that. But it's just as effective to represent the resort alongside my brother, since he and Lizzy and I run things together now.

Besides, I like hanging out with Connor. I've missed it.

"I wonder if Lizzy and Brett are here yet?" he asks as we step forward in the line.

"I'll check." I pull out my phone intending to send Lizzy a quick text. My email is open in the window, and I spot the subject line of that damned email I received this morning. A cold pit of dread drops through my stomach, same as when I first read it.

This could be trouble for me, no question about it. Trouble for all of us, if it goes far enough.

I close the app, text Lizzy, and we get our drinks. As we wander toward the first display, Connor remarking that there seem to be a lot of new artists here this year, I consider telling him about the situation. I almost told him when we were in the car on the way over, but ultimately decided against it.

Even if we weren't in public right now and at risk of being overheard, I'd probably make the same decision. It's a dick move to keep this from him, but I'm already the asshole for getting myself into this mess to start with, so what's the difference?

I don't want to worry him. That's part of it. But I don't want to admit what I've been hiding, either.

He already knows some of it. Seven or eight months after Mom and Dad died, he found out about an affair I was having with one of our employees.

It's not something I'm proud of. Not to make excuses, but I didn't handle Mom and Dad's deaths too well. Aside from the shock of it all, my siblings and I were left to keep the resort running. Those first several months were so chaotic, I barely remember them. It was all we could do to keep Mom and Dad's life's work from crumbling to dust.

And I blamed myself for all of it.

I got a call from Mom that day. The day they died. She called from the boat, but I didn't answer because I was busy with work. I figured I would call her later.

Later never came.

I spent the next seven months convinced that she had been calling for help. And me? I couldn't be bothered to answer the phone.

I couldn't handle it, and didn't have the luxury of trying to deal with something as inconvenient as my feelings anyway. I had to keep my family and our business together.

I could've turned to alcohol. Or drugs. Instead, I indulged in self-destructive behavior of a different sort. I had a total of three affairs with lower-level employees, which is firmly against resort policies, not to mention the family code. The fact that it was wrong was part of the appeal. The riskier the location, the dirtier the sex, the cheaper the woman the better. It was the only escape I had from the red-hot guilt and agony constantly snapping at my heels. It was as addictive and destructive as anything else I could've decided to do.

When Connor figured out what was going on, he managed to pull me out of it. He found my walls, took a sledgehammer to them, and broke me into a hundred little pieces. All in the space of five minutes.

That was the beginning of climbing out of the dark place I let myself fall into, the beginning of the grieving process I'd tried so hard to escape, and the end of my affairs. I broke things off, promised Connor I would never put the resort at risk like that again, and have kept my nose clean since.

I should've told him at the time that she wasn't the only one. But I didn't know how to admit that to my kid brother.

Besides, I have no intention of repeating past mistakes. I can only hope that's good enough and that they're not going to come back and bite us all in the ass.

I get a text from Lizzy informing me that she and Brett are at the food table on the first floor at the same time we come around the corner of a display and spot them grabbing their little plates and napkins.

When she sees us, she sets them down and comes to greet us. She gets to Connor first, giving him a hug. I clap Brett on the shoulder in greeting while I wait my turn. I'm pleased to see he's wearing a quality suit. Not that I think he wouldn't, but he'll be part of the Rivers family soon, and the face we show to the world matters, like it or not.

"Good to see you," he says with a smile.

"You too." I like Brett. Of course, sometimes people surprise you, but he seems to be a good guy and treating my sister well.

He'd better, or he'd have me to deal with. I wouldn't take kindly to anyone mistreating my sister.

Lizzy comes over and gives me a hug. She's warm and affectionate, my sister. So like our mother, though I don't think she sees it.

She looks like our mother too, more and more so as she gets older. Her long brown hair falls past her shoulders, the way Mom's did. She resembles Mom, too, aside from her green eyes.

Of course, as we've heard our entire lives, we all resemble one another. Lizzy teases us that the only reason people can tell Connor and I apart is because I'm the serious one and he's the carefree one.

She's not far off the mark.

I give her a kiss on the cheek before letting her go. "Been here long?"

She retrieves her plate and napkin. "Fifteen minutes?" She looks to Brett for confirmation.

He nods. "Something like that."

We make our way down the line, artfully stacking our items so as to allow room for a little bit of everything. The food at this event is always spectacular, and beautifully displayed with crystal vases full of flowers and luxurious linens draped over the various tiers they set up on the table. It's a spread worthy of the Rivers Paradise Resort, actually.

There are broad wooden trays with gourmet meats and cheeses, olive tapenade with mini rounds of sourdough, silver platters with an assortment of grapes and strawberries and other fruits, seared salmon crostini, stuffed mushrooms, and prime rib tapas. The sights and scents alone are enough to get the mouth watering.

Connor tosses me a mischievous smile. "This is better than the fifth night in a row of Guido's, huh?"

"You can never get too much Guido's."

Guido owns the pizza place at the bottom of the hill from the resort, is an old family friend, and makes the best damn pie in California.

Connor isn't remarking on my choice of pizza. He's harassing me because I never cook. Almost never. Well, no. Never. I subsist on fast food, meals from the restaurants at the resort, and the dinners my family prepares when we get together. Though they give me a hard time about it every now and then, it's not that big of a deal.

"Hey, speaking of that," Lizzy says, "I haven't told you yet. Alice has some new blood."

I groan. All right, my disinterest in cooking is not a big deal to *most* people. Our banquet manager, Alice, however is another matter.

"Great." I take a little spoonful of olive tapenade. "Yet another employee who promises to repair my dietary deficiencies."

Lizzy laughs and tucks a little stuffed mushroom onto her plate. "She actually didn't say anything about that. But you know it's just a matter of time."

"Maybe she's finally accepted the fact that I don't need a personal chef."

"You may not <u>want</u> one," Connor pipes in, taking a grape from his plate and popping it in his mouth as he waits for the line to advance, "but that doesn't mean you don't <u>need</u> one."

"Don't you start in, too."

He grins. "I'm telling you, just let her give someone a trial run. It'll satisfy her and then she can let go of the whole idea."

"Not interested."

If it were anybody else, I would just tell Alice 'no' in a way that means business. But she's one of the resort's original employees and part of my earliest memories. She's been mothering the three of us ever since Mom and Dad died a year and a half ago. It can get tiring, but her heart's in the right place. It's hard to get too upset about that.

"I agree," Lizzy says, glancing at Connor. "Do it for a week and tell her you didn't like it."

"Or maybe you will like it," Connor says. "It'd be better than the crap you eat now."

"I like the crap I eat now."

"You can't subsist off chicken nuggets and French fries forever, old man."

I'm pushing thirty these days, and lately Connor has taken great pleasure in reminding me of it.

"You're only three years behind me, kiddo."

He gives me a look. "Don't call me kiddo."

Lizzy and I both laugh.

We make our way toward one of the tall cocktail tables scattered about so we can eat before we make the rounds. The conversation turns to Lizzy and Brett's upcoming nuptials. They're getting married in just three months.

At first I wasn't too happy about the timing. It'll still be busy at the resort, for sure, and I thought she should work around high season. We're the owners, so business comes first. But she and Connor convinced me it won't be too bad now that we have an executive assistant helping out. They're probably right.

"Do you know who you're bringing yet?" Lizzy asks.

I'll definitely need a proper date for her wedding. "I don't know. Maybe I'll bring Sarah."

"I like Sarah," Lizzy says.

"You like everybody." She does, too. My sister has a heart the size of California.

"Don't you like her?"

"I like her fine."

Sarah's fine. They're all fine. There's nothing spectacular between us, but maybe some people don't get to have spectacular. I've seen the way Lizzy looks at Brett, and the way Connor looks at Whitney. Not to mention the way my parents looked at each other. I'm fairly certain I've never experienced such emotion a single day of my life.

I had a few girlfriends in college, and another one briefly when I was getting my Masters, but there were no big fireworks like my siblings seem to have. There's been nothing of significance since then. I don't have time for significant anyway. Business and family keep me plenty busy.

We spend the next couple hours meandering through the rooms on each floor, occasionally picking up desserts or fresh drinks along the way. There's a little bit of hobnobbing with some people in our Swan Pointe network, but for the most part I get to enjoy the show and my siblings. Occasionally we'll separate as one person lags behind to make a purchase, but we catch up with each other eventually.

By the time we've left the second floor and have scattered to examine the offerings on the third floor, we've each found at least one painting to add to our collection, an investment habit instilled in us by our parents.

It's when we catch up with each other at the booth of a new artist from Florida that a harmless conflict ensues.

"I'll take that one," I say to the woman, who's probably in her late twenties but has artificially-gray hair with a pink streak that weaves in and out of the thick braid she wears over her shoulder.

I point to the painting in question, a large landscape at sunrise, perfectly executed, and something I like well enough to find a place for at my house, rather than putting it in the bowels of the resort so we can rotate it through the collection there.

"No, no!" Lizzy puts her hand on my forearm. "I want that one."

"Too bad, sis."

"No, no, no. I wanted it for the dining room. " Still hanging onto my arm, she steps slightly between me and the artist. Lizzy looks at her. "I'll pay you more."

I laugh. "It's too late. I already said I'm buying it."

Connor laughs, too. "I should get in on this just to make it more interesting."

Lizzy holds a finger to him in stern warning. "Don't you dare."

Connor and I exchange amused glances.

She turns back to the woman. "I'll pay you $500 above your asking price."

"Six hundred."

"Rayce!" She spins on me, her green eyes blazing.

Brett is laughing too, now. "You guys are so competitive."

Lizzy looks at him, all seriousness. "Are not." She turns back to the artist. "Eight hundred."

The artist is looking between us with a mixture of disbelief and glee, like she doesn't know if she can take this seriously or not, but sure as hell hopes that she can. She'll find out soon enough. Lizzy and I could go on like this for a while. Anyway, it's a fantastic painting and worth the money. This young artist hasn't figured out her value yet and is undercharging.

I assume she could use the money, too. Our father cautioned us against talking down an artist on their price. He said the starving artist cliché is pretty close to reality for most working artists, and to never take advantage of their possible desperation by bargaining.

"One thousand," I say.

"Noooooo." Lizzy bends her knees slightly as she turns to me and hangs on to both my arms. "Please, please, please. I love it so much."

Still hanging onto me with one hand, she makes a broad gesture toward the colorful canvas, melting a little as she looks at it. "Wouldn't it look perfect in my dining room?"

She turns those big doe eyes of hers on me.

Uh-oh.

"Please, big brother."

Connor laughs out loud at that one.

This battle is lost. Sneaky thing. I have a soft spot for my sister, and she knows right when to press her little finger on it.

"You're shameless," I say. "You're also the new owner of that painting."

Her face lights up and she clasps her hands in front of her chest, grinning first at me, then at the painting.

"You'd better top my last bid though."

She comes up on tiptoe and kisses my cheek, which makes it all worth it I guess, then grins at the artist. She starts digging her credit card out of her purse. "Add $1100 to your price."

You've never seen an artist whip out a card reader so fast.

"Big softy," Connor says grinning. He takes a sip of his drink, looking down the aisle toward the booths we've yet to check out.

I open my mouth to respond, but the words disintegrate on my tongue as something catches my eye. Or I should say, someone.

She's standing at one of the cocktail tables on the other side of the room. In between us are the food tables, more cocktail tables, and probably a couple dozen people. But I can't take my eyes off her.

She has soft blonde hair that flows just past her shoulders in silky waves. She's by herself, her forearms resting on the table and her hands wrapped loosely around her glass. She's just standing there, not talking to anyone. Not even looking at the artwork. It's like I've caught her in a moment of calm, right here in the middle of the art show.

She exudes this presence, simply from the way she's holding herself. What is it? Confidence? Poise?

She's wearing delicate, strappy heels and a soft burgundy skirt that flows just past her knees. It has an angled hemline, and a subtle slit that reaches up her thigh. Her sleek, fitted top has buttons down the front, and a silky fabric tie at the base.

The slit on her skirt seems perfectly positioned to give a glimpse of the thin, intricate tattoo on the outside of her left thigh. The bottom of the tattoo is a thin wisp that reaches almost to her knee, and the rest disappears beneath her skirt. I wonder just how far up that curving, flowing design snakes up her body.

Her sleeves come to her elbows. I wonder if she has tattoos on her shoulders. Or back. Or anywhere else on her body.

I'm not one to care for tattoos. A woman's skin is more beautiful untouched, in my opinion. But this woman, and her tattoo, are different. It's slender and delicate and lacey, almost in the style of a henna tattoo, but more fluid and elegant.

That is a word I have never used to describe a tattoo before. Elegant. Maybe it's the tattoo, or maybe it gains its elegance from the woman wearing it. She holds herself like a woman of class, but without the arrogance that often goes with it.

Still, though she's nicely dressed and well put together, she's not wearing high-end clothing. The impression of high class doesn't come from the quality of the cloth she's wearing. It comes from her.

<u>Graceful. Beautiful. Intriguing</u>. These are the words going through my mind as I look her. I've never seen a woman like this, and want to know what kind of person she is on the inside to make such a striking, unique picture on the outside.

I take a step in her direction, but Connor's hand on my arm stops me and I realize he's been talking to me but I have no idea what he's been saying.

"—remember Ted from the Swan Pointe Business Summit, don't you?"

Now I see there's someone standing next to Connor. He smiles and extends his hand.

I do recognize Ted. We met last fall. He has the potential to bring a lot of conference business to the resort. I smile and shake his hand, saying something pleasant and polite, but keep one eye on the woman at the table.

She takes an unhurried sip of her drink. Not many people can look so relaxed and comfortable alone in a social situation like this. Who is this woman?

"I'm glad you tracked us down," Connor says to Ted. "Rayce is definitely the one to ask about this."

"Your brother tells me I need to consult with you about an art investment," Ted says. "What do you think of this painting over here?"

He gestures towards a painting in the opposite direction of the woman who's caught my eye. He takes a few steps in that direction, with Connor following. They're obviously both under the assumption that I will come along, too, and very concerned about the painting this man wants to buy. I couldn't care less.

Buy whatever damned painting you want, I'd like to say.

But my professional training takes over. I juggle the task of politely giving this man some assistance and keeping an eye on the woman at the table. It's a challenge, because to look at Ted and his painting of choice, I have to face in one direction, and to check on her I have to face in another.

A frustrating ten minutes go by. I tell him this is a reputable artist and a fine painting at a good price, but he insists on asking question after question after question.

Meanwhile the woman at the table is clear across the room and I'm still here. I take a solid swallow of the full-bodied red I'm drinking, eyeing her over the rim of the glass as Ted drones on and on.

Finally I've had my fill. "You'll have to let me know how it looks in your study, Ted." I clap my hand to his and shake firmly. "If you'll excuse me."

He yields with a smile, the way people do when I decide that's how things are going to go. "Yes, of course. Thank you for the advice."

"My pleasure."

As I turn to leave, Connor gives me a look. I'm sure I haven't been rude, it isn't that. He's probably wondering what's up.

However, I don't care what he's wondering, because when I look to the table, she's gone.

I comb all three floors. The crowds are thinning, and I fear she's simply gone home. On my second circuit through the second floor, Connor comes up. "There you are. Where have you been?"

I barely look at him. I'm too busy scanning the room, and coming up empty, yet again. "I saw a woman."

"Which one?" Connor asks, looking around the room himself.

"None of these. She isn't here." Saying it out loud only irritates me further. She isn't. She isn't here. "Dammit."

Connor laughs and claps me on the back. "I think you'll be okay. You have plenty of women."

"None who matter."

He raises his eyebrows at me. What's he surprised about? He knows there's no one I'm serious about.

I scan the room again, as if I don't already know she's not here. I let her get away. She's only ever going to be a vision I saw once, and that's it.

"Let's just go."

# Chapter 3

## Emma

It's been a couple weeks and I'm getting a better feel for things at work. I've received my first partial paycheck and tried giving some money to Aaron and Pierce, but they insisted I wait until I have a full check. Pierce did well at the art show so he's in no hurry. Aaron said he wouldn't care if I never paid him back. He wants me to worry about replacing the car I was forced to sell, but I can't stand the thought of being in debt to them. I have to pay what I owe first.

I've exited the service elevator and am making the long walk down the underground parking garage. Up ahead are the spaces reserved for the owners. Their spots are right next to one of the glass-backed elevators that's for guests and upper management. I've been dying to take one to the tenth floor at the top so I can check out the view, but that's a big no-no.

All three of their vehicles are here, a couple BMWs and a shiny black Jaguar. This time of day they usually are, but when I get off late at night, the only one I see from time to time is that Jag that belongs to Mr. Rayce Rivers.

Though all three siblings own the resort, the only one I've seen is the youngest, Mr. Connor Rivers, because he's over the restaurants and banquet, among other things.

I've heard Mr. Rayce Rivers has come through banquet a couple times recently. I wasn't around, but heard about it later. When the elder Mr. Rivers comes through for inspection, people talk about it.

Well before I reach their cars, the elevator doors ding open. Two people exit, Mr. Connor Rivers and the woman I can only assume is his sister, based on appearances alone, Ms. Elizabeth Rivers. They resemble one another for sure. Such a handsome family. Young. Rich. Some people get it all.

Another man steps out after them. This has to be Mr. Rayce Rivers. Aside from the family resemblance, he carries himself in a way that practically screams "Boss."

He cuts a fine figure and wears that expensive-looking suit as if it were made just for him. Which, I realize, it probably was.

The three of them make their way to their cars, continuing whatever conversation was going on in the elevator. I take him in, my blood starting to run thick. He has dark hair, a smooth jawline, and lips that probably stop hearts all over Swan Pointe.

Well, fuck me. That's the owner? Of course it is. Because fate is out to get me, clearly.

I mean, no. His GQ hotness is irrelevant. This place is ginormous. There's a billion people working here. I could probably work here for years and never interact with him.

Not that he'd be interested anyway.

Why is my brain going there when all I'm doing is looking at him from across the parking garage? What the hell is wrong with me?

Maybe I can't be trusted around men. Especially men like this. I should've tried for a kitchen job at a nunnery or something. Nuns gotta eat too, right?

My eyes drift down his form again. He's a sight, from the way he fills out his suit jacket, to his smooth, purposeful stride, to the expensive-looking shiny shoes. Apparently I'm a sucker for a man who knows how to wear a suit. My eyes travel back up his body, wondering what he looks like underneath it all.

Ms. Rivers says something and he breaks out in a broad smile that actually slows my steps. Fucking gorgeous, that smile. I'd bet anything he's not the sort of man to give that kind of smile easily. I feel I've been given a glimpse of something private. Hidden.

Still unnoticed, I watch as he and his sister wave goodbye to their younger brother, who disappears inside his car. The remaining two continue to talk as he walks her to her door. I keep my head down as Mr. Conner Rivers' car passes me. As soon as it does, my eyes fly back to the older brother.

He opens the door for her and gives a slight wave before shutting it. He casually approaches his driver-side door, smoothly extracting his keys from his pocket.

The sound of Pierce's motorcycle is so loud, I realize he's been approaching for a while before it finally got my attention. The sound draws the notice of Mr. Rivers, too. When he calmly glances up to find the source of the noise, his eyes land on me. He halts.

All I hear is the sound of my heart beating in my ears. It's a long, long second that Rayce Rivers and I look directly at one another. I'm vaguely aware of Elizabeth Rivers backing out of her spot, of Pierce approaching as she drives away, and of my insides growing hot and still.

I pull my gaze away, forcing myself to stop staring at the owner of the Rivers Paradise Resort like he's some guy at the end of the bar.

Pierce makes a U-turn in front of me and comes to a stop, the scent of exhaust heavy in the air. Eyes on the ground in front of me, I chant to myself, <u>Don't look, don't look,</u>

<u>don't look</u>. I grab the helmet off the back and look just before I put it on. He's not next to his door anymore. He's wandered several steps closer, hovering near the trunk, staring at me. He seems surprised to see me. Not surprised to see a person, or surprised that the person was looking at him. No, I get the feeling that he's surprised to see <u>me</u>.

I don't understand it, but I drop my eyes, plop the helmet over my head, straddle the bike, and wrap my arms around Pierce's waist.

I don't allow myself to look again, even when we pass right by him. As we drive away, headed for the service ramp, I catch a glimpse of Mr. Rayce Rivers in the side mirror. He's still standing by the trunk of his car, both hands in his pockets, watching us drive away.

Over the next week, I see Mr. Connor Rivers several times, usually chatting up Alice or one of the other managers. I see Ms.

Elizabeth Rivers once, from afar. I don't see Mr. Rayce Rivers again at all.

Thank God. Once was quite enough. That moment in the garage has been darting in and out of my thoughts ever since as it is.

I still catch myself looking for him, and my heart rate speeds up every time I pass his car in the garage, but I'm sure that will go away with time. Won't it? Meanwhile, I'm just glad our paths don't cross more often. Men who look like that are dangerous.

I'm past the formal training stage, but still have a few things to learn about how things are done here. My coworkers have been helpful about showing me the ropes, but half the time I wonder if Alice is out to get me. She seems to put more work on me and have higher expectations of me than the others.

I don't know if she's trying to find out how much I can handle, or if this is to make up for being hired under dubious circumstances. But in spite of being a hard ass, she's a pretty good teacher and I'm a quick learner, so I've been able to pick things up well enough, I think.

Several times, she's asked about the personal chef services I used to do and how that works. At first I thought she was just curious, but something about the way she keeps bringing it up has me wondering. Do they pay the management well enough that she could afford it? Because if so, maybe this wouldn't be a bad place to try to make a career. I mean, I'll have to settle in somewhere.

I'm putting away warm, freshly laundered table linens on the bottom shelf of a storage closet when Alice sticks her head in the door. "Emma." She curls her finger, beckoning me over, then disappears into the hall.

I straighten and close the cupboard doors with a soft thud before following her out. She's waiting in the hallway next to a room service cart. It holds two trays, one with a plate covered by a silver dome and one holding a single set of silverware wrapped in a black cloth napkin, a little bowl of nuts, a tall wooden pepper grinder, and a collection of other condiments. There's also a small carafe of ice water, but no glass.

"Take this upstairs to Mr. Rivers," Alice says.

My heart begins to thump. <u>Mr. Rivers? Me? What? Why?</u> "Which one?"

She gives me a look, because it's a stupid question. I've been here long enough to know that employees distinguish between the two brothers pretty simply. Connor Rivers is Mr. Connor Rivers and Rayce Rivers is simply Mr. Rivers. As if he is *the* Mr. Rivers and no further distinction is necessary.

Still, a girl can hope.

"Mr. Rayce Rivers."

<u>Fuck. Fuck. Fuck.</u> I recall the image of him standing next to his car, our eyes locked. My heart flutters into my throat. "Why me?" Another misstep, but I can't help it.

She gives me a sharp look. Though Alice is generally good to her employees, she has exacting standards and we are expected to live up. She's the kind of person who doesn't need to snap her fingers to make people jump. The look she's giving me is usually sufficient.

"Sorry."

"Since you're new here, I'll explain. If Mr. Rivers orders lunch from one of the restaurants, we use banquet staff to deliver whenever possible to reduce stress on the kitchens."

I'm nodding contritely, because I know I'd damn well better. This explains why I've seen the occasional banquet server wheeling away a cart like this. I've always been busy with something else, and it didn't concern me, so I've never asked about it.

"If his office door is open, you may knock briefly then go directly inside. If it's closed, knock and wait for his answer."

Crap. Is this really happening? My mind spins trying to come up with a way out of this.

"There's a credenza on the right-hand side of his office. Park the cart in front. Ask if he would like you to place his meal there or on the desk. If he wants it on the credenza, unload this tray only."

She places one finger on the tray with the domed plate.

"Set the remaining items directly on the credenza next to it. Tray, carafe, silverware, condiments, nuts." As she goes through each item, she shifts her hand over an imaginary flat surface, indicating where each item should be placed.

Through her little speech, my eyebrows are slowly rising, temporarily distracted by these fussy instructions. "He's very particular, isn't he?"

"No." I'm getting the look again. "I'm particular about how the owners of this resort should be served and cared for."

I press my lips together, giving her an obedient nod. It didn't take long to figure out she thinks pretty highly of the Rivers family. She proceeds to tells me precisely how to place everything should he want his lunch brought directly to his desk. My skin tingles at the thought of getting that close to him. I bite the inside of my cheek to make it stop. There are specific steps for dealing with the carafe of water, everything. I feel like I'm being given instructions for serving a king.

A really hot, sexy king who I'd rather avoid, if it's all the same to everybody else. Not that I think he'd be interested anyway.

Then I remember the way he looked at me in the garage and my cheeks warm up.

Knock it off, Emma. Men like him aren't interested in girls like you, and when they are it's for the wrong reasons.

I've been down that road already.

"Bring the cart back with you. Do not leave it in his office. Should you be sent to pick items up when he's finished, load everything neatly onto the cart without disturbing him. There is no need for discussion during pickups. Oh, since you're new, be sure to introduce yourself when you arrive. That's very important, but no need to make a fuss. Simply say, 'I'm Emma and I have your lunch, Mr. Rivers.' Do you have any questions?"

Yeah. Can somebody else please do this?

I shake my head.

"Good." She turns smartly on her heels and heads for the Starlight Room. "Make it snappy. His food's getting cold."

# Chapter 4

## Rayce

I've managed not to look for her purposely, because that's too much like stalking. But fuck. The mystery woman from the art show is an employee here. In banquet, based on the uniform she was wearing. That was jarring as hell, once I realized what she had on. Not only because that makes her off limits, but because that intriguing woman should be a guest at a place like this, not working in the bowels of banquet.

I don't have a set pattern to the rounds I make. I like to keep an eye on things and don't want people to know when I'm coming. But since seeing her a week ago, I've been to banquet twice. Even though I have no idea what good could possibly come from it, I couldn't help but look for her.

Hell, everywhere I go, I look for her. Even picking up a pizza at Guido's, I'm looking for her. It's right at the bottom of the hill so I see employees in there often enough. But she's been nowhere. Vanished, just like after the art show.

And now, as if the universe is serving her up on a silver platter, she appears right at my open office door.

I would think it was fate, if there weren't just one problem.

"Excuse me, Mr. Rivers." She has one hand on the service cart. "I have your lunch?"

She's in slim black slacks and a button-down, white shirt. Her blonde hair is pulled into a neat ponytail, leaving the smooth, pale skin of her neck exposed. Even in uniform, she's beautiful and poised.

The slight blush on her lovely cheeks does not escape my notice. I could be wrong, but I think I know what that blush is about. I would play it to my advantage, in any other situation.

This thing about her working here—and now getting ready to serve me—is every kind of wrong. This isn't how things should be. Not at all.

It has not escaped my notice that I've thought more about this woman since seeing her at the art show than all the other women combined over the last year. Yet, I have to keep it under wraps because I'm the boss. It's irritating.

"Come." I gesture slightly with my left hand.

As she wheels the cart toward the credenza to my left, the situation annoys me more and more. She's an employee. Bringing my damned lunch. I don't want her to serve me and leave. I want to talk to her.

She brings the cart to a stop.

"What's your name?"

She startles slightly. "Oh right. Sorry."

I've no doubt made her realize she forgot introduce herself, something Alice instructs new employees to do the first time they serve one of us. Alice is unnecessarily particular about the whole thing.

"Emma."

Emma. Something squeezes inside my chest.

"Emma what?"

She hesitates. For the briefest moment, she looks as she did in the garage. Like she's as interested in me as I am in her. She tucks it away under a professional mask and raises her chin slightly. "Emma Swanson. Would you like your food here or on your desk, Mr. Rivers?"

She's strong-willed. I like that. And I'd bet not the kind of woman to throw herself at her boss.

Clearly, God is getting even with me for my sins.

"Bring it here." I gather some papers and set them to the side. As she wheels the cart over, she seems unable to stop herself from casting one quick glance after another in my direction. The color on her cheeks is deepening, but she clearly has her guard up. Like she thinks I might make a move on her no matter who I am or how many times she calls me "Mr. Rivers" in an attempt to keep things in line.

It's my own fault. I didn't hide my reaction very well when I saw her in the parking garage. It didn't occur to me to try. I was too astonished to see her. I didn't realize she was in that uniform until after she rode away with the beefcake who probably has more tattoos than she does.

I glance at her shoulders, wondering how many tattoos she <u>does</u> have, underneath those clothes. She comes around to my left side, bends over the desk slightly, and places the tray on top.

An unwelcome mental image brings my past back to me: me hastily bending an eager employee over my desk, late at night when the office was empty. That's how the sex was, too. Empty, and only a temporary relief from my demons.

She was standing right where Emma is now. Not that my draw to her is anything like the others. I don't want to take her like that. I want something different. But does it matter? Thinking of my past mistakes reminds me of the promise I made to my brother. Not to mention that damned, threatening email.

I look toward the broad windows and the lush resort grounds beyond, briefly pinching my eyes shut as my vow to Connor swirls around in my consciousness with Emma's scent: mild floral notes with a hint of citrus.

"May I, Mr. Rivers?"

I open my eyes. Her hand is out, palm up. I want to put my hand on hers, lace our fingers together, and pull her onto my lap.

Fuck.

I don't even know her. What is she doing to me?

In Emma's other hand is the carafe of ice water. "Your glass?" she prompts, her raised hand gesturing to my empty glass, which is on the other side of my desk, beyond her reach.

I hand her the glass. She seems careful to make sure our fingertips don't touch. I lean back as she pours.

I'm trying to remind myself that she's an employee, that I've made promises that matter, that I can't go back to my past, but there's a larger part of me taking over. I can't seem to stop myself. She doesn't feel like an employee as much as she feels like the intriguing woman across the room.

I allow myself to examine her face, visually tracing the curve of her cheek, the line of her nose, the soft swelling of her lips. Her eyes flit to mine. I examine her eyes: sky-blue rimmed in dark cobalt.

She hastily drops her gaze, finishing with the water. I know I'm crossing lines. But what if I don't want to care about that?

"I've seen you before," I say.

Avoiding my eyes, she sets my glass on the desk, then puts the rolled silverware below it with slightly fumbling fingers. "Well, I work here."

"Not that."

Her hand, reaching for the little dish of nuts, pauses in midair and her eyes return to mine. This time, they linger.

"I saw you at the art show."

"You did?" She drops her hand, straightening, her eyes still on mine.

I nod and smile slightly. Her eyes dip to my mouth momentarily.

"Were you in the market for a new painting?" I ask.

"Hardly. My roommate was one of the artists there."

"Ah." For some reason this makes sense to me. "Which one? Maybe I know her."

The corner of her mouth hitches up, an almost-smile. I find myself badly wanting to see the rest of it. "He. Pierce Lindholm." The name sounds familiar, but I don't know him. One of the new artists, perhaps. But that's not the most important consideration right now.

"Your roommate is a man?"

"Yes."

"Is he your boyfriend?"

A little voice reminds me that I have no business asking my employees their relationship status.

But this isn't boss to employee. It's me to her. And I need to know.

She's hovering in place, still looking at me, trying to put her guard back up, but failing. As we look at one another, not speaking, there's a passing acknowledgment between us about what's really happening here.

"I'm not exactly his type."

"Then he's an idiot."

"He's gay."

"That's no excuse. Was he the one on the motorcycle?" Because if he wasn't, and that was her boyfriend...

"Yes. And I don't think you're supposed to be asking questions like this."

She breaks eye contact at last and I lean back. She picks up the little bowl of nuts intending to place it on my desk, in the same damned spot they always place it. I gently take her by the wrist, stopping her.

Her blush deepens and she holds her breath. The vein at the base of her neck pulses rhythmically.

Touching her had an unexpected effect on me as well. My blood starts to run hot. I take it back. I do want to bend her over my desk.

I remove the bowl from her hand and release her. "It's not necessary to serve me like that."

"Alice says—"

"I trump whatever Alice says."

Our gaze holds another heartbeat before she stubbornly removes the plate from the tray and places it on my desk. Fuck, she needs to stop serving me.

"Leave the items on the cart."

"I've been instructed to bring the cart back, Mr. Rivers."

"Call me Rayce."

I'm crossing line after line, but I don't want her to be so formal. Not in this context anyway. My dick twitches at the thought of her calling me Mr. Rivers in a darkened room with her clothes off, but right now I just want to hear my first name on her lips.

She removes the dome from the plate, the steam rising from the fajita strips and the scent of sautéed onions and peppers accenting the air. She places the dome on the cart.

"I need to follow her instructions." She looks at me pointedly. "I need this job."

I exhale and drop the little bowl on my desk with a thunk. She needs this job. She needs to not put it at risk by crossing lines with me. I should want the same damned thing. But I don't.

She starts wheeling the cart away.

A hard knot grips my chest. She's going to walk out of here, and who knows if I'll see her again unless I purposely go hunting her down. Which, I realize, I'm no longer above doing.

"Wait."

She stops with one hand on the cart and looks at me. "Do you need anything else, Mr. Rivers?"

Do I need anything? Good lord. I need her not to vanish again. I need this to not be the last I see of her today.

"I'd like a piece of that new lime cheesecake from Sweetbrew."

"All right."

The knot in my chest loosens. This gives me a minute to figure out where to go from here. "Then I'll see you when you get back."

She straightens, dropping her hand from the handle of the cart. She looks at me openly. She knows what I'm doing.

I don't care.

"Alice may send somebody else."

I lean forward slightly, resting my forearms on the desk and lacing my fingers together. I give her a look that shows I mean business. She's coming back and that's the end of it.

Now that I've given her this look, she's struggling to maintain her façade. And not because she wants to resist me, but because she doesn't. I know enough to know when a woman wants me, no matter how hard she's trying to hide it. The vein at the base of her throat is pulsing rapidly. I want to run my fingertips over it.

Before I can respond, she adds, "She can send whoever she wants."

As if what Alice wants makes a difference. Alice does what I tell her to, and is all about giving me and my siblings what we want anyway. Right now, what I want is for the woman standing in front of me to come back to my office before the day is over.

"Then tell Alice," I say slowly and deliberately, "that I request you."

# Chapter 5

## Emma

My heart is pounding and my blood is galloping through my veins. This can't be happening. It's like the universe is determined for me to fuck myself all over again.

And oh, how I want to. I've been in his office all of five minutes, and I already want him more than I can stand. He's nothing like that pansy ass Chad was either. He's not someone who storms around demanding employees respect him. Mr. Rayce Rivers is the sort of man who earns respect on sight.

Warmth licking down my center, my thighs clench at the thought of touching him. Feeling his arms come around my body. Allowing him to claim my mouth and anything else he wants.

But, fuck it all, none of it matters because I absolutely cannot under any circumstances go down this road again.

I'm not ignorant to the fact that he's wise to me. He sees what I want. I could take the sexual tension between us, put it on a plate, and serve it to him steaming hot.

Still holding my eyes, he nods ever so slightly. A reminder. He's not the kind of man to repeat himself, I'd wager, but that little nod is all it takes for the command he just gave to repeat itself in my mind. <u>Tell Alice that I request you.</u>

I step closer to his desk, squarely opposite him. I hold his eyes and grab an almond from the dish. He watches as I slowly bring it to my mouth, the salt shocking my tongue. I take my time chewing. Like I have all damn day. All the while, I'm looking him straight in the eye.

I swallow, and when I finally speak, I somehow manage to keep my voice calm and steady. "I'll do no such thing."

A slow smile emerges on his face. It happens so gradually, that I'm momentarily frozen by it. He's smiling at me like I just threw down the gauntlet, and he's picked that fucker up.

Like an idiot ignoring her own peril, all I can think of is how stunning that smile looks on Rayce Rivers' face.

# Chapter 6

## Rayce

Sure enough, another employee brings the lime cheesecake.

I didn't even want it.

I instruct him to leave the rest of my dishes, pretending I'm not done with them yet, in the hopes that when someone returns to retrieve them, that someone will be her.

Of course, it isn't.

I don't know what that would've accomplished anyway. What am I going to do? Ask her out? Invite her back to my place? Ask if she'll be my date to Lizzy's wedding?

To top it off, this afternoon I received yet another email from Taylor Norrell. It's just as concerning as the last one was. She hasn't come out and said she intends to go after me for sexual harassment, but every time I read one of her emails, that's where my brain goes.

It wasn't sexual harassment, of course. Sure, I was fucked up at the time, but not a monster. I'm always mindful of consent, but in those cases I made extra damn sure every encounter was consensual. But that doesn't change what they were: torrid affairs with lower-level employees.

The relationship with Taylor, if it could be called that, was as devoid of emotion as just about everything else in my life was back then. The sex was rough and dirty, the way we both wanted it. Sure, it was consensual, but I didn't care about her, or any of them. Not really.

It was the local gossip columnist, that damned Rita Becker, who somehow caught wind of things. She published a condemning article filled with speculations both true and false. At least she failed to name names. That's when Connor asked me point blank about it, and I lied straight to his face.

It was my new low point. Worse than anything I'd done yet.

When Connor saw what was really happening and called me out on it, I tried to fight it, like I'd done for the eight long months since our parents drowned at sea. But Connor wouldn't let me hide anymore. That little brother of mine saved me.

That's why I couldn't bear to tell him that it wasn't just one employee, but had been a string of them. Why hurt him further?

Thank <u>God</u> Lizzy doesn't know anything.

When I promised Connor that was the end of it, I meant it. It was a mistake I intended never to repeat.

And now here's Emma.

There's been no shortage of women in my life—employee or otherwise—but none of them have caught my attention like this one has. She's the only one who's stood out, and I'm supposed to sit in my office like a good boy and never find out <u>why?</u> Never find out, <u>what if?</u>

If God is a vengeful god, he more or less excels at it.

By the end of the day I'm so irritated by the situation, that when Connor comes into my office and deposits a folder on my desk, I only grunt in acknowledgment.

He was turning to go, but this stops him. "What's wrong with you?"

"Nothing."

What am I going to say? Should I ask if he thinks I can make an exception and go after the stunning new employee who served my lunch today? No. Not an option.

He scratches at the back of his neck. "You sure?"

I pick up the folder, open it, and start flipping through the papers inside. I've made the mistake of taking things out on my little brother before, and don't want to do it again. I make an effort to keep my voice calm and friendly. "Is the Harrison report in here?"

"At the back." Judging by the easy tone of his voice, he's going to let things go. Because he's a good guy like that.

"Thank you."

Connor's appearance is only a more forceful reminder of all the reasons behind my promise. I didn't make that promise lightly, and I know he didn't take it that way either. My siblings and I co-own this resort, and if someone brought a lawsuit against me, I'm not the only one who would be hurt by it. They're invested in this, too.

Not to mention the public shame I would bring to the family name. That actually means more than the potential financial losses. Maintaining the integrity of the Rivers name is critical. It's even more important now that Mom and Dad are gone and we're left to represent everything they stood for.

Trying to remember all that's at stake, I firmly tell myself to forget about Emma Swanson. There are other women to be had. I don't need that one.

I repeat those words to myself over and over, trying to make them sink in.

Which they flat refuse to do.

So when Alice comes to my office at a quarter to six, chastising me yet again about my plans to pick up Guido's for dinner on my way home, telling me she's found the perfect person to be my personal chef this time, a certain Emma Swanson, I do something I've never done before.

I agree.

It happens in a heartbeat. All my self-chastisement gone to waste.

Alice looks too surprised to be happy, apparently thinking I'd never say yes to bringing a personal chef into my home. She was right to think that, of course, because that's not what I'm really saying yes to.

"Only for one week," I add, remembering the advice Connor has been giving me for quite some time, and feeling guilty as hell about it. Nevertheless, that will be my alibi. If anybody asks, that's my reason for finally going along with this.

"Only one week?" In spite of her lack of joy at my initial 'yes,' she still manages to seem disappointed about this restriction.

I turn to my computer, place my hand on the mouse, and act as if I'm able to concentrate on work and still have this conversation at the same time. My blood is racing with guilt, but eagerness too. This will give me a chance to figure out a solution to this problem. Because there has to be one.

"I'll try it," I reply. "That's all I'm agreeing to."

Though if Alice can get Emma on board with this, I doubt I'll send her home after a week.

"Thank you, Mr. Rivers. One week isn't really enough time, though. Wouldn't you say? Will you give it two?"

"Fine." I click open a new email, not really reading it.

"Thank you. I don't think you'll regret it. She has prior experience and has proven herself here in the time that she's been with us. I've talked to her about how this would work—"

My gaze flies to her.

"—and I'm certain she could accommodate you without getting in the way."

"You talked with her about doing this for me?"

"No, sir, I would never do that without speaking with you first. I only asked about what she used to do and how it worked. They know how to make it as easy on their clients as possible. I have confidence that she'll know how to treat you right. As for pay, I asked her about that as well, so I think

I have a good understanding about a fair wage."

I straighten slightly and clench my jaw. "A fair wage" just hammers home the problem. Emma is an employee here, and now thanks to my agreeing to this when I know I shouldn't, she'll be my employee twice over.

In my house. Just her and I.

Who am I kidding? Even if Alice doesn't know what this is really about, Emma will. She'll never agree.

Alice continues. "I could get it set up so there's nothing you have to do. Would you like me to write up the details and bring them to you?"

I wave my hand and lean in closer to my computer. "Just email it."

"Yes, Mr. Rivers," she says, gleeful at last. And this is a woman who tends to be short on glee. She hustles out of my office, calling over her shoulder, "I'll take care of everything."

Still not seeing whatever's on my screen, I'm a churning mix of guilt and exhilaration. Regret and anticipation. I've just tried to set us both up for potential disaster, but my heart beats thickly wanting it.

If, that is, she agrees.

# Chapter 7

## Emma

By the time I get off work, I've relived the incident in Mr. Rayce Rivers' office about a hundred times. I'm dripping with the guilt of it. I should <u>know better</u> than to feel like this about the fucking boss.

And not just my immediate supervisor. No, no. The. Boss.

It doesn't help that I stood up to him at the end, because every time I think about things, I may start off feeling guilty, and I may end up feeling guilty, but in the middle? In the middle my heart pounds, and my skin tingles, and I fantasize about all the other ways today could have gone.

Him taking me on the desk. Me straddling him in his chair. Him fucking me upright, pressed against the glass of the large windows, for anyone out in the gardens to see.

My fantasies are straight up hardcore.

When I'm not fantasizing about what didn't happen, I'm fantasizing about what did.

His fingertips touching mine and the electric shock I feel just remembering it. The way he looked at me, heat simmering just beneath the surface of those intense eyes. And that smile.

The energy of it all bounces around in my stomach, betraying me.

That's when the guilt starts up again. Because even though I stood up to him, I didn't want to.

This just proves yet again, that I can't trust myself to be close to things that harm me. I have to keep a distance miles wide. I mean, why on earth am I attracted to a man who's obviously the typical boss slime ball? His behavior was totally inappropriate, as I've firmly reminded myself over and over.

It doesn't matter that it didn't feel inappropriate. It felt exciting and intriguing and almost... natural. As if we've been exchanging that kind of banter and those kind of looks for years. Which only proves how fucked up I am.

Because no matter how it felt, it *was* inappropriate.

It was.

He was. Bosses shouldn't say and do things like that. I don't need to be someone's plaything. Again.

I get started on dinner as soon as Pierce and I get home. For now, home is their second-floor loft located on the edge of an industrial section in Swan Pointe. It's an old warehouse, with a chop shop down below. Their loft takes up the entire second story, all 4500 square feet of it. At the far end is a small living area that includes a tiny, outdated kitchen, a closet of a bathroom, and a sleeping area partitioned off with wooden screens. The rest of the space is open, with exposed rafters and pipes twenty feet above us.

Floor to ceiling windows cover the length of the north wall. Pierce says that's the sole reason he chose this place. He installed remote-controlled shades—the fanciest thing in sight—so he could adjust the lighting at different times of the day. Almost the entire space acts as his studio. He has three different easels scattered about, a few work tables holding coffee cans filled with paint brushes, giant tubes of paint, and framing supplies, and a rickety metal drafters table he uses as a desk.

Paintings in various stages of production are stacked against almost every wall. Other than the living area, the only truly clear space is one corner that's nothing but glossy hardwood flooring, Aaron's portable dance barre, and a fifteen-foot mirror that's so old its reflection has turned antique matte.

I take a wide berth of it every time I go by.

Next to the dance floor—inconveniently—are a few stacks of my boxes I can't unpack. I'm trying to keep my footprint here as small as possible, so I live out of the two suitcases I store behind the chair in the living area. A chair, a coffee table, and a couch. That's the living area. There isn't even a TV, not that either of them seem to miss having one.

What they probably do miss is full access to the couch, considering how limited the seating accommodations are here to start with. That's why I put away my linens as soon as I wake up in the morning.

After I landed the job at the resort, I did a budget to calculate how much longer they'll be stuck with me. It seems like an eternity. They're being good sports about it, but I can't wait to get out of their hair.

To make up for my presence here, I prepare the meals as often as my schedule allows. Aside from giving me a way to make a contribution to the household, I feel better any time Aaron gets a decent meal.

As I'm putting the casserole in the oven, he walks through the door. He's wearing black dance pants, a snug gray tee, and worn tennis shoes. He keeps his blonde hair short, in an attempt to tame his thick, natural curls, but the wave of his locks come through anyway.

He grins at us. "Hey."

Pierce and I both give him a hello in return.

He heaves his duffle bag off his shoulder and drops it by the door. He kicks off his shoes. The socks follow. He leaves the entire pile of stuff by the door and crosses the room toward us, his bare feet padding across the cement floor.

He stops to compliment the latest painting in progress—a gorgeous piece Pierce declares is "absolute shit"— then comes into the kitchen to see what I'm up to.

"What's cooking?" Ever with that suspicious tone in his voice.

"Something that smells like heaven," Pierce says, tapping his brush into some paint on his palette. He's in jeans and an old paint-splatted T-shirt that pulls across the length of his massive chest. Even at the easel, he gives off the biker vibe.

"Zucchini and eggplant Neapolitan," I answer.

"Hmmm," is all Aaron says, which is good enough. He's familiar with this dish so he knows just how much he can have and stay within his calorie range. It's delicious, packed with nutrients, and pretty low-cal so it's a win all the way around. I make it probably once a week.

"How were rehearsals?" I grab the head of lettuce off the counter and start rinsing it at the sink.

He eyes the multi-grain bread I picked up at the Co-op yesterday—something I know he won't touch, no bread for him—and gets a glass out of the cupboard. "Fair. We should be ready in time, for the most part."

He's waiting for me to finish at the sink. I step out of the way, hating that I'm so often underfoot here. He fills his glass as I dry the lettuce with paper towels.

"Sergei is happy?" Pierce asks from the easel.

Sergei is the choreographer and a drill sergeant in rehearsals.

Aaron downs his glass right there at the sink, then turns on the water to fill it again. "Hard to tell, but I think so."

Pierce presses on. "How's Natalia's ankle?"

I look over my shoulder to glare at him, but he just taps away on his canvas with the brush, oblivious to the opening he just gave his boyfriend.

"She's trying to dance on it, but it's giving her problems." Aaron eyes me carefully.

I know that look.

Thanks a lot, Pierce.

I tear into the lettuce. "I'm sure she'll be fine," I say sternly. We're not having this conversation again. This is another reason I need to get out of here. Living here puts me too close to the world Aaron still inhabits.

"We could use a backup," Aaron says.

"Then Sergei should go get one." He doesn't need a backup. That's not what any of this is about.

"Emma…"

"I'm not changing my mind. I like my job." I ignore the tingling up my spine that comes from remembering today's encounter with the damned boss. "Everything's fine."

I blame fucking Sergei for this. Aaron has been willing, more or less, to support my decision and let me live my own life. But once Sergei Petrov heard I was his roommate, he's been putting ideas into

Aaron's head. Pressuring him. Now Aaron's pressuring me.

But I'm not going back to that world. I'm not. It's been too long anyway. I don't know what good he thinks I'd be after over a year off. I've kept up a solid workout regimen, but I certainly don't train anymore. Yeah, my first post-dance job blew up in my face, but that has nothing to do with anything else. My life might be a bit of a disaster now, but leaving dance isn't the reason why.

"If it's because you wouldn't be principal..." Aaron says.

"That has nothing to do with it."

"You wouldn't need to be embarrassed."

"That's not it."

"You'd get back there so quickly, Emma. I know you would. You're so fucking talented."

The way Aaron says this stops me. It stops Pierce, too. I'm looking at Aaron, and Pierce is looking at both of us, his paintbrush hovering in midair.

Aaron doesn't just want this for me. He wants it for himself. It's strange sometimes, the attachment people can have to someone else's abilities.

"I was good," I acknowledge.

"You <u>are</u> good."

"I had my time. It's okay, Aaron. Everyone has to move on eventually." No dancer gets to dance forever.

I think he's going to say that I moved on too soon. That I left in my prime, and not because of age or injury. That's what he said when I first left. But dammit, it's not like he doesn't know my reasons.

"Okay." He rubs my arm briefly. "All right." He heads to the couch and lets out a deep breath as he sits down. "I'll leave you alone about it."

"Thank you."

"Just don't tell Sergei I'm giving up." He gives me a slight, teasing smile. "I swear he likes me better now that he thinks I can get Emma Swanson in his company."

I turn the light on the oven to check on the casserole. "I doubt that." I'm lying and he probably knows it. We both know perfectly well how these things work.

After dinner I'm cleaning up the dishes, frustrated that Aaron left way too much on his plate. Apparently today Sergei told Aaron he needs to slim down some for one of his costumes. As if. That fucker.

Not for the first time tonight, my mind wanders back over moments in Rayce Rivers' office. Like right now I'm remembering how it felt when he caught my wrist in his strong grasp and the way he smiled at me when I stood up to him, like he wanted me even more and wasn't afraid to let it show.

I shove those thoughts away. It's stupid to keep dwelling like this. It was just a weird, one-off incident anyway. I'll probably never be alone with Mr. Rivers again.

My phone buzzes. My breath shortens in nervous anticipation when I see it's Alice calling. Why would she call me?

I dry my hand on my thigh and answer. "Hello?"

"Hi, Emma. This is Alice."

"Uh. Hi."

"Would you meet me in my office at 2:30 tomorrow?"

Oh, shit. My shift starts at three. Is she having me go down early so she can fire me? Did Rayce Rivers say something to her? Did my little act of defiance get me canned? I am instantly both terrified that I've lost a job I so desperately need, and pissed at the idea that he may have told her to let me go.

Fuck him, I think. Fuck him if he would do something like that.

Though... I don't think he would.

I shake my head at myself in frustration. Why don't I think he would? I don't even know the guy, so how do I know what he would or wouldn't do? Yet, if I had to place money on it, I'd say he isn't the kind of person to fire me out of spite.

Because apparently I'm an idiot who never learns.

"Sure. Okay. No problem."

"Thank you," she says in her usual clipped tone. Or is she being more stern than usual? I can't tell. "See you then." And the line goes dead.

"You want me to do what?"

I'm sitting in Alice's little gray box of an office even more freaked out than I was the first time I was here. She's just asked me to be Rayce Rivers' personal chef, a request so out of the blue it's almost surreal. Surely, she doesn't mean it. Aside from being alarmed for the obvious reasons, I'm also confused. If he's looking for a personal chef, why doesn't he set it up himself? Why is his banquet manager doing it? And why the hell is she asking <u>me</u>?

Then I remember.

Oh geez. <u>This</u> is why she's been asking me all those questions?

"I've been looking for the right person a long time, Emma. I think you're perfect for the job. In fact, it's one of the reasons I decided to give you a try here."

I blink at her.

"I didn't want you to contact my last boss, but you hired me with the intention of having me work directly for <u>your</u> boss?"

Holy fuck, I did not mean to say that. It just slipped out. Still though. Alice is a pretty sharp tack and weirdly protective of the owners. What gives?

She leans back, her swivel chair squeaking slightly, and smiles. "Rose has been with us a long time and I trust her. I told you. She didn't tell me what happened at your last job, but she says she knows what it was and there's nothing I need to worry about. I trust her, and now I trust you, too."

You. Absolutely. Shouldn't.

"This isn't really in my job description."

I know I need to stay on the good side of someone who has the power to let me go, but I am not going to be personal chef to Rayce Rivers. I'm absolutely not.

"This would be handled separately." She puts her fingertips on a piece of paper in front of her and slides it to me. "Of course, you would be compensated appropriately."

I'm still in shock as I glance over a contract of services, instructions on how to coordinate around his schedule, pertinent contact information for both her and him, and... my eyes bug open when I see the weekly pay. "Is that supposed to be per month?"

"Per week."

I look at the paper again. That's for a single week? I lean in, reading things more closely. Okay, this contract includes both breakfast and dinner during the workweek, plus dinner on Saturdays, but damn.

"Wait, this doesn't include the cost of food? I'll be honest. This is way too much."

"It is not. The pay represents compensation for your skills, <u>absolute</u> flexibility for Mr. Rivers' schedule, and a willingness to adjust on short notice. It also represents your <u>complete discretion</u>. The Rivers family is subject to public scrutiny, and anyone entering their homes to provide a service must be trustworthy."

She slides over another piece of paper. A nondisclosure agreement.

Okay, this is just getting worse and worse.

But I'm looking at that number, and thinking about the couch I sleep on, and the rides I'm always having to borrow, and how this could get me out of my friends' hair so much more quickly. Still, this would be such a bad idea.

"He's only agreed to this on a trial basis, for now. Two weeks."

Okay, Emma. Say no. Just say the word. That's all you have to do.

But I'm doing the math and practically salivating at having that much in my bank account so quickly. Two weeks. Too little weeks and I'd have enough to pay them back and put down a deposit on a crappy apartment somewhere.

Plus you want to do it. You want to see him again.

I shove those thoughts aside. Mr. Rivers can piss off. He's a slime ball.

Probably.

"Even though you should be prepared to be flexible both now and if this turns into a permanent position, his schedule is pretty routine for the next couple weeks, so yours should be as well."

"Uh-huh."

Say no. Say no, Emma.

"I've purposely scheduled shifts that mainly put you there when he's gone."

He wouldn't even be there? Okay, I did not just feel disappointment about that.

Alice continues. "I want this to be as nonintrusive on his personal time as possible."

"Well, I'd need to talk to him about menus." I'm an idiot. An idiot who never learns. "I need to know what kind of food he likes. Stuff like that."

She smiles, straightening. "That's no problem. I gave you extra time here."

She taps on the piece of paper, pointing to the first day's schedule, which I notice starts tomorrow. The two-week contract runs midweek to midweek. "You said that usually takes an hour, right?"

I nod. How am I letting this situation get so far away from me? But all that money...

She grabs a pen and puts it next to the contract. "Do you have any questions?"

I pick it up, rolling it in my fingers as I pretend to read through the contract again. Dammit. I really shouldn't agree to this. I glance again at the pay.

Two weeks, and I'd only need to get through the first meeting. After that, I won't even see him. I can do that, right? I can get my money and get out.

"No. This sounds fine." But I don't sign yet.

She leans on her forearms, smiling at me in an unusually open way that I find rather disarming. "Thank you. I'll tell you in confidence that I worry about Mr. Rivers sometimes. The way he eats." She shakes her head. "Well, you'll see. Just do everything you can to make this as easy on him as possible. I've been trying to get him to do this for a long time and I want it to stick. And that would be good for you too, wouldn't it?" She gestures to the piece of paper. "That's not a bad little raise."

"So I'm not in banquet anymore? What if he doesn't want more than two weeks?"

"We'd like to keep you on call, if you're agreeable to that. "

I nod.

"But don't worry. You still have your job here if he doesn't like it."

"What if I don't like it?" I desperately need this money, but I can't do this long term. I need an exit strategy, especially if he decides he <u>does</u> like it.

I think of that smile he gave me when I stood up to him. Maybe I'm slow on the uptake, but I just now realize something. If she's been trying to get him to do something like this for a long time, and he's just now agreeing, I know why. And it's not for the reason she thinks.

I don't care what her schedule says. He's going to make damn sure our paths cross.

My heart flutters in my chest.

"Why wouldn't you like it?" Alice asks. "I thought you enjoyed that kind of work?"

"I did. But…" But what? "It… depends on the client sometimes. Sometimes someone isn't a good fit."

She starts to scowl.

"Through nobody's fault," I hurry to say. "But I…" I swallow hard, realizing I'm probably making no sense to her. Why would anybody turn down this kind of pay? "I like working banquet, too."

For far, far less money. Uh-huh. Sure.

She furrows her brow at me. "No one's making you do this, if that's what you're asking. But please, get him to like it. It's taken me almost two years to get him to try this. That boy needs to eat better."

I smile slightly. I've never heard her refer to the great Mr. Rayce Rivers as 'boy' before. Somebody once told me that Alice has been here almost twenty years. She used to work for his parents. Maybe she saw him and his siblings running around the resort when they were just little rug rats, and not the powerful executives they are now.

She cares for him. Maybe even feels a little motherly toward him. Is it strange that makes me like both of them even more?

I look again at the number on the piece of paper. I really fucking need this and it would be money honestly earned. I can say that much at least. Two short weeks would make a huge difference, not just to me but to my long-suffering roommates.

I bounce the pen slightly in my fingers, then resolutely bring it to the contract, the tip hovering slightly above the paper.

Last chance to back out. Are you sure you want to do this?

I sign both papers before I lose my nerve. That kind of money is a lot walk away from when I'm living off the charity of others.

Maybe he knows it, too. Maybe the price has nothing to do with flexibility and discretion, but was rather to make sure I'd sign. Maybe this really is my past repeating itself.

I set the pen on the desk with a click and keep my eyes on Alice. I know how risky this is, but I'm desperate. And if I've learned one thing, there are plenty of things I'm willing to do when I'm desperate.

# Chapter 8

## Emma

I was nervous to tell Aaron what I've done, and I was right to be so. Unlike Alice, he knows my story.

"Why in the hell would you agree to this?"

We're sitting in the living area, he and Pierce on the couch and me in the chair. We're balancing our dinner plates on our laps, but Aaron has been mainly picking at his. I put a small amount of lean steak in the stir fry to appease Pierce, but Aaron has pushed all his meat to the side. He's not touching the brown rice either. He's eaten a few vegetables, but that's it.

"Did you not hear how much I'm getting paid?"

"Still, Emma."

"I can't stay here forever. I need the money."

"We're in no hurry. You don't have to do this."

"What's the problem?" Pierce interjects. "Just because he's the boss, doesn't mean the same thing's going to happen again."

"Exactly. It's not like I have this insatiable urge to sleep with all my bosses."

My cheeks grow warm as if I've just spoken a lie. But I didn't, right? Just because I find Rayce Rivers attractive—I mean, who the hell wouldn't?—that doesn't mean I'm going to sleep with him. I just need the money.

That's what I keep coming back to. I do need the money, but now that it's done, it's more difficult to convince myself the money was the only reason. I keep thinking about Rayce Rivers and the way he kept trying to reel me in and wondering what in the hell is going to happen once I'm inside his home.

My thighs clench with a hot swoop of wanting.

No, Emma. No.

Aaron's eyeing me. It's like he knows. Or maybe I'm just being paranoid. "I didn't say that. But this is the kind of situation where false accusations can arise."

"I don't think he's the kind of person to do that."

He raises eyebrows.

"Just because Chad was that sort of asshole, doesn't mean every boss is the same way."

"Okay." He's narrowing his eyes at me like he's trying to figure something out.

I try very hard to keep my expression innocent. Well, I am innocent! I haven't done anything wrong. In fact, I stood up to that Mr. Rivers, and would do it again if I had to.

I would.

"Why take a chance at putting yourself in that situation again? Is it really worth it to you?" He starts to stand with his plate.

I point one finger at him. "No, you don't!" He freezes, not even having straightened all the way up. "You've barely touched your dinner."

"Knock it off, Emma. I'm not starving myself." He gets up the rest of the way and heads into the kitchen, setting his plate on the counter. "There's too much oil in this. I'll have an apple."

"There is not too much oil." What bullshit. I try not to push him when he gets like this because it only makes things worse, but I'm on already edge. Why is he acting like I've done something wrong when all I did was take a job? Nothing's happened.

Another thought that feels like a lie.

Rayce Rivers and I may not have laid a hand on one another, but I can't think back on things and honestly say nothing happened. Maybe I couldn't say <u>what</u> it was, but it wasn't nothing.

But that's where it's going to end. I'm in it for the money. That's it.

"Hey, don't get mad just because I'm not going to say I think this is okay."

"Aaron," Pierce starts quietly. "It's her decision. Besides, it's done."

Aaron's back is to us and he's silently cutting his apple.

"I needed the money, Aaron." My own desperation is coming through my voice. It's not like I <u>wanted</u> to be in this mess. It's not like I wanted to lose everything I had or be in debt to my friends and invading their home.

And I can't even think about the thing that really started it all, the genuine fucked up mess that made me desperate enough to borrow money from my old boss in the first place. I can't think about <u>that</u> at all.

All I know is this is the situation I'm in, regardless of the reasons why, and I have to do something to make things better. Anything.

"Okay," he says, softer.

"I won't really see him, anyway. I'm just cooking his meals and getting out. It's only for two weeks. Then I'll have enough to pay you guys back and get my own place."

He turns around, resting one hand on the counter. "Don't let him take advantage of you."

"I won't."

I hope I won't.

"Give her a little bit of credit," Pierce says.

Aaron picks up an apple slice, his sorry excuse for dinner, and takes a bite. I take another bite of my dinner too, chewing and stewing.

"I just don't want to see you get hurt again."

I nod and glance up at him before looking back to my plate and taking another bite. "I know."

"Just be careful. Keep your distance."

"I know, I know."

Picking up another apple slice and leaving the rest on the counter, he comes back to the couch and sits down. We chew in silence for a few more minutes.

"I miss the days when you didn't have time for boys."

I glance at him quickly, hoping I didn't mistake the teasing tone in his voice. He's giving me that look, making things up with me.

I smile. "Okay, Dad."

That's the end of it. We've been friends too long and through too much to let things drag on. He said what he had to say.

And I heard him.

I'm driving Aaron's old Honda Hatchback through an upper class, coastal neighborhood toward Rayce Rivers' house. I didn't think through how my new job would affect Aaron and Pierce's schedules. Coordinating transportation for what's basically a split shift, once in the morning and once in the early evening, turned out to be a logistical hassle. Eventually we figured out that I'll take Aaron to class in the morning, pick him up after rehearsals in the evening, and use his car to get back and forth to work in between.

It makes me wish I'd agreed to three weeks instead of two so I could get a cheap scooter or something, too. Just some way to get around, because this transportation arrangement isn't going to fly very long. God, I hate being a burden on everyone.

I miss having my own car, but what choice did I have? At the time, I needed the cash more than I needed a car. Here I am still needing cash, and look where it's coming from. My boss. Again.

But this is legit. It's not like before.

The GPS on my phone brings me to a sprawling modern, two-story home with smooth, straight lines and bold architecture. It's white and practically glimmering in the bright, California sun. There's a huge front landing with tall double doors, the large window above them giving a glimpse of the Art Deco style chandelier hanging in the foyer. The broad, sloping front lawn is covered in bright, green grass and has been expertly landscaped with mature Monterey pine and a few clusters of low bushes. The white house is on a slight hill, set back from the road, and a good distance from the neighbors.

The entire setting exudes a sense of power and confidence, without being overly flashy about it. Sort of like the man who owns it.

Tingles climb up my spine, and I take a deep breath. *It's just a job.*

There's a circular drive, which breaks off to the left side of the house. I navigate Aaron's oh-so-humble Hatchback down this side drive. The house is to my right and a row of hedges are to my left. Before I reach the freaking six-car garage ahead, there's a break in the hedges, just as I was told there would be. I turn through them and see there is, indeed, a small concrete parking area big enough for three cars.

I'm surprised to see a little red Acura, probably at least ten years old, parked in one of the spaces. I pull in next to it and kill the engine. In the silence that follows, the thumping of my heartbeat seems to echo inside the car. I couldn't say if I'm nervous or excited or what. Everything's bouncing around inside me and all mixed up.

I'm acutely aware of the fact that I refused to bring him a piece of cake, but he got me to agree to serve him two meals a day, day after day.

Point Mr. Rivers.

But if I'm going to do a job, I'm going to do it. Last night I spent three hours re-creating the kind of forms we used at Powerhouse Personal Chef, coming up with menu options, and in general trying to make sure I didn't show up looking like an amateur. I stopped by the office supply store after dropping Aaron off this morning, and got everything organized in a little half-inch binder. It helped me feel that this is a real job. All I have to do is focus on the work, and everything will be okay.

But now that I am out here, sitting in my car knowing Rayce is inside that big, beautiful, white house, and I'm about to go into it?

I can't seem to make myself open the door and get out.

What if I set a gigantic trap for myself? What if I make the same mistakes all over again? I doubt Aaron and Pierce would come to my rescue this time.

Who could blame them? If I did something like that again, I'd have no one to blame but myself.

This thought strengthens me somehow. This is in __my__ control. All I have to do is watch my own actions. I cling to my resolve, grab the binder, and get out of the car.

I go through the break in the hedges and toward the side entrance near the garage. The sound of ocean waves is coming from somewhere behind the house. This neighborhood is on a bluff overlooking the Pacific. I caught several glimpses of it in between houses on the way here, but I haven't seen what his view looks like yet.

I approach the door. I don't hear any sounds coming from inside the house. I hesitate, then knock and drop my hands.

I take a deep breath, inhaling the scent of fresh, salty sea air. I focus on making sure I have a professional, neutral expression on my face.

The handle turns, my heartbeat speeds up slightly in anticipation, and the door swings open.

It isn't Rayce on the other side. It's a tall, thin woman, who looks to be in her upper forties. She's wearing tan slacks and an orange polo shirt with the logo of a cleaning service on the left breast.

Oh. Right.

I remember the red Acura.

She's wearing cleaning gloves and has a rag in one hand. She offers me a warm smile. "Are you Emma?"

I nod.

"I'm Lilith. Come on in." She backs up, opening the door wider, and I step inside. "Mr. Rivers explained that you'd be working here. He asked me to show you to the kitchen."

Well, all right then.

Maybe I have nothing to worry about after all.

Which is good. Totally not disappointing.

We go down a broad hallway that's well-lit and inviting. We pass a massive utility room and another door that's closed. Further down, there's a gorgeous formal dining room to the right and an open entryway into the kitchen on the left.

Lilith indicates that I'm to go into the kitchen. "Here you go. He said for you to familiarize yourself with things."

"Okay."

She hustles off deeper into the house and just like that I'm left alone.

I take a shallow breath and slowly breathe it out.

I wander into the kitchen, my senses alert for any indication of where in the house he might be. Part of me expects him to jump out at any moment. But there's no sight or sound of him.

Not surprisingly, the kitchen is gorgeous, with marble countertops, tall, luxurious cabinets, and professional-grade steel appliances. There's a huge central island with a little sink on one end, high-backed barstools at the other, and an assortment of fruit in a heavy ceramic bowl in the center. The kitchen opens to the living room, which is so large there's two separate seating areas, with room to spare.

I set the binder on the counter and go into the living room, and it's here that I get my first glimpse of his view.

Through the floor to ceiling windows that cover the entire west-facing wall, there's a spacious backyard that looks like it belongs to a resort, with covered cabana-style patio areas on either end of the deck and a massive infinity pool. Beyond that, a stunning panoramic of the Pacific Ocean.

"Holy shit," I mumble.

I long to go outside to get a better look. Paradise is mere steps away. Instead I hover there for a moment, taking it all in. What would it be like to enjoy this view every day? I imagine sitting under the patio, a glass of wine in hand as I watch the sun set over the ocean. He's there too, his legs propped up on the table, his warm arm draped over my bare shoulders as the wind brushes through.

Oh my god, Emma, seriously? What's wrong with you?

I turn away from the fantasy scene to examine the rest of his home. In the center of the living room is a cluster of large, comfortable-looking white chairs gathered around a low stone coffee table.

In the far end of the room, a second seating area includes a couch, a loveseat, and a couple chairs, and is faced away from the windows and toward a curved wall. Centered on this wall is a large, flat screen TV that curves along with the wall. God, even the TV looks fancy in this place.

Above the TV is a massive painting that must have cost a pretty mint. It's not the abstract, modern art I would've expected. It's an Impressionistic painting of the ocean at sunrise, and is almost as compelling as the real thing. It's the only touch of color in the entire room.

From the living room I can see the large entryway, with its tall double front doors and soaring windows above. This foyer leads to other rooms on both sides, one of which is the dining room I passed on my way in, but I don't know what the other room is.

The foyer's floor is stunning. There's a large, circular pattern in the middle: an intricate, swirling, tile mosaic of tans, blues, and greens. The movement of the swirling pattern actually reminds me of my tattoo.

I'm dying to walk all over that gorgeous entryway. Bare foot. Maybe do a spin or two.

Centered above the mosaic, hanging from the tall ceiling, is the massive chandelier I saw through the windows from outside. Someone coming in through the front doors would come through that stunning entryway and to the living room's centralized sitting area with its pristine, comfy-looking white chairs, all the while presented with a million-dollar view of the ocean.

On the far end of the living room, next to the windows, a stairwell disappears into the basement. Near this is another curving stairway that leads, I can only presume, up to the bedrooms.

I wonder if that's where he is.

I hear someone coming up the basement stairs and my heart leaps into my throat. I jolt back to the kitchen, realizing I haven't been doing what I was told. I hurry to open a cupboard door, willing my heart to settle down.

Inside are an array of large serving dishes and platters. Hand gripping the cupboard door, I glance over my shoulder. The person who comes into view on the stairs isn't Rayce Rivers. Yet again. It's another cleaning woman, wearing the same outfit as the other one and carrying a little caddy full of cleaning supplies.

Disappointment drops into the pit of my stomach.

I chastise myself for being foolish. I remind myself that Rayce Rivers is the downside to working here, not the upside.

When she gets to the landing, she gives me a glance and a smile, which I return. She doesn't say anything to me, just crosses the living room and disappears down the hallway.

I return to the open cupboard, my hand still on the knob. Okay. I'm here to do a job. I need to stop screwing around. I spend the next few minutes going through some of the cupboards, admiring the state-of-the-art appliances and cookware, and trying not to anticipate his appearance.

Everything is neatly put in its place and well organized. It's all spotless and looks brand-new. Does he actually *use* anything in this kitchen?

There's a pantry in the back corner, but before I get that far, something in the corner of my eye gets my attention.

My heart stops momentarily. There he is, nearly at the bottom of the upper stairway, which I'm sure I correctly guessed leads to his bedroom.

He's wearing black suit pants and a white, button-down shirt. His untied tie is around his neck and his suit jacket is draped over his arm. He's not wearing shoes, but is padding over to me in black dress socks.

Fuck, that's hot.

"Good morning, Emma." He hangs his jacket on the back of one of the barstools.

"Good morning, Mr. Rivers." My blood is pumping thickly.

But it doesn't matter how sexy he looks. I retrieve the binder, grateful for an excuse to turn my eyes away from him. I locate the checklist I printed out last night. "I thought we could start by discussing menu options."

I'm forced to turn back in his direction and am immediately distracted as he lifts his collar and starts to tie his tie with strong, decisive hands.

He wraps one piece smartly around the other. He's fast and precise. I already know this knot will turn out perfectly.

"I'm sorry, but there's no time for that this morning. I had to schedule an early meeting."

My eyes go to his. "Oh?" I hope I don't sound as disappointed as I feel. In addition to feeling disappointed, I'm also confused. I wonder why Alice didn't change what time she told me to be here. "I could've come earlier." Geez, my first day and he's already leaving hungry.

"No need. We can discuss things later." He lifts his jaw slightly as he flips the tie up and through a loop. "For now, look through the pantry and decide on something for tonight. I already had breakfast."

He finishes a neat Windsor knot, and tightens it snug against the top button of his shirt. It somehow makes his shoulders look even more broad, his chest even more inviting.

Dammit, Emma! Knock it off.

Determined not to gawk, I turn my back to him and open the pantry. It's a large walk-in and has plenty of food for just one person I suppose, but it's such a big space it still feels a little bare. I take quick stock, my eyes landing on, unbelievably, several boxes of sugary, multicolored breakfast cereals.

I grab one and turn toward him. "Is this what you ate?" I'm giving him an incredulous look.

That beautiful smile of his emerges and my heart stutters.

"Yes."

I glance at the box, then back at him. "It's no wonder you need help."

He laughs and turns away. I'm delighted by his laughter one second, and let down by his exit the next. I watch him cross the living room and pad quietly back up the stairs. Is that all I get for today?

Gee. I was clearly worked up over nothing.

I put the box away and take another deep breath. Feeling a little irritated, I continue to assess what he has in the pantry. It's a motley assortment of things like Flaming Hot Cheetos and Oreos alongside bags of quinoa and little jars of gourmet pesto.

I've advanced to a slender cupboard full of spices when he makes another appearance, this time the muffled step of his shoes announcing his entrance. I look automatically, then quickly return to the cupboard, refusing to ogle this gorgeous specimen of a man as he crosses his living room paradise.

"None of these spices look like they've been opened."

"I don't use them. Lizzy bought them for me."

I watch him grab his suit coat and slide it on. "Lizzy?"

"My sister."

"Oh." Well, isn't that cute? I've only thought of her as Ms. Elizabeth Rivers, but him calling her Lizzy makes them both a little more adorable. And more human.

"She mistakenly thought I wasn't cooking because I didn't have the stuff."

I close the cupboard door and cock my head at him. It's starting to come together now. "Did she buy the pots and pans, too?"

He nods, adjusting his suit coat so it sits squarely on his broad shoulders.

"Don't you cook at all?"

"Not if I can help it."

"You just eat Fruity Pebbles all day, Mr. Rivers?"

There's that smile again, but it falters as his eyes skip over my body. "Why are you wearing a uniform?"

I'm wearing the same kind of shirt and slacks I would wear to work. "Wasn't I supposed to?"

"Not in my home, you won't."

"But they are." I gesture toward the hallway, indicating the cleaning ladies.

"That's different. They work for a service. You work for me."

I cross my arms, suddenly feeling prickly. I should be glad of the reminder that I work for him, glad he's not flirting with me, glad this is going down just as it should. When guys like him are interested in girls like me it's for the wrong reasons anyway. Hell, if I'm going to come here as his employee I *want* to be in uniform. But I'm inexplicably annoyed with him.

"Yes, I know that, Mr. Rivers. But shouldn't I—"

"Look, Emma." He comes around the island toward me.

The closer he gets the more my body temperature rises. I can't stop the hot blush from blooming on my cheeks, but I hold his eyes and stand my ground, arms firmly in front of my chest.

"There's really only three things you need to know here. One, no uniform. Two, cook whatever you want so long as it's not spinach. I'll eat anything else. Three, call me Rayce. Understand?"

"Yes, Mr. Rivers."

I'm not trying to be obnoxious, I swear. It just slipped out.

At the same time, I shouldn't call him by his first name. We need boundaries, and that one is so basic.

He gives me a look. We both stand here not saying anything, and shift into a stare down. He's close to me. I could reach out and run my fingertips down the front of his shirt, feeling his chest underneath. The heat in my cheeks is slowly creeping down my neck.

It's not my defiance that's making me edgy. It's the way he's looking at me. Not like someone who's only ever seen me a few times, but like he's known me for years and has had to deal with my stubbornness over and over again.

Also, definitely not the way a boss looks at an employee.

"Does this mean you're serving spinach for dinner?"

I smile, then press my lips together quickly, chasing it away. "Of course not. I just... want to keep things appropriate."

"There's nothing inappropriate about my given name. It's not as though my parents decided to call me Dick."

I stifle a laugh. I shouldn't encourage this familiarity by laughing, but God, he deadpanned it so perfectly.

He comes a fraction of an inch closer. He's not close enough to be directly in my personal space, but plenty close enough to make my heart race. "Alice assured me I could trust you to make this a painless experience," he says in all seriousness.

"Yes. Yes, of course." Dammit. I've made him uncomfortable in his own house. That's breaking rule number one in this business.

"I'm not Mr. Rivers here. I'm Rayce. That's what you'll call me in my home."

He's the client. He gets to decide these things. He does. I still hesitate because, and this feels ridiculous to say, it feels like we'd be taking a… step. Still, what can I say? "All right."

He waits. Raises his brow. That damned demanding brow. I know what he wants. My heart is pounding so soundly I wouldn't be surprised if he could hear it.

"Rayce."

I was right. His name on my lips does feel different. More intimate.

*So* nice.

There's a glimmer in his eye. Point two, Mr. Rivers.

He smoothly fastens the first button of his suit coat. "Thank you, Emma. Serve dinner at six."

With that he grabs an apple out of the fruit bowl on the counter and exits into the hallway. He's heading for the garage, I assume. Leaving for real this time. Before he disappears from my sight, Lilith passes him in the hall.

"Thank you, Lilith."

"You're welcome, Mr. Rivers."

But no correction is forthcoming. So <u>she</u> can wear a uniform and call him Mr. Rivers, but I'm to wear jeans and call him Rayce? I'd call him out on it, but I hear the door leading to the garage close behind him.

I check the time, cursing myself for feeling disappointed yet again.

I got here just sixteen minutes ago and it's already over.

# Chapter 9

## Rayce

Today has been the longest day of my life. Usually, time flies when I'm at work. I love it here. I love everything about it, from overseeing meetings with our excellent management staff to analyzing cash flow projections. Business is in my blood, and when I stay too late or work too long, I never mind it.

But today? The minutes are crawling toward six o'clock. Time is playing tricks on me. It feels like an hour goes by, but when I look at the time in the corner of my screen, I'm lucky if fifteen minutes have passed.

Between the time I agreed to let Emma be my personal chef to when I saw her this morning, I came to two conclusions.

One, I saw her before I knew she was an employee, and would have spoken to her if she hadn't disappeared on me. That makes her fair game.

Two, the fact that she is an employee is definitely a problem that needs to be solved. But there must be a solution, and I intend to find it. This is a temporary glitch. A momentary obstacle. I smooth out glitches and overcome obstacles all day long. I get paid handsomely to do it, too.

This isn't anything I can't fix.

So yes, I have a plan with Emma. And no, I won't feel guilty about it.

She's mine. She just doesn't know it yet.

The farther along I get on this path, the less I care that she's an employee. I should care. I want to care. But even when I try to feel guilty, to make myself stop what I know I'm doing, I can't get it to stick.

Because if I thought I wanted to know more about this woman before, it's even worse now. We had maybe five minutes together this morning, and what did she do? She drew me in even more. She moved through my kitchen with a graceful confidence I can't describe. She smiled at me with such openness and not a trace of guile. And she's so damned beautiful.

She stood up to me, too. God, her spunk is attractive as hell. She's not like other women I know, whose tactics are varying degrees of annoying. She doesn't cower before me. She doesn't pout and manipulate like a spoiled princess. She doesn't try to lure me in with sexual prowess.

She faces me like an equal.

So, yes, six o'clock can't come quickly enough. Because if there's one thing I want from Emma Swanson, it's more.

# Chapter 10

## Emma

Even though dinner is at six, I start anticipating his return well before then. He said dinner was at six, but does that mean he comes home at six, or sooner? It's not unreasonable to think he might come home at five, is it? Because that's exactly when I start listening for the side door.

Okay, 4:42, but no earlier, I swear.

I'm at the gas stove in his gorgeous kitchen, using a top-of-the-line, eight-inch, All-Clad, stainless steel skillet for the first time. This is seriously nice cookware. The pork tenderloin filet is browning perfectly, sizzling and smelling divine.

I'm in the house alone. Before Lilith left this morning, she gave me a sealed envelope with my name on the front. Inside were instructions to operate the security keypad, as well as a code that's just for me.

I find the way he's handling things a little confusing. In some ways, he's kept his distance. He didn't answer the door, and left it to Lilith to give me instructions upon my arrival and a way to get back in before she left. But he also insisted I don't wear a uniform and call him by his first name.

Maybe he really does just want to feel comfortable in his own home? Maybe he doesn't want to be served dinner by someone in uniform? I can understand that.

Then there's the whole thing about figuring out the menu. That would have given him the perfect excuse to talk to me, if that's what he wanted to do. But instead he said, 'Anything but spinach.' If he really does intend to leave it up to me, that gives us nothing else to talk about.

Did I imagine everything that happened in his office? I mean, what was it really? He didn't overtly say much of anything.

Well, other than asking me if I have a boyfriend. And he did say Pierce was an idiot to think I'm not his type. And that his being gay was no excuse.

Maybe he was just trying to give me a compliment? Maybe I misinterpreted his looks, both in his office and in the parking garage?

No. I turn off the heat and transfer the skillet directly into the preheated oven, shaking my head. No, I'm not doing this. That's when I get into trouble, when I start questioning myself.

Maybe Mr. Rayce Rivers has lost interest in his little employee, but I'm not going to convince myself he wasn't looking at me like he wanted me, when I know he did.

But if he's already bored with the idea? Well, that's great. I don't want things any other way.

I look at the clock on the sleek, black microwave. Twenty-one minutes to six. There's a fluttering in my chest. Probably just... pre-performance jitters. Well, the only way around jitters is through them. I don't even have to think about it. I focus on what needs to be done.

While the tenderloin is baking, I assemble the salad and clean up so there's no sign of my prep work. I go to the refrigerator and pull out the bowl of date and cilantro relish I made ahead of time and set it by the stove.

I glance at the clock. Eight minutes to six. The pork only needs another minute, and still no sign of Rayce. Maybe he's going to be late. He certainly has plenty to do down there. I come up with a plan in case I need to keep his dinner warm, ignoring the foolish disappointment I feel at the possibility he may not be on time. I continue with my preparations in case he does, in fact, walk through the door when he said he would.

When the pork is ready, I pull it out of the oven and lay the meat on a wooden cutting board to rest. Meanwhile, I set his place at the end of the bar. He has a few sets of dishes, and I chose the one that best complements his meal.

I've been debating whether to set things for him here or in the dining room, but one person in that large dining room seems so lonely. I don't like the idea of him eating by himself anywhere, but at least the kitchen feels more cozy.

I turn the heat on the drippings in the pan to warm them, and this is when I hear the door open at the end of the hall. Gripping the handle of the skillet, I look toward the opening to the hallway, holding my breath. The tapping of his dress shoes on the floor gets closer and closer.

Breathe, Emma.

I turn back to the stove before he comes into view. For a split second I lose track of what I was doing... then gratefully remember. I scoot the bowl closer, and pour the pan drippings over the relish.

"Good evening, Emma."

I keep my back to him. "Good evening." I don't call him Mr. Rivers, or Rayce. If he notices, or cares, he doesn't comment.

I glance at the time. Two minutes until six. Perfect. I'm right on schedule. I give the relish a quick toss. "Dinner is about ready."

There's some sort of shuffling at the bar, which draws my attention. He's placed a briefcase on one of the stools and is hanging his jacket on the seat back.

I don't remember him leaving with a briefcase, but maybe it had been by the door to the garage or in his car. He didn't have a briefcase when I saw him in the parking garage either.

"Working tonight?"

I regret it as soon as the words come out of my mouth. It's not my business what he does. I don't need to get familiar with him. <u>Stay focused.</u>

I retrieve his plate from his place at the bar.

He places his phone face up on the counter. "There's always work to be done." He doesn't sound unhappy about it. If anything, he sounds like he's looking forward to it.

I wonder if he's going to disappear like he did this morning, but he lingers, one hand casually resting on the counter as he watches me work. "What are we having?"

Does he mean 'we' as in 'he and I'? Or 'we' as in the royal 'we'?

"Seared tenderloin with date and cilantro relish." I've laid the tenderloin on his plate and am drizzling the colorful relish down the center. "The relish has dates, cilantro, orange juice, and a bit of sliced cranberries." I grab the salad and begin placing it on his plate with tongs.

I tuck the dirty dishes and tools in the dishwasher as I finish with them. I gave this some thought ahead of time. I wanted to make sure I wasn't disturbing him with clean up while he was trying to eat. By the time I've placed his plate back on the placemat, the kitchen is clean. Other than the wooden cutting board, which I'll wash by hand, there's no sign that I've been here.

He's still standing, but looking over his meal. My jitters return with abandon. What if he doesn't like it? I purposely picked a meal that was a favorite for many of our clients. It's usually a no-fail option. But still, we always have the menu discussion with clients first. Always. All he gave me was "no spinach."

Why couldn't he have given me ten minutes to talk? About the menu, I mean. Now I get to wonder day after day if I'm giving him what he wants.

He bends over slightly, getting a closer look. "This is beautiful, Emma. If it tastes as good as it looks, you could work in one of our kitchens."

His words swell inside my chest more than I'd like them to. He catches me smiling at his complement and rewards me with a smile of his own. That handsome smile does something it shouldn't to my chest.

Grateful for something to do, I take the cutting board to the sink and begin rinsing it off. "I already have more work for you than I can handle."

"It seems you're handling things fine. It's a shame there's not enough for two. You should be able to enjoy the fruits of your labors."

My heart flutters at the idea of having dinner with him. It's such a pretty image, the two of us sitting together, talking and enjoying a meal like we were on a date. Knowing this could never happen, and would be trouble if it did, I try to push the image from my mind.

I'm having zero luck with this.

"Well, as long as you eat it, I'll be happy." If I made something like this at home Aaron would never touch it.

"I promise to eat every bite."

I glance over my shoulder at him. He's taken his seat, in front of the only plate in the kitchen.

I don't like this. I don't want to leave him to eat his dinner by himself. Maybe I should join him, just to keep him company. But that's stupid. He lives alone. He eats alone all the time. I'm sure he doesn't give it a second thought.

That's not really why you want to join him, anyway.

God, why can't I just keep my head screwed on straight?

I tap the faucet off, snatch the dishtowel, and start forcefully drying the cutting board. I can pretend to myself that I don't know why I'm irritated, but I do.

I've been looking forward to seeing him all day, and here I am just seconds away from leaving. I've been wondering what would happen the next time we saw his other, and the answer is nothing. I made his dinner, and now I'm going home.

It's exactly how it should be. But I wish it weren't.

Because I'm a fucking moron. I still can't believe I'm fantasizing about my boss <u>again.</u>

Not that I exactly fantasized about Chad. It was different. Very different. I mean, Rayce still has sometimes seemed like a spider spinning a web. But the difference is, this time I <u>want</u> to get caught.

Is it because there's so much more to desire about this man?

Or am I just hell-bent on self-destruction, and that's what's really drawing me in?

As I'm putting the cutting board away, the clink of his silverware on the plate tells me he's cutting into his meat. Preparing to take a bite.

Jitters again. I really want him to like this.

"Damn, Emma."

I turn, towel still in my hand. He's nodding appreciatively, cutting off his next bite while still chewing.

"You like it?" I didn't mean to sound so vulnerable.

He gives me a warm smile. This isn't the sexy, devious smile I've seen before. This is open and friendly and reassuring. "It's fantastic."

I smile back, bouncing on my toes slightly. I've always cared whether or not a client was happy with their meal, but I've never cared this much.

"How long have you been cooking?" He takes another bite.

"A little over a year."

His eyebrows raise. "Is that all? What were you doing before?"

My heart thumps uncomfortably in my chest. Not because he asked, but because I almost told him. "I know you said you're not picky, but I'd feel better if we could talk about menus. It's kind of stressful to have to guess."

"Hmm. That makes sense." He sets his fork and knife on the edge of his plate with a soft clink, and gets up from his chair, heading for the wine cooler beneath one end of the counter. "Have a seat. We can talk about it now. And don't think I didn't notice the subject change."

"Now?" Don't sit down, Emma. Don't you do it. "But you're eating."

He pulls a bottle of red out of the cooler, then retrieves two long stemmed wine glasses hanging upside down from the rack above it.

He starts to pour a glass. "Don't you want me to eat?"

"I don't want to disturb your meal. No, none for me thanks." I hold out my hand to stop him from pouring the second glass. He gives me a smirk like he knows I really do want that glass of wine, but doesn't press.

He's sits back down and gestures with his fork that I'm to take a seat.

Do. Not. Sit. Down.

He begins to cut another bite.

"Won't you feel weird if I'm watching you eat?"

"No. But if it helps you feel better, I could feed you bites from my fork. That way you're eating, too."

Oh, he's back to playing now, because he gives me a devilish look that makes my toes curl. "Now that's exactly the kind of thing you shouldn't be saying!"

He laughs. "Why not?"

I cross my arms, thrown off guard by that laugh. It's so light and free of malice. Not like Chad, who half the time seemed to be teasing and belittling me. Rayce is playing, having fun, full of confidence that I'm having fun, too.

How does he know that?

Still, we can't keep doing… this. We need lines and can't cross them. Well, he can't cross them. I'm just doing my job.

"You know why not."

He's still chuckling, apparently realizing I'm not near as angry as I should be. His laugh is so warm and rumbly. It makes me want to squeeze him.

I do want to sit with him. I don't want him to be alone and I do want to sit with him and I don't even care what we talk about. I want to ask him about his day and tell him about mine. Then I want him to pull me onto his lap and bring me into his arms and show me what it feel like to be attended to by Mr. Rayce Rivers.

Jesus, how are we ever going to get through two weeks if he breaks down my walls so easily and I just let him?

This is exactly what you want him to do.

But what I want doesn't matter. I need to stay strong.

"I'm here to cook and serve your meals. That's it." I wanted to sound firm, but don't think I pulled it off. If he tells me to sit down one more time, I know I will do it.

Ask me.

He's unfazed, still in control. "Then we'll talk menus in the morning. Does that suit you, Emma?"

No, make me stay with you.

Yes, let me out of here.

I keep my arms tight in front of my chest and nod.

"Good."

I don't move. He sets down his silverware. He takes a sip of his wine, watching me over the rim of the glass.

My breath shallows and my thighs clench. He has a bit of stubble on his jaw, just a hint of it, and I long to brush my fingertips over it.

It would be so easy. I know he wants it, too. All I have to do is give in.

He puts down his glass and gets up slowly, his eyes still holding mine. My heart pounds and my skin tingles as he approaches. He stops just in front of me, close enough that I have to look up at him. Close enough that I smell the slightest hint of aftershave on his skin.

I'm a whirlwind of thought and sensation. I crave the touch of his mouth against mine, and betray myself by licking my lips slightly.

He notices me do this. I try to correct the mistake by pressing my lips together firmly, keeping my body in place. It's only years of training my body to obey that keeps me from leaning into him like I want to.

It's unfair. If we had just talked at the art show, who he is wouldn't matter. Who I am wouldn't matter. I could've chased my desire for him in any direction.

But would he have wanted me? Why didn't he talk to me then, when he said he saw me? Why is he so interested now?

My gut sinks a bit at this thought. Guys like forbidden fruit. That's what Chad had said when I found out he was married.

Those deep blue eyes are holding me in place, and there's no question that Mr. Rayce Rivers wants me. But why does he want me? And why do I want him, after the hell I've been through?

Yet.

If he leaned down right now, what would I do?

His eyes dart to my lips, but he doesn't move. I'm barely breathing. I'm tortured wondering what he's going to do next.

When I speak, it's almost a whisper. "Are you going to kiss me?"

He nods slightly. "Eventually."

A little thrill skitters through me. I shake my head slowly. "You can't."

That smile again. That smile that says he will do whatever damn thing he wants, and I'll like it. I probably would, too.

"You can't," I make myself say. "I work for you. That's all."

I want to say, Don't you know I've been down this path before? Don't you know the only thing at the end of this road is heartbreak? Why do you have to be so sexy and charming and demanding and appealing?

He nods slightly, like he understands my torn desires better than I think. "Then you'd better get going." He says it gently, but there's a firmness to his voice, too. It is a command that will not be questioned. He just brought an end to any wondering, or fantasizing, about what happens next.

What happens next is I go home.

Disappointment pools at the pit of my stomach.

Well, I got what I wanted, didn't I? I can't just say this is only a job. I need to act like it.

"Right."

We go our separate ways, him to his seat with his usual suave, and me to my purse and keys on the far counter. My legs are a little soft, like half-cooked noodles. I'm already imagining what would've happened if he'd kissed me instead. The image is so strong I can almost feel the stubble against my chin. I can definitely feel the swooping in my chest.

Still, it's better that I'm leaving. It is. He may be the most intriguing man I've ever met, but he's my boss and that's all there is to it.

Just before I enter the hallway, I say, "Goodnight, Mr. Rivers."

"Emma." That commanding voice again.

I stop and face him, hoping he will summon me back to him and hating myself for it.

Eyes on his plate, he presses his napkin to his lips with both hands and sets it on the counter. He leans forward slightly, resting on both elbows.

He looks me in the eye, and it is our strongest connection yet. In this moment, he's not my boss. He's not Mr. Rayce Rivers, King of the luxury resort on the hill. He's a man, one I feel I know better than makes any sense.

"You will call me Rayce," he says quietly but firmly, "or call me nothing. That is non-negotiable. Do you understand?"

I press my lips together. I nod.

"Thank you. Good night, Emma."

"Good night."

I silently go down the hallway and let myself out of the house, wishing I called him

Rayce like I wanted to, and leaving him to finish his dinner alone.

# Chapter 11

## Rayce

In the five minutes Emma and I were in the same room together, I went from one desire to the next so quickly it's a wonder I didn't get whiplash. I wanted to run my hands over every curve on her body. I wanted to eat dinner with her and ask all the things I want to know about her. I wanted to pull her into my arms and suck on that full, bottom lip. I wanted to say, "Stop fucking around. We both know where this is going." But I also want her to come to me without all the guilt and hesitation I see in those lovely blue eyes.

When she was standing right in front of me, so clearly torn, and looking up at me with that trusting, open expression that made my heart squeeze, I longed to give her a kiss that would've said what I was feeling: I promise not to hurt you. Come away with me.

I wanted to do everything except what I did do. It just about killed me to send her off. There will come a time when I kiss Emma Swanson, but that time was not tonight.

I eat a few bites more after she leaves, but the kitchen feels more quiet and empty than it usually does. The ticking of the clock on the dining room wall punctuates the air with relentless tenacity.

I rub a thumb along the edge of the woven maroon placemat. It's part of the stuff my sister picked out when she insisted I "set up house like a real person." I don't think they've ever been used.

Emma put a lot of thought into giving me a beautiful place to eat. It seems a shame to abandon it.

But I can't stop hearing that damned clock.

Setting my fork and knife on my plate, I pick it up and leave the rest on the counter, including the wine. Before leaving the kitchen, I tuck my phone in my pocket. Because I never, ever go anywhere without my phone. Plate in one hand and briefcase in the other, I make my way through the living room and foyer to my office.

It has wood paneling, mahogany furniture, and a large window that keeps the room from being too dark. It's a more welcoming place than the stark emptiness of the rest of the house. Besides, it has a good history. This is where I do my best work.

Though, as I pour myself some brandy from the decanter on the sideboard, and settle in at the computer with the scent of Emma's fine cooking in the air, I'm not sure how much I'll be able to concentrate on work tonight, regardless of where I'm sitting.

# Chapter 12

## Emma

I'm working my way through the aisles of the upscale grocery store close to Rayce's house, and irritated by everything. The wine bottle clinking in the cart. The miles and miles of artisan cheese you'd never see in my local store, with price tags that only make them affordable because I'm buying them for <u>the boss.</u>

Even the fact that the cart's wheels are apparently perfectly aligned and don't squeak or rattle at all.

Who knew grocery shopping could be so luxurious?

Faux wooden shelving for boxed goods? Check.

Classical music piped in over the sound system? Check.

Five hundred dollar bottles of wine? Check.

I was tempted to pick that one up with his credit card, just to spite him, but he probably wouldn't care. I doubt Mr. Rayce Rivers would look twice at that bill.

All he cares about is making sure I prepare dinner for two. That's what his text said earlier. Please prepare dinner for two.

It's not that I care that he obviously has a date. I mean, it's Friday night and he's Mr. Rayce Rivers, Swan Pointe's most eligible bachelor. Why shouldn't he have a date?

What did I expect? Since that first dinner on Wednesday, our interactions have been brief enough that I could almost believe this is just business, if my boss weren't such a flirt. Though, I've seen him in such small doses I'm not sure it counts. I didn't see him at all this morning. Not that I care.

I toss a bundle of garlic cloves into the basket, where it rolls and rolls backward until it hits the paper bag of artisan rolls that are so fresh they're still warm.

No, I don't care that he has a date. I care that he's a cad. As if I didn't already know. I wonder if his hot date knows how much he's been flirting with his newest employee lately.

"Eventually," I mutter under my breath. He thinks he'll kiss me eventually? Oh no, sir.

I cross my arms, eyeing the heads of red leaf lettuce. All of which look absolutely fucking perfect. Do employees hover nearby waiting for the edge of a leaf to brown so they can ship it off to the stores in my neighborhood?

I wonder what that job pays. Lettuce shipper.

I grab a head, shove it into a bag, and try to chastise myself. Again. Because nothing about this situation is irritating me more than the fact that it's irritating me. I don't want it to irritate me.

But every time I think, I'm not irritated or I don't care what he does or It's not any of my business, I only get more irritated.

It's like my body knows I'm lying to myself and won't stand for it.

I reach for a bundle of asparagus just as the misting system turns on, drenching my hand. I snatch the bundle away and shake it, sending the cold droplets flying. I wrangle it into the plastic bag, which is not cooperating, and toss it into the cart.

Stupid, rich asparagus.

# Chapter 13

## Rayce

At first, I don't notice what Emma's done.

When I come home and into the kitchen, all I see is her. She's at the counter filling two little burgundy ramekins with what looks like a yellow cream of some sort. Her hair is pulled into a soft knot at the base of her neck, and a loose strand is resting on her shoulder.

I don't know if it's crazy, but I'm in love with this woman's neck.

She's wearing a cute burgundy top that flairs at the waist, over black skinny jeans. This no uniform policy was a good plan.

"Evening, Emma." I set my briefcase on a stool at the bar.

She's leaning over the little ramekins, focused on her task apparently, and doesn't turn or pause in her movements at all. "Evening."

Other than that first time, she still hasn't called me Rayce. I said it was Rayce or nothing, and apparently she's chosen nothing. Not that she's had much opportunity for either. I've purposely given her some space so she has a chance to adjust to things, and maybe want what's going on between us more than she wants to resist it.

Tonight I'll find out if I've waited long enough. It's sure as hell been long enough for me. The last two days have felt like an eternity.

There's a rich, meaty scent in the air that gets my stomach rumbling. "Smells delicious."

"Thank you." Again, she doesn't look in my direction. Her tone seems a bit tart, too. I head in her direction, intending to find out what's wrong, but now the dining room is in my line of sight again and I see what I missed before.

"What's all this?"

I wander into the room. The table is set with my fine china—another Lizzy purchase—covered with an actual tablecloth, and sprouting an impressive arrangement of pink and white roses smattered with day lilies and chrysanthemums.

"It's for your date." She zooms by, a ramekin in each hand, and sets each on the table with a smart thud.

"My date?"

"I thought things should look nice." She faces me at last, clasping her hands in front of her and raising her chin. "If you're going to have a woman for dinner you should attempt to impress her."

A grin tugs at the corner of my mouth. Oh, this is adorable.

She gives my emerging grin an impatient glance, then continues. "I've prepared cinnamon and almond crusted roasted duck, steamed asparagus with gorgonzola cream sauce, and chilled beat salad."

"Wow."

"The salad tastes better than it sounds." With that she zips past me, back into the kitchen.

I follow her, fully smiling now. "That sounds wonderful, Emma. Thank you. I have a question for you though."

"Hm." She's back to not looking at me, pulling a covered bowl from the refrigerator.

"I told you to prepare dinner for two and you thought that meant I have a date?"

She straightens and blinks at me, the refrigerator still standing open. "What?"

"Why did you assume dinner for two meant a date?"

"Uh…" A beautiful blush is creeping over her cheekbones. The refrigerator is still standing open.

"How did you know it's not my brother?"

She glances at the huge bouquet of flowers on the table. "Oh god."

"Or a business colleague."

Her eyes leap to mine. She's properly mortified now. "Oh shit. I mean, sorry. It's not is it?"

I laugh. I'm tempted to torture her a bit more, but I can't bring myself to do it. "No."

She drops her hands, still holding the bowl. "Well, who is it? Why do you look so happy?"

"Why shouldn't I be? You thought I was bringing a woman over here and got jealous."

"I did not!"

"Oh no? So you won't be happy when I tell you that my dinner companion tonight is you?"

She blinks, the blush on her cheeks deepening. "I... huh?" Her beautiful face goes through a series of emotions: shock, embarrassment, pleasure, faux irritation.

"You *are* happy." I draw closer to her.

"I'm..." she glances at me, clearly wondering what my intentions are as I come nearer, and trying to decide if she should be wary... or yield. "I'm... only here to cook your dinner."

I take the bowl from her hands, which are slightly chilled because she's still standing in front of the open refrigerator.

"And I wasn't jealous."

"Uh huh." I set the bowl on the nearby counter.

"Why would I be?"

I go back to her.

"We're not in a relationship. I mean, obviously. So, no. No. I wasn't—"

I come up right in front of her, my arm brushing her shoulder as I grasp the door behind her. She stops talking and we both stand still. That little vein is fluttering at the base of her neck.

Her eyes are on my lips. I'm looking at hers, too. I'm dying to know what she tastes like. "We can't do this," she says softly.

"It's just dinner, Emma."

Her eyes slowly raise to mine. She doesn't know if she should argue or not.

"What's the harm of dinner?"

"The harm is I don't think I can trust you."

A smile tugs at the corner of my mouth. "Why? What do you think I'll do?" I move half an inch closer, wanting so badly to close the gap between us.

"I… think you'll kiss me."

I keep my eyes on hers. She's no fool. "I promise I won't kiss you tonight. Is that better?"

Neither one of us move. She glances at my lips again. She nods slightly, like she's not sure that makes things better at all.

I smile and straighten, taking her by the hip and gently tugging her out of the way as I close the door. Her cheeks bloom red. A timer goes off on the oven but she doesn't react to it.

"Now where do you want this bowl?" I grab it and gesture toward the table, grinning at her flustered expression. "On the table?"

She bats the loose strand of hair off her shoulder. "Oh, give me that. Go clean up."

She grabs the bowl and puts it back on the counter like she can't decide where it goes.

I laugh. "Did you just send me off to wash my hands like a little kid?"

The timer beeps again.

"Seriously. Go away. You're distracting me." She hustles to the oven and opens the door.

I grab my briefcase off the stool. "You're staying for dinner, right?"

She ducks her head, trying to hide her smile. "If you insist. Go on now. If this duck burns it'll be on your head."

# Chapter 14

## Emma

We're sitting at the table, leaning forward on our elbows, talking and picking at the remnants of our dinner.

"This was really fantastic, Emma. Thank you. The table's set so nice, too."

He gives me a sly grin, and I prepare myself to get teased. God, I was so mortified when I realized what I'd done. But, I guess it's turned out all right. He wasn't upset, and what's the harm of dinner? He hasn't tried to kiss me once. In fact, it started out almost business like because we finally got to talk about menu options. Since then it's been an enjoyable conversation, going easily from one topic to the next.

The food *was* pretty damned good too, if I do say so myself.

"So many nice touches." He gestures to his ramekin. "Where did you get this?"

"It's yours."

"It is?" He picks it up to examine it more closely.

I laugh. "Don't you go into your kitchen at all?"

"Of course I do. It's where the Coca Puffs are."

He sets it back down and steals a bite-sized piece of roasted duck, right off the platter. "I shouldn't eat any more, but I can't get enough of this duck."

"Better than Coca Puffs?"

"Better than Fruity Pebbles, even."

"Wow. I guess I scored a home run." He winks at me and I smile back. God, it really has been such a nice evening. "Thanks for…"

I feel the blush rising on my cheeks. I lean on my palm and just smile at him. I can't seem to finish my sentence.

He nods, pleased. "You're welcome. All week I've been enjoying your phenomenal cooking and not happy about the fact that you weren't able to enjoy it yourself."

How sweet.

He swipes another piece of duck off the platter. "That's what I don't understand about someone cooking your meals for you."

I cock my head at him. He's no stranger to people working for him. Why should hiring a personal chef be any different? What *was* his reluctance to the idea? "Well, restaurants cook meals for people."

"Not in their homes though."

Hmm, that's true. "But you have people clean your home."

"It's not the same thing."

"Why not?"

He eyes the platter of duck, then sits back as if to distance himself from the temptation. He takes longer to think about his answer than I expected. Finally, he looks at me and says bluntly. "Meals are supposed to be about family."

"Ah."

Dammit, I was right that he doesn't like eating alone. I hate to think of it.

"When I was growing up, both my parents cooked. We had to as well, or at least help."

"You? Cook?"

He grins and shrugs. "I know some stuff. I just don't enjoy it as much as other people seem to and I'm happy to pick something up, so why bother? Anyway, we'd help make dinner then sit at the table and eat together. That was something my parents insisted on. Even when we were teens and our schedules got more hectic, the rule was, you never eat alone."

Wow. I couldn't count the number of times I ate alone growing up.

"Even if it was just me and Mom at Guido's after a track meet. No eating alone."

His eyes roam over the flowers on the table. He has the soft, far-away look of someone reliving nice memories, but with a dark edge to them. I've heard about their parents' untimely deaths, but not until this moment have I felt any pain over it. I hate that he's hurting.

"My parents were busy, but they always stopped for dinner." He looks at me. "For us. There were times it was fun because we were talking and laughing, and times my siblings and I were acting like brats and squabbling and driving our parents crazy. But still. Dinnertime was sacred. We could count on having their attention one hundred percent."

I want so badly to put my hand over his, to chase away the shadow I see lingering over those memories.

"I guess that's why the idea of a hired person in my home making my dinners has never appealed to me."

"That makes sense." We hold each other's gazes, and the outside world and this crazy situation we're in disappears. It's only me and him, and me wanting him to know I see his pain. "I'm sorry you lost them so early."

"It's not your fault," he says quietly.

"That's not what I'm sorry for."

His face softens. He nods and lightly brushes my arm with his fingertips. "Thank you."

I don't move, react, or change my expression, but a dangerous fluttering starts against my chest. It's a different kind of wanting for him than I've had up to now.

"What about you?" He smiles and grabs another piece of duck. "What were dinners like for you growing up?"

I'm inclined to share the truth with him, as he's done with me. But it would only feed that fluttering in my heart, and that would be a bad, bad thing.

"They were fine." I shrug. I start to clean up, the plates and silverware clinking as I stack them. "Normal."

"What's normal?"

"Well…" I stand with the dishes and he follows suit, grabbing the platter and the bowl. The switch in activity has changed the sense of intimacy and my heart is settling down. See? I'm fine. It's all fine. "I don't know. We didn't have the Leave it to Beaver thing you had."

Heading out of the dining room, I glance over my shoulder to make sure he didn't take that the wrong way. He's right behind me, and just grins at me. I smile back and go into the kitchen, setting our plates next to the sink.

"We had dinners like that sometimes, but more often dinner was on-the-go or every man for himself. Our schedules were kind of busy."

"Really? What did your parents do? Are they still married?"

"Um…" Again, I want to tell him everything, and I mean <u>everything.</u> Which is weird, because I don't talk about that with people. But of course I keep my mouth shut. He's not my confidant. He's my boss.

I start rinsing our plates with warm water and he retrieves some containers for the leftover food. "Yes, they're still married." Miraculously. "My father is a CPA." Well, he *was* anyway. "My mother's a receptionist for an airplane parts manufacturer." A job she was lucky to get and she's still struggling like hell to get by, thanks to my father.

I'm trying to forgive him. I guess I'm still working on it.

Time to change the subject.

"Are you and your siblings close?" I start loading our plates into the dishwasher. "I mean, I know you work together, but do you hang out, too?"

He nods, dishing the rest of the duck into a square container. "We have dinner together

158

once a month and do other things together sometimes, too."

"Do you have just the two siblings?"

"Yes. But we have a cousin who's practically a sister. Corrine. We keep her under wraps and out of the public eye, though."

"The public eye?" I take the now-empty platter from his hands and start to rinse it.

He grabs the bowl of beet salad, which is nearly empty, and gives me a wry look. "You don't read the The Voice, do you?"

The Voice is a free Indie newspaper that's in stands all over town. "No."

"Good." He empties the remains of the salad into a smaller container. "You're not missing much."

I examine his grim expression. "Why? What do they say about you? Just news, right?"

"If there's real news, the regular papers will cover it. That, we don't mind. When we remodeled and re-opened the Cottages, the press was helpful. But there's a gossip columnist who seems to take pleasure in causing trouble for certain people around town."

My heart is pounding uncomfortably now. I know what it's like to have your family name smeared through the papers. "Are you one of the people she likes to make trouble for?"

A hard look flashes across his face and he pops the top onto the salad. "Me and my family, yes. Often enough."

I load the platter into the dishwasher. "Sorry. It's frustrating to have people gossiping about you."

He sighs. "Most of it's not true. Just drivel." He joins me at the sink and starts to rinse the bowl. Our shoulders are almost touching. I resist the urge to scoot closer. "We've been dealing with it since we were kids, because our parents were such visible members of the community. So we're used to it. But yes, it can get frustrating."

I'm curious what kind of rumors that gossip columnist has spread about him and his family, but I vow never to try to find out or give that column the time of day. Not that I have before, but I definitely won't now. I wouldn't want him finding things out about me and my family that way.

Course, most the crap published about my father was, unfortunately, completely true.

I realize something. "Wait! You're not supposed to be helping!"

I try to take the bowl out of his hand, but he pulls it out of my reach.

"No," I protest again. "This is <u>my</u> job."

He loads it into the dishwasher. "It's not a problem. Don't worry."

"Well then, what are you paying me for?"

He laughs. "I know how to load a dishwasher. That doesn't mean I know how to make roasted duck. Speaking of which…" There goes another piece out of the container. He should just have another helping for real and be done with it. "How about you?" he asks. "Any siblings?"

I grab a clean fork and hold it out to him, along with the duck leftovers.

"No, I shouldn't."

"Sit down and eat." I point at a bar stool with the fork.

"No, this is going in the fridge." He takes the leftovers and tries going for the lid, but I'm done with him doing my work.

I take the container back, put it on the counter, and press both my hands against his chest, steering him toward the bar stool. That gets his attention. Oh, that grin!

Well, my hands on his chest is affecting me, too. He's so deliciously firm, I want to feel around a bit, but I'm on a mission and refuse to let his muscles distract me.

"Sit or I'm not answering any more questions."

He sits, laughing, and I busy myself putting the leftovers away, hoping my cheeks cool off before I have to face him again. It's as bad as when he grabbed me by the hips to scoot me out of the way and close the refrigerator door. I felt that in more places than just my hips.

"You didn't answer my question," he says.

"What question?"

I need another minute for my blush to disappear, so I go into the dining room to retrieve the rest of our dishes: the wine glasses that are nearly empty and the little ramekins.

"I asked if you have any siblings," he calls from the next room.

"Oh." I wait until I'm back in the kitchen so I don't have to holler. "Just one." I set the ramekins next to the sink and head over to give him his glass. "A half-brother who's sixteen years older than me."

Rayce raises his eyebrows, reaching for his wine. "That's quite a gap." He downs what's left in his glass and I do the same. It's this delicious pear wine he had in the wine cooler that went perfectly with the duck. Sweet and smooth.

"He's from my father's first marriage." I load my glass into the dishwasher, and make an asking gesture toward his. He hands it over, indicating he's done. "We weren't raised together or anything, but we try to keep in touch."

I load his glass and start looking around the kitchen. It's pretty much clean now, but I grab a rag to wipe down the counters anyway. I need something to do.

"Are you close?"

I shrug. "Doug hasn't been much a part of my life. He's got his own stuff going on. He's in Virginia. Works as an accountant. Has a wife and three daughters. He has his hands full."

Too full to help when things got tough, that's for sure. Who could blame him, though? He has a family to support, and like he said, Dad got himself into that mess. Let him suffer the consequences.

I've asked myself if I should've let Dad suffer the consequences.

I wouldn't be in the mess I'm in now if I had.

But as sideways as things have gone, I can't say I regret doing what I could to help. I couldn't stand by and do nothing, no matter how disappointed in Dad I was.

"I can't believe you've only been in the chef business for a year"

I glance up at him tentatively, working my way over the already-clean counters. "Well, I'm not a real chef."

"Could've fooled me. Did you cook a lot when you were younger or something?"

"No. But it's really not that hard. And I had a good teacher at my last job."

Well, shit. Why did I mention my last job? I need a quick diversion. I turn my back on him to rinse out the rag. "You've been in the resort business your whole life, right?"

"Mmm-hmm."

Silence.

I glance over my shoulder. Amused, he narrows his eyes at me. I know he knows what I did. I just don't know if he's going to let me off the hook.

I dry my hands and start to circle the island, looking for something else that needs to be done. "Do you like working the family business or was it thrust upon you by default?"

I glance at him again. He definitely knows I'm trying to change the subject. Oh that evil grin.

"Don't bother asking. My last job ended badly and I don't want to talk about it."

Nice, Emma. Real smooth. Way to dodge that land mine. I swear, it's like I have no boundaries with him.

I lean one hand on the counter, not knowing what else to do with myself. Too late, I realize how close we are. Why didn't I pick a different place to stand? I'm forced to look at him and pretend he's not making me all fluttery.

"I'll agree to that if you tell me about your roommate," he parries.

"Um... okay. What do you want to know?"

"Is he really gay?"

Now it's my turn for an evil grin. Hey, fair's fair.

"You don't have a boyfriend?" he asks playfully, as if he already knows the answer. Because come on, if I did, would I even be here?

"Why should you care?"

"You know why."

"Um, employee. Boss." I point first at myself and then at him.

"Yes, I'm aware. It's unfortunate. But we can't really help that, can we?"

There is one way around it, as I know too well. "You could always fire me."

Another land mine successfully dodged. *Score.*

"Why would I fire you?" He looks genuinely perplexed.

"I don't know. Why are we talking about whether or not I have a boyfriend? Why did I just have dinner with you?"

He puts his strong hand over mine. That gesture both settles me and gets my heart pumping.

"You're here because I want you to be and because you want to be."

I open my mouth to protest but he goes on, saving me from the lie. My heart is still pounding and my skin is humming against his touch.

"We're talking about this because we're both thinking it anyway. But if you have any fears of being fired, that's not going to happen. Unless you do something like steal my car or attack me with a meat mallet, your job is in the bag. What happens between us is not a factor."

I'm shaking my head. "We can't. You know we can't."

He squeezes my wrist gently, then lets go and leans back in the stool. He grins at me. "If you say so."

"Now cut that out."

"Cut what out? I'm agreeing with you."

"You are not."

He laughs. It's a big, warm laugh that I long to crawl inside of. Lord help me, *why* am I doing this to myself.

"Okay, no talking about jobs, roommates, or the inevitable."

The inevitable? The thought gets me tingling in more places than just my wrist. Once more, I open my mouth to protest, but again he goes on before I can interrupt.

"What about our childhoods? Can we talk about that? How about movies we like? Video games we like to play?"

I laugh. "Yeah, sure. Let's talk about all the video games I like to play. I have a long list."

He purses his lips. "Are you teasing me, Emma?"

"About what?"

"I happen to be a video game aficionado."

I laugh, but a little uncertainly. His eyes have that mischievous twinkle, but I somehow don't think he's kidding. But... surely not.

"You own and run one of the top luxury resorts in the country."

"That's what they say."

"And you're a video game aficionado?"

"A person has to unwind somehow. I prefer the retro games. Spyro. Crash. Mario Bros. The classics."

"You're serious."

He grins. "You have to admit. Those are fun games."

"I wouldn't know. I've never played them."

Now it's his turn to look like he's trying to figure out if I'm serious or not. "You've never played Super Mario Bros?"

"No."

"Crash Bandicoot?"

I shake my head.

"What did you play growing up?"

"Nothing."

I wasn't the kid with that kind of time.

"You've never played anything?"

"Oh no, wait! I played Candy Crush once."

He stares at me in disbelief. "What kind of childhood did you have?"

"Apparently the boring kind." I grin at him.

"And you don't play games now?"

"Well…no." I lean forward slightly and give him a sly look. "I'm an <u>adult.</u>"

"Yes, but there has to be a kid in there somewhere. A really deprived kid." He pops up from his seat and heads for the stairs. "Come on. Let's go."

My hand drops from the counter. "Uh…"

Ten seconds later he's disappeared into the basement and I'm left wondering what he has in mind. Should I follow him down there? I mean, this night has already gotten out of hand. First dinner, now the basement? Isn't that where things like making out happen? In basements?

My traitorous body gets tingly at the idea of making out with him in his basement.

Eventually.

The inevitable.

But… he promised he wouldn't kiss me tonight.

"Emma?" he calls up. "Are you coming?"

"You promise," I call down. "Right?"

His warm laugh drifts up the stairs. "Yes, I promise. Get down here."

But I'm already heading for the stairs. He could've said, <u>No way. Deal's off. Get down here so I can kiss the fuck out of you,</u> and I'd still be descending the soft, carpeted stairway.

I'd follow that warm laugh anywhere.

# Chapter 15

## Rayce

I do not do this with anyone I didn't grow up with. Ever. I hope to God Emma keeps this little bit of trivia to herself. Who knows what that damned gossip columnist Rita Becker would do with it.

I couldn't help it though. Emma does something to me. So much I can't hardly keep track of it all. She's a constant presence tingling on my skin and pumping through my bloodstream.

It's taking a hell of a lot of willpower not to kiss this woman. The only thing keeping me from it is the promise I made.

But it isn't just physical. Her confidence, her ease, her smile… it's all settling down into me and making me pay attention. She's bringing out the side of myself I don't often show. With Emma, I'm not "Playboy Rayce Rivers", as Rita Becker sometimes calls me.

Which I have to admit is fair.

Not just because I've been with a lot of women. But also because—and I'm just now realizing this—I have a dating <u>persona.</u> No matter who I'm with, I'm not just Rayce. I can't seem to forget that I'm Rayce Rivers, Resort Owner and Bearer of the Rivers Family Legacy.

The women I've dated have all factored into that image in one way or another. I didn't realize this until now, but... maybe I've been evaluating how they could help... or harm... the family image?

But that's fair. My siblings and I have to be aware of the same thing. Image matters, like it or not.

But it's different with Emma.

I couldn't care less what other people think of her because I think she's amazing, and my dating persona is nowhere to be seen.

It's just her and me. The real me. The me who likes to be playful and flirty and a little bit naughty and, yes, entertained with the occasional game of Super Mario Bros.

With Emma, I'm starting to see where I've gone wrong in the past. She's making me think about what might really matter in a relationship with a woman.

And it's nothing like what I thought.

"Come on, come on, come on!" she says.

We're in the game room in my basement, sitting next to each other on the couch, the familiar Super Mario Bros music playing in the background. We've both kicked off our shoes and she's sitting cross-legged, leaning forward in concentration, trying to get Mario over a Piranha Plant.

Aaand… failing.

"Dang it!" She sits up and scowls at the screen. "I died again."

"That's okay. Next time, wait for the flower to open, then run for it."

"Shouldn't I wait for it to be closed?"

"It'll be closed by the time you get there. It's all about figuring out the timing."

She goes for it at the first opportunity—she's bold, I like it—and makes it over.

"Yay!" She bounces up and down on the couch. "Good tip."

She likes to narrate as she goes. "Oooh, I'm big! ... Oh no! I'm little again."

I chuckle. The only thing more entertaining than playing Super Mario Bros is watching Emma do it.

"Oooh the star! I want the star!" She's leaning her controller and her entire body to the right as she tries to make Mario catch the star.

"Watch out for the—"

"Dang it!"

I laugh.

"I hate those stupid mushroom things. They keep killing me."

"It's okay. Try again."

"I only have two lives left."

"You're doing fine."

A few seconds later she's down another life and handing me the controller. "Get me through? I don't want to go all the way back to the beginning again."

"Just this once," I say in a teasing voice. "You have to practice if you want to get better."

"I'll practice all day long for the things that matter," she says grinning.

"Oh yeah?" I get her past the Goombas and hand the controller back. "What matters more than this?"

"Mmmm…" She doesn't answer for a moment, then finally gives a half shrug. She's concentrating on the screen and moving along better now. It could be she's just wrapped up in the game, but I think she didn't answer that question on purpose.

She's a mystery, this one. She gets tight-lipped about certain things and I'm trying to figure out the pattern.

There's something Emma's not telling me. Funny thing is, there aren't any red flags going up about it. I still feel the way I have since the moment I first saw her: intrigued and captivated. I want to know more about her. What's her story?

She finally gets to the flagpole and I watch her face light up as Mario slides down the flag pole and goes into the castle. She plops back in satisfaction as the little fireworks go off. "I have to admit. That was fun."

"I told you."

She leans her head back against the couch and looks at me, smiling. God, I could do this with her forever. I couldn't even say how long we've been down here.

"Your turn."

"Go ahead. I can play anytime. Can I get you anything? More wine?"

She gives me the side eye. "Are you trying to get me drunk so you can break your promise and kiss me?"

I grin. I'm tempted to show her that I need no such assistance to get a willing kiss out of her, but I'm staying true to my word. "No. I'm trying to get you to relax so you'll tell me more about yourself."

"I've told you things about myself."

"I mean without changing the subject."

She sets the controller on the seat next to her and bites her bottom lip. She doesn't admit it, but she doesn't deny it either. "You don't want me to go on and on."

"Sure I do."

She pulls her knees to her chest and turns toward me slightly, leaning against the back of the couch. "But why?"

<u>Why?</u> I mute the TV and turn toward her as well, resting my arm on the back. "Because you interest me, Emma. Ever since I saw you at the art show, I've wanted to get to know you."

"Then why didn't you come talk to me then? When it would have been..." She seems unwilling to finish her sentence. Suddenly she seems vulnerable. Worried.

I lightly brush the tip of my finger on her shoulder to nudge her. "What?"

"When it would've been okay."

<u>Ah</u>. She thinks I didn't approach her when I had the opportunity.

"I wanted to. I tried. But by the time I had the chance you were gone."

She gives me a skeptical look.

"Really. I saw you across the room, then my brother cornered me with a potential client. By the time I got away, you were gone. I searched every floor looking for you."

She chuckles, giving me a searching look. "Now I know you're full of it. You don't strike me as the kind of guy to search every floor for anybody."

"I'm not."

Our gaze locks, and her smile falls away. My body is throbbing with her presence. I want to brush my fingertips down her cheeks, run my fingers through her hair, pull her into my arms.

"You were standing at a table, alone, wearing a burgundy skirt and a silk top with a tie at the base."

Her eyes don't leave mine.

"You were so calm and sure of yourself, in the middle of all those people." So beautiful. Just like she is now. "I wish I would've gone over when I first saw you, but instead I just…" I shake my head slightly, my heart beating thickly in my chest. "…looked at you."

Her lips part slightly, and her face softens with that look of longing and restraint I'm becoming so familiar with.

"I couldn't look anywhere else."

# Chapter 16

## Emma

I'm breathing shallowly, my heart <u>thump thumping</u> against my chest. I'm holding my knees close to my body, even though I want to unfold, open up, scoot closer and let him be right about the inevitable. But I don't move.

I can't keep the pleasure out of my voice though. How can I not be pleased at the idea of drawing the attention of this amazing man? "Really?"

He nods, and I believe him. Is that dangerous? Because I believe him. Oh, how I wish that night had gone differently. If only he'd come over sooner or I'd stayed longer, then we wouldn't be in this situation.

"I thought sure I'd never see you again." He smiles. "Now here you are, in my game room."

"Yeah." Thump, thump, thump. "But I shouldn't be." Dammit.

He doesn't respond to that. We just keep looking at each other, and I am both glad and not glad that he made that promise about no kisses.

"I should go," I say quietly.

He glances at the clock on the wall. I told myself, and Rayce, that I would only stay a few minutes down here. That was over an hour ago. Now I'm pushing right up against the time I have to leave to get Aaron from practice.

"Because you have to pick up your roommate, right?" He winks at me.

"I really do." But I don't move. "If I wait any longer, I'll be late."

Then he'll ask questions.

"Well, we don't want that." He's slow to get up, but he does it. He holds his hand out to me.

I look at his hand, so strong and inviting. I long to take it. But I dare not touch him. This is already hard enough.

"Thanks." I stand up on my own.

He drops his hand easily, still looking so sure and confident. "Let me walk you out." He retrieves his phone from the table, drops it in his pocket, and starts to take a step toward the stairs.

"No." I raise my hand slightly and he stops.

Tell him this is as far as this goes. Tell him you're not staying like this again or eating meals with him or doing anything other than being his employee. Tell him this just isn't a line you're going to cross, and to stop pushing things.

I don't say any of that.

"I'll let myself out."

He doesn't argue and I don't say any of the things I should. I go up the carpeted stairs, cross the beautiful living room with windows darkened by the night, and head for the side door. It doesn't feel like a fantasy house anymore. It feels more like a home, maybe because I'm getting to know better the man who lives in it.

I climb into Aaron's little Hatchback, drive out of the luxurious neighborhood, and hurry across town. I am, in fact, late picking him up, and lie as to the reason why. I lie to Pierce about where I was all night.

I don't feel as guilty about this as I should, and know it will hit me later when the high from my evening with Rayce wears off and I'm left with the reality of the situation.

I'll straighten myself out tomorrow. Tonight I let my exhilaration linger.

The fantasy of Rayce Rivers feels too good to chase away just yet.

I was right. The guilt did kick in later. It's Saturday, and I've spent all morning and afternoon oscillating between texting Mr. Rayce Rivers to say I quit, and counting down the minutes until I get to see him again.

Especially because this time when I arrive to cook dinner, he won't be at work. He'll be home.

Two words keep crashing around my head: <u>inevitable</u> and <u>eventually</u>.

But he made a promise, too, so there's that.

I want to quit, but I need the money.

I want to see him, but I don't want to make another mistake when I haven't even recovered from the *last* one yet.

I finally devise a compromise. I can't walk away from this job—I've started to scrounge through apartment listings and found a few I might be able to afford after paying Aaron back if I stick this out—but I don't want to be there cooking dinner when he's there, too. And I really shouldn't eat with him again. I'd hate for him to eat alone, but… I shouldn't.

I can't accept that making the same damned mistake all over again is inevitable. I just can't. Anyway, it'll probably be different once we're not in such close proximity all the time. Maybe once I'm back in banquet, I won't really see him anymore.

My heart squeezes painfully at this thought.

I head to the store yet again for ingredients and fresh bread, and put together a lasagna in the nicest baking dish we have. It'll be enough to feed him tomorrow night too, my night off, and all I'll have to do is throw it in the oven when I get there and tell him to take it out when the timer dings.

In. Out.

I'll barely see him.

Which is completely depressing.

# Chapter 17

## Emma

When I get to Rayce's house, there's no sign of him. I put the lasagna on the counter and the salad in the fridge, then turn on the oven to preheat.

The house is still. I cross the living room to the stairs leading to the basement, listening for video game sounds coming up from below. Nothing.

I walk lightly across the intricate foyer floor, and even go so far as to peek into the room across from the dining room. It's an office, elegant and impressive and full of light from the front windows. But he's not here either.

I'm not bold enough to explore different levels of the house, but as I head back into the living room, I notice the patio door is unlocked. He's not in his backyard paradise, as far as I can tell, but decide to go out anyway. I've been in his basement. Surely he wouldn't care if I took a look around his patio.

I step outside and am greeted by fresh sea air, calm blue sky, and sparkling ocean reaching back to the horizon. I can actually feel my blood pressure drop.

The patio furniture is topped with luxuriously thick, colorful cushions and I damn near sink into one of the lounges as if I owned the place. I don't think he'd care. I really don't. But I'm not crossing any more lines with him. No more.

I'm going to just stick this out so I can get my apartment money and see what happens when we're not in each other's path so much. One more week. I can do that.

As I circle around the side of the pristine pool, the sound of crashing waves far below the cliff's edge drifts up in a soothing rhythm. When I get to the end of the massive patio, I see what I couldn't before: stone steps leading down the cliff side. I can't see how far down they go, and don't have a chance to find out, because I hear footsteps coming up.

I hustle back into the house. Once I'm safely inside, I watch him ascend the steps and cross the patio. He's clearly been working out.

He's wearing black, athletic shorts and his white shirt clings to his muscular body in a V of sweat.

He hasn't seen me, or at least I think he hasn't, but I'm seeing plenty of him. He lifts the hem of his shirt to wipe the sweat off his brow, giving me a perfect view of tightly honed abs, firm pecs, tanned skin.

I can't stop staring. And I thought he looked good in a suit. I just want to take a bite out of him.

I take several steps backwards as he comes in the house and spots me. I'm a flustered mess, trying to not look like I've been <u>looking.</u> "Ah." His face lights up in a panty-melting smile. "I wondered when you'd get here."

He grabs a towel that was sitting on one of the bar stools—a detail I'd missed earlier—then uses it to dry the dampness in his hair. His bicep flexes as he moves.

"What's for dinner tonight?"

His shirt is still clinging to his amazing chest, and now I can smell him. That deep masculine scent of a man who's just had a hard workout.

My thighs clench.

"Uh… Emma?"

My eyes snap to his. <u>Oh shit.</u> I've been <u>staring at his chest.</u> "Lasagna! It's lasagna."

He's grinning. He's on to me. Shit.

"There's enough for you to have leftovers tomorrow." My tongue feels awkward in my own mouth, like speaking is too much of a challenge after the sights I've just seen.

He's giving me a knowing look.

Oh, please don't comment on what an idiot I'm being. Let me out of this gracefully.

"I figured it'd be nice for you to have extra since I'm not here for dinner tomorrow. I mean, I'm not here to cook your dinner tomorrow. I mean, not eating with you. Cooking. For you." He's grinning at me in amusement. "I mean, I just I thought it would be nice."

You said that already. Stop talking, Emma.

I clamp my mouth shut.

He chuckles. "My family is having dinner here tomorrow but that'll be perfect for lunch. Thank you." He turns and heads up the stairs, trotting lightly and giving me an even better view of his lithe body. "Actually..." he turns and I snap my gaze from his rear to his face. "Is it a full-sized pan of lasagna?"

I nod, not trusting myself to speak again.

"How about we save that for tomorrow's dinner? It's as close to a home-cooked meal my family will ever get in this house. And that will give me a chance to brag about your cooking." He winks. "Tonight, we can order something in."

"Uh..."

We? In?

He turns and continues on up the stairs.

"But..." I say weakly.

"I'm taking a quick shower. Be down in ten."

I stare at the place he disappeared with a pounding heart. This is getting out of hand.

And I'm definitely not imagining him naked in the shower with water running down his bare chest… along his tight abs… and… other parts. I'm really not.

Two voices quibble in my head.

Aaron was right. This was a big mistake. This is starting to feel inevitable.

I'm just looking. It's fine. We haven't even touched each other.

Yeah, but you want to.

Shut up, you.

By the time he gets downstairs from his shower, I've pulled myself together and am ready to be firm about not staying here for dinner. I think I am.

No, I definitely am.

I'm just finishing up a little note with cooking instructions for tomorrow when he comes down the stairs and into the kitchen.

For the record, Mr. Rayce Rivers looks good in everything. Suit? Check. Athletic clothes? Check. Casual slacks and a short-sleeved maroon polo that hugs his chest just the right amount? Double fucking check.

"The lasagna's in the fridge," I say in my most professional voice. "Heating instructions are here." I tap on the note. "The salad should be fine for tomorrow but you may want to pick up some fresh bread. This loaf won't be as good."

"You don't mind, do you?"

"No. It's your dinner. You can do whatever you want to with it. But about dinner tonight—"

"I was thinking Guido's. It's been too long."

I forget to say no, and instead ask, "What's Guido's?"

He raises a disbelieving brow. "What's Guido's? Only the best pizza place in Swan Pointe." He pulls out his phone. "You're about to discover pure pizza heaven." He seems to be sending a text or something.

"But…"

He puts his phone on the counter with a satisfied grin. "Should be here in 45 minutes or so. You don't mind waiting, do you?"

"Do they have an app or something?"

"No. Guido is an old family friend. All I have to do is text him the usual and he sets it up for me. Except this time I told him to make it a large."

"But, I'm not—"

"You're going to love it."

I cross my arms and scowl at him since I know he won't let me speak until he's sure he's getting his way.

He grins, yet again seeming to sense I'm not really upset. Which I *totally* should be.

He heads to the pantry and pulls out a bottle of olive oil and another of balsamic vinegar. "I do owe you an apology, though."

Now this gets my attention. I drop my arms. "An apology? For what?"

He retrieves two beautiful little dipping bowls and pours a bit of olive oil into each. "For not inviting you to dinner tomorrow." He follows the olive oil with balsamic vinegar. "I would love to, but my family wouldn't approve. I'm not supposed to be involved with employees."

"We're not involved."

"If we're not, we should be."

"But you just said you're not supposed to."

He tears off a piece of fresh French bread and holds it out for me. "This is different. You can't tell me this doesn't feel right."

I've never known someone to just put things out there like that, with complete confidence it will be received in kind. He's not dancing around things at all either. He hasn't from the first time we talked.

Maybe that's because he's used to seeing what he wants and getting it. I don't know. But I like that he goes after what he wants. I even like that what he wants is me, if I'm honest with myself.

And maybe it does feel different, like he says. But no matter how this feels, it has to be wrong.

I glance at the bread, but don't take it. "It shouldn't feel any way. We're not even dating yet."

"Ah!" His eyebrows shoot up and he raises one finger in victory. "You said 'yet'."

My stomach drops. "No. No, no, no. That's not what I meant."

"Yes, it is."

"It is not."

He laughs. He sets the bread in front of me and scoots one of the bowls closer. "You're so fucking adorable."

My heart swoops up inside my chest, but I throw my hands up. Surviving a week of this is starting to feel impossible. "Is there no line you're not willing to cross?"

He was getting ready to tear off a piece of French bread for himself, but he sets it back down and gives me a serious look.

"Yes, Emma. There are lines I'm not willing to cross. The ones that matter. But here's the thing." He faces me, leaning one strong arm on the counter and gesturing between us with his other hand. "There shouldn't be a line between us. It's a temporary obstacle, this boss employee thing. There's a solution to this problem and I intend to find it because pretending that some arbitrary line matters in this situation..." He shakes his head. "It doesn't."

My heart is beating right out of my chest. God, I wish I didn't want this so much.

"You know, you really shouldn't talk to me like this."

"Tell me you don't like it, and I'll stop."

"I've told you to stop a hundred times."

"No, you haven't."

Now, it's my turn to be incredulous. "Yes, I have."

He shakes his head. "No. You've said 'we can't' and 'we shouldn't'. But you've never said no or told me to stop."

I'm staring at him, my mind running through our past interactions. It's challenging though, because his expression is morphing into something new. Something that's heating up my insides. I may have thought he wanted to kiss me other times, but I've never seen this look before. It's not just desire, it's determination, and I already know what happens when Mr. Rayce Rivers is determined about something.

My whole body starts to tingle and I feel the heat rising to my cheeks.

He comes off the counter and starts slowly coming my way, looking sexy as fuck. "I haven't stopped, because you haven't asked me to."

Uhhhh…

"And you haven't asked me to because you like it."

He's getting awfully damned close. "I…" I swallow.

"You can't deny it."

"Uh…."

He puts one hand on my hip. My body lights up with the electricity dancing over my skin.

The tiny part of me that's being reasonable is clinging to the last line we have left—at least we haven't kissed. "You promised you wouldn't kiss me."

He slides his other hand around my waist and pulls me into his arms. My hands are on his chest. Because I should push him away.

But I don't.

"I promised I wouldn't kiss you *yesterday.*"

He comes closer, almost to me, the scent of aftershave on his skin.

"And I didn't."

His chest is warm and firm and his arms around me are intoxicating. He leans in. His mouth coming closer. His intention clear.

We can't. We can't. Say no, Emma.

What I say instead is this: "Rayce."

Instead of a reprimand, it comes out like a wish. A request. A desire.

I tip my mouth up to meet his, and when we touch, whatever line there was between us is obliterated. Hot molten slips through my body and my bones turn to butter.

My hands flatten against his chest, because I have to push him away and make this stop. But I'm weak. So weak. This is why I can't trust myself.

Because I'm kissing him back.

Because I want it so badly. The weak side of me is trying to get all I can in the seconds before I do what I know I will. What I know I must.

His hands cup my face, weakening my resolve. Our mouths part and his tongue sweeps against mine.

I manage not to whimper. I exhale deep and slow as I'm lost in what would be the world's most perfect kiss, were it not for one thing.

Emma, you know how to walk away from the things you want. Just do it.

God, he feels so right. Why can't this be right?

It was never like this with Chad. It paled in comparison. That first rushed, awkward kiss was nothing like this one. But I thought he could rescue me from the turmoil in my life like he promised he would.

Then he turned against me, and I never saw it coming.

Rayce is different. Everything about this is different.

Except the fact that he could crush me as efficiently as Chad had and it would do him no harm.

My hands grip the front of Rayce's shirt in desperation, needing to push him away but needing to fall deeper into this kiss and into his arms.

I want to believe that Rayce is safe.

That he's not going to hurt me.

That he's not using me or just getting his thrills with the help.

That this feels as real to him as it does to me.

Rayce cups my face so gently, almost lovingly, and is kissing me with such tender intention… such simmering passion. It's deliriously intoxicating… and wrong. No matter how wonderful he's making me feel, this has to be wrong.

My boss. A mistake. Again.

The reality is I'm kissing Mr. Rayce Rivers. Owner of the Paradise Rivers Resort. A powerful, unflinching man. If he turned on me, I would be helpless in every way.

I have to stop this.

But I can't.

I can't do this again.

But I want him so badly.

My past is too recent not to haunt me. Chad's words come back to me: Every now and then guys need something a little nasty on the side. Were you stupid enough to think it was anything more?

I'd never felt so small and worthless and never saw it <u>coming even though I should have.</u>

Our mouths still working together, I'm at the cliff's edge. My shame about my past and confusion about the present solidifies into a hot mass at the base of my throat.

At that same moment, he tightens his hold.

Heart fluttering in panic, I break away with a hard shove against his chest. That only scoots me backwards more than it pushes him. He doesn't even budge.

So strong. So powerful. He could destroy me if he wanted to.

Yet, my heart twists at the hurt expression on his face. In spite of that hurt, he seems much more concerned about me. Like he genuinely, even deeply, cares for me.

You should know better, Emma! He kissed me and he shouldn't have. He knew it was wrong and did it anyway. What does that say about him? About either of us?

I never, ever should've taken this job. It stops now.

"Emma..." He moves slightly as if he's going to come and console me.

"No—" I choke out.

He stops instantly.

"Don't come any closer."

His hands rise into the air, that universal gesture that means I'm not going to hurt you. He even takes a step backward.

"Emma..." He's never sounded so vulnerable. He's killing me.

"No..." I say again, remembering now what it feels like to walk away. I forgot how much it hurt. But I'm finally doing it. I back up, unsteady on my feet.

"Emma, wait..."

I turn and hurry to the far counter, scooping my purse into my arms, the strap dangling. "Stay away," I whisper, aching for both of us. "Please."

I rush to the door on trembling legs and actually stumble a bit. My limbs have never been so fucking uncooperative. I exit the house and flee across the darkened driveway. I duck inside the cold and empty shell of Aaron's car, hurrying to close the door.

I glance behind me, toward the break in the hedges.

He hasn't followed me.

Come get me, that weak woman inside of me thinks. Save us from this.

But some things cannot be saved. Not my dancing. Not my father. Not this.

I make myself start the car. I make myself drive away from the white house on the hill vowing I will never return. I don't slow down and I don't look back. When I'm miles away, I'm stunned to realize that I've left part of my heart back there.

I didn't mean to give Rayce Rivers a piece of myself. I didn't even know I had until just now.

But it's not the first time I've left a piece of myself somewhere else. It's all for the best.

But I have to wonder... what will be left of me if I keep this up?

# Chapter 18

## Rayce

I hover in the kitchen, one hand gripping the counter. What did I get wrong? What did I miss? I knew she didn't like the idea of breaking rules, but I also knew she just needed me to take us to the next step. Or I thought that's what she needed.

Did I do something wrong? I mean, really wrong? The thought makes me physically ill. Have I completely misread this entire situation?

But the way she kissed me...

It was purposeful, full of wanting and tenderness and desire. It was practically an out-of-body experience. As I held her in my arms, I thought, <u>I'm kissing my future wife.</u>

I swear to God, that was the thought running through my head.

I've never felt so terrified, or so exhilarated. When I cupped her face, I wasn't just trying to show her what I felt. I was holding on, needing her to steady me. I didn't know I could feel anything like that. I've never been one to believe in fate, but kissing Emma felt like destiny.

But I was wrong.

I completely fucked this up. Maybe I pushed her someplace she didn't want to go. Maybe I read everything wrong because I needed to think she wants me as much as I want her.

I've never needed that from any woman.

My heart clutches in pain at the thought that I caused her pain.

But the way she said my name... with such longing.

Even the way she looked at me when she said no... with such regret.

It's confusing. Am I just desperate to believe she wants me, too? Is that why I see it in her eyes?

I'm still standing here in my empty

kitchen, the air vibrating from her presence even though she's gone. I'm not moving at all.

I have no idea what to do next.

# Chapter 19

## Emma

I didn't think it was possible, but I think this is even worse than quitting dancing. I barely slept last night. It's almost three in the afternoon and I haven't showered. I've done little more than lie on the couch, still covered in blankets, and binge watch <u>Orange is the New Black</u> on my tablet.

"What's going on with you today?" Pierce calls from his computer.

I don't look at him. "Nothing."

His chair squeaks when he gets up, and he comes over and sits across from me. He's watching me, clearly not accepting my 'nothing' as nothing.

"Something's going on."

"You're just trying to procrastinate working on your painting," I say flatly, not even caring if it's harsh.

I've been here long enough to learn his patterns. Every painting seems to go through a phase where he'll dabble on it for a minute or two, then be on Facebook for an hour, then dabble on it for a minute or two, then wipe down one of his work tables, or show me trailers for the latest movies, or fuss over the weeds in his garden even when there aren't any.

"Yeah, probably," he admits easily. "But something is clearly wrong."

I lose track of what's going on in the episode, barely watching it. As I imagine confessing to Pierce, I'm surprised to realize I like the idea of it. It's a lot easier than disappointing Aaron. I hit the off button on my tablet and let the screen fall onto my stomach. "Aaron was right. I shouldn't have taken the chef job."

"Why," he says slowly, giving me the side eye as if he already knows.

"It's…" I rub my thumb along the cool edge of the tablet, "…maybe gotten a little bit inappropriate."

Pierce sighs. I look at him sideways, nervous about what I'll see. He's leaning forward on his knees, large hands clasped in front of him. He's all business. "Are you sleeping with him?"

I shake my head. "He kissed me. I stopped him, but… not right away."

Because it was the most amazing kiss any woman has ever experienced.

He sits back in the chair. " Well, good for you. It's common for women to feel like they can't stand up for themselves when a guy tries to take advantage like that. You did good, Emma."

"No," I say firmly, putting the tablet on the table and sitting up for the first time in hours. "It's not like that. I mean he shouldn't have done it, but he wasn't trying to take advantage of me."

"You don't have to justify his behavior."

"I'm not. He shouldn't have done it. I shouldn't have done it. But this isn't sexual harassment or something. We're both attracted to each other and he knows it. If he weren't my boss, there wouldn't be a problem."

"But he is your boss."

"Yeah." I sigh and lean back into the couch. "I can't believe I let this happen again."

"You have to get out of this situation, Emma."

"I know. I'm… probably going to quit."

"Probably?"

This is the other thing that's making it more difficult than when I walked away from dance. I'm wavering.

"I don't know."

"Emma," he says, exasperated.

I hide my face in my hands. "It feels different with him. I'm so confused."

"Well, let me clear it up for you. It's not different. He's your boss and he should fucking know better."

I groan. "I know."

"I know you know. You wouldn't be so obviously miserable if you didn't know this was a mess you need to get out of *right now*. If he's the kind of guy to do this—"

My phone rings and saves me from hearing the rest of whatever he was going to say. It's not like I haven't thought all these things myself, but it's bothering me to hear Pierce saying it.

I look at the caller ID. It's not a number I recognize.

"Hello?"

"Is this Emma Swanson?" a heavily-accented male voice asks.

"Yes."

"This is Sergei Petroff."

Oh my God.

"From the Swan Pointe Dance Company."

"Yes, I know who you are."

If he's calling to try to get me into his company, I swear to God I will hang up on him.

"You need to come get Aaron."

"Why? What happened?"

"He passed out."

I sit straight up. "What?"

"He'll be fine, but he's useless right now. He's not to come in tomorrow, but I want him back Tuesday. That gives him two days. Make sure he's ready."

I'm not one of your dancers, you know, I want to say. But his bossiness is the least of my concerns. I hop off the couch. "I'll be right there."

"What's going on?" Pierce asks as I stick my phone in my purse.

"I don't know. Aaron passed out. We need to go get him."

Pierce stands up, too. "Is he all right?"

I grab some clean clothes from my suitcase by the couch. "Sergei he says he's fine. He probably just got dehydrated or something."

I don't say any of the other things running through my mind, because I don't want to worry Pierce. I don't want to worry myself either. It's not like I've never seen this kind of thing before. He could just be dehydrated.

Or it could be a sign that his food dysfunctions are worse than I've realized.

I throw on some clothes and pull my hair into a hasty ponytail. As Pierce and I head down to the dance studio, I try not to let all the horrible possibilities I'm imagining get out of control. It's difficult, but once I get down there it gets easier because I let my anger take over.

This is why I left. Exactly why.

I have to actually go into the building, which I haven't done the entire time I've been living here. I only ever wait for Aaron at the curb. In fact, this is the first time I've been inside a dance studio since working in one. It's sweltering, too. Is Sergei too cheap to turn on the fucking air conditioning?

There's music pouring from the classroom. My body starts humming, longing to move, but I clamp that down hard. I march down the hall, heading for the back office where we were told Aaron is lying down.

The whole thing pisses me off. Everything about this pisses me off. Keeping my eyes straight ahead as we pass the open classroom door, my peripheral vision catches a glimpse of a familiar sight: dancers in leotards, echoed in the floor-to-ceiling mirror at the front of the room.

Sergei, the last person I wanted to see, must have spotted us walking past because I hear him stop the class and call my name. I keep walking. Sergei angers me more than anyone.

Less than a minute after we enter the back office to find Aaron lying on a dance mat, looking pale and clammy, Sergei appears at the door. He has a long face, arched nose, and thin blonde hair hanging past his shoulders. "I've been wanting to talk to you."

I turn my back to him, heading for Aaron. "I know what you want. The answer is no."

He humpfs. I'll bet he wasn't expecting that. I don't care.

"Yes, I've heard you're difficult," he says with a smooth accent. My face is burning as Pierce and I kneel next to Aaron and help him slowly sit up. "You know, you would do well to remember that few people would put up with you after that stunt you pulled."

I know this game. I'm not playing it. "Forget it. I'm not joining your company."

He straightens and his face twists into a condescending knot. I can practically see the peacock feathers bristling. "Who said I wanted you?"

"Well if you don't want me, then we don't have a problem."

Pierce and I help Aaron get up off the mat. He sways a bit and Sergei scowls. "Get him some vitamin water. It'll help him rehydrate faster."

"I know what to do."

"Make sure it's the sugar-free kind."

"Piss off," I mumble, as we start heading for the door.

"What?" he asks.

I actually don't think he heard and I'm not repeating it. With Aaron leaning on Pierce for support, I follow the two of them out of the room. As I pass by Sergei I say, "Why don't you turn on the damned air conditioning?"

"It's broken." He's on his way back to the classroom, back erect and nose in the air.

Then send everybody home, I want to say. But I know better. I'm sure that never occurred to anybody. I sure as hell wouldn't have gone home over something as inconvenient as a little heat.

215

Still, though I'm vaguely aware that my anger at this might be a touch out of proportion, I'm steaming all the way out of there. I'm steaming all the way home, as Pierce sits in the back with Aaron and interrogates him to determine the exact cause of his fainting spell— dehydration and heat exhaustion, he claims.

Maybe. Maybe not. I have a few questions of my own, ones I'll ask as soon as I get Aaron alone.

We get Aaron home and Pierce gets him settled in bed while I pour some orange juice and get a slice of wheat bread. When Aaron sees what I have for him, he tries complaining, saying he wants to follow Sergei's instructions for sugar-free vitamin water.

"Sergei can go fuck himself," I say. "I'll go to the store and get something with electrolytes in a minute, but I want you to get this in your body first."

I only get him to eat half the bread, but he does at least drink the juice. Pierce goes into the kitchen for more, and I take my opportunity to find out what I want to know. "Are you purging?"

He shakes his head, still looking clammy and weak.

"Laxatives? Tea?" There's a special tea some people use to get things moving through their system before they can absorb too many calories. That shit is dangerous sometimes, too. He shakes his head again.

"Are you lying to me?"

"No, Emma. Fuck. I just didn't drink enough today, all right? Sergei was pushing us hard and it was hot as a fucking sauna in there. I can't eat anymore though. I feel too sick. I just want to sleep."

I know he could be lying to me, but since heat exhaustion actually is plausible, I'm hoping that's all this is. Aaron doesn't exactly have a healthy relationship with food and he needs to eat more than he does, but I've never seen any signs that he's gone beyond that either.

"All right. Get some rest."

Finally starting to calm down, I go back into the kitchen. Pierce looks shaken. I rub his broad shoulder. "He'll be okay." He's leaning on the counter, bracing himself with both hands.

"I heard you."

My stomach drops and my hand freezes. "I was only making sure."

He looks at me. "Do you believe him?"

I lift one shoulder. "I think so."

"He doesn't eat enough."

"I know."

"I've talked to him about it. It doesn't help. If anything, it seems to make things worse."

I nod. "I know."

"I feel so helpless. I just want to knock some sense into him sometimes."

"It could be worse. A lot worse. And it'll probably be different when he retires."

Pierce gives a humorless laugh. "Yeah, *years* from now."

"It was just heat exhaustion. He'll be okay." I might be trying to comfort myself as much as Pierce.

He doesn't seem comforted at all. Pierce isn't stupid. Even if it was just heat exhaustion today, that doesn't change everything else.

218

I shrug again. "Look, it's not something we can control."

He pops off the counter, and starts marching back toward the studio. "You're right. I can't stop him from hurting himself and I can't stop you from hurting yourself either."

"Hey!" Well that sure as hell came out of left field. I hustle out of the kitchen, following Pierce and lowering my voice. "It's not the same thing."

He gives me a firm look. "It's exactly the same thing. You're both hell-bent on destroying yourselves. What the fuck am I supposed to do about that?"

"I'm not. I just..." I sweep my arm around me, "Look where I'm living. I have nothing. A few boxes full of crap and a suitcase. I need the fucking money."

He shakes his head and says softer, but still firmly. "Not as much as you think you do."

Easy for him to say.

He goes to my purse that's sitting on the table, and opens it.

"What are you doing?"

He retrieves my phone and holds it out to me. "You have a place to stay and food to eat. And friends willing to help you until you can provide those things for yourself. That's more than some people have."

I look at my phone. I know what he wants me to do. But even after what happened yesterday, the thought of quitting makes me physically ill to my stomach, and not just because giving up a week's worth of pay hurts. In spite of everything, walking away from Rayce feels... wrong.

But that's probably my messed up feelings throwing everything out of whack, right? As an outside observer, Pierce has to see this situation with more clarity than I do. This is just... me making the same mistake all over again.

So why does it feel so different?

"Tell him you quit."

I open my mouth to protest.

"Give me one fucking victory today, will you?"

I press my lips together. After what happened yesterday, I should've quit already. Maybe I really am like Aaron, hell-bent on my own self-destruction. Pierce is right. He has to be.

I take my phone and pull up Rayce's number.

# Chapter 20

## Rayce

I can't work for you anymore.

That's what her text says. I fucked this up all the way around. Not only have I pushed her away, I've cost her a job.

Me: You don't have to do that. I'm sorry.

Emma: I can't see you again.

Me: Then I'll stay away.

Emma: You won't.

I can't blame her for thinking that. I'm not even sure she's wrong. I toss my phone next to me on the couch. I'm in the game room but the TV isn't on. After I put Emma's lasagna in the oven, I came down here as an escape but it's not working. I'm too turned around to think about anything else. Normally, I look forward to dinner with my siblings and my cousin. But right now, all I want to do is sleep.

Me: You shouldn't lose income over this. I'll stay away. Really.

But I don't hear back. I manage to avoid responding for seven whole minutes. You're doing such a good job. This isn't your fault. I'll let you work in peace.

Still no reply. I don't know if she's thinking about it, or just ignoring me because she's made up her mind. I still can't believe I screwed this up so badly.

I lie down on my side, exhausted from too little sleep and too much stress. I consider half a dozen different texts I could send her, but even though I want to, I don't send any of them.

It feels too much like begging, and I don't beg.

A light <u>pat, pat, pat</u> on my cheek wakes me up. I open my eyes to find Little Max, Lizzy's future stepson, blinking at me, maybe a foot away from my face. He's probably the sweetest six-year-old boy I've ever met. Not that I've met many.

"Uncle Rayce?" he whispers loudly. "Are you sleeping?"

Not anymore.

"No."

"Daddy said I have to be quiet so I don't wake you."

"You're being very quiet."

He grins, proud of himself. His grin widens as I sit up and rub my eyes. I can guess what he's thinking.

"Can I have a piggyback ride?"

I must have really crashed out, because I come up into the living room to discover everybody's already here. Lizzy with her fiancé Brett, Connor with his wife Whitney, and my cousin Corrine with her boyfriend Mason.

Everyone's paired up and happy. And for the first time ever, I resent it.

This is not like me. All the people I love most in the world are in my living room, and it's made me happy to see my siblings and cousin find people who love them so well.

I've been accused of being overly protective, and as the oldest brother, that's probably true. But someone has to look after them, and if that means watching for signs that anything is amiss, well then that's what I'm going to do. No one gets to hurt my family.

But all I see is the spark in Lizzy's eyes when she looks at Brett, the sense of wholeness and well-being Whitney has brought to Connor, and the way Corrine snuggles into Mason like he's the living incarnation of safety and peace.

This is the kind of stuff I look for, because these little clues are the kind of things you can't fake. They're the kind of things that reassure me that their happiness is real and there isn't trouble brewing behind closed doors.

It truly makes me happy.

So never before have I been with them and cared at all that I was the only one who's still single. I've never resented it. I've just been happy for them.

But today?

Today it hurts. Because there's only one woman I've ever wanted by my side in such an intimate, family setting, and I may have broken things between us forever.

I let little Max off my shoulders. He spots Corrine's new puppy in the dining room and runs off to play with him.

"There he is," Corrine says. She looks like a delicate sprite of a thing, thanks to two battles with cancer, but she's a pretty tough cookie. Even though she's a cousin, she feels more like another sibling because we were all raised so close together. "We were wondering if we should call an ambulance," she teases. "It's not like you to sleep in the middle of the day."

"I didn't sleep well last night."

"Everything okay?" Lizzy asks.

"Fine."

"I don't know," Connor says in his teasing voice. "Things are pretty weird around here. Did you know you have an actual meal cooking in your oven?"

"Ha ha." I sink into a chair. Normally I enjoy our monthly sibling dinners, but I'm in no mood for this today. Smelling Emma's lasagna cooking is not helping matters. Why didn't I just order pizza?

"Is that something your personal chef prepared for you?" Whitney asks.

I nod.

"What's her name again?"

"Emma." My heart tightens as her name passes over my lips.

"What do you think of Alice's little experiment?" Connor asks.

"I think I can prepare my own damn meals."

Light laughter skitters around the group. I'm feeling prickly, but apparently that's not coming across. It's just as well. This isn't their fault.

"Texting Guido does not count as preparing a meal," Connor says.

I don't respond to this.

"So are you going to tell Alice you've tried it and didn't like it?" Lizzy asks.

"Not so fast," Connor says easily, his arm on the back of the couch and his fingers absently playing with the ends of Whitney's dark hair. "Let's see how her lasagna tastes first. If it's good enough, I say we take a vote and overrule Mr. Pizza over there."

Whitney gives Connor a gentle jab with her elbow. "Stop picking on him. Look how tired he is."

"I'm fine."

But Whitney's comment seems to have kicked in Lizzy's radar. My sister cocks her head at me, a more serious expression on her face. "Are you sure you're all right?"

"Fine. I just couldn't sleep last night, for some reason." Time to redirect the conversation to a safer topic. "How's the wedding planning coming?"

This does the trick. My sister's face lights up. "Really well. In fact, yesterday Renée and I got the flowers picked out." Renee is the resort's Events Manager, and is helping Lizzy put things together. I have no doubt it will be a grand affair.

She turns her attention to the women in the room. "You have to see the bouquet." She grabs her phone, which has been sitting on the coffee table. "Here, I have a picture." The girls shuffle around and gather next to Lizzy while she shows them the various pictures on her phone.

Things are moving on and I'm happy to fade into the background and take on the role of overseer. Mason asks if anybody wants a drink and gets up to retrieve some beers. Brett goes into the dining room to check on Little Max and the dog.

I think I'm safe from uncomfortable topics, when Lizzy hits me with this. "Oh, Rayce. You're not allowed to keep changing your mind about who you're bringing to the wedding, like you did with Connor. I'm not getting table placards printed three different times."

"They didn't even have table placards." They got married too quickly for that.

"Still. I know you," she says with a teasing glint in her eye. "I should lock you down right now. Who are you bringing?"

I want to say, It's still two months away and I'm not bringing anybody anyway, so stop asking.

No, strike that. What I really want to say is, The woman I'm bringing is Emma Swanson and you'll more than like her, you'll love her, because she's the most remarkable woman I've ever encountered.

"I'll figure it out later."

"I think you should bring Sarah," Lizzy says. "I like her."

It doesn't surprise me that that's who Lizzy would suggest. I mean, sure. Of all the girls on the roster, if there was a 'front runner' it was probably Sarah. We make the most sense, on paper anyway. Her family has been in Swan Pointe for three generations and owns more prime California real estate than anyone I know personally. She knows what it's like to grow up with certain expectations and understands how to handle being in the public eye.

If it weren't for her tendency to fall into gossip, I'd tolerate her a lot better. She's fine. Really fine. But any time I've thought of a long-term future with her, it's felt more like a business deal than a matter of the heart.

I suspect she feels the same about me. She once said we'd make a 'fine match' with the same tone she'd comment on a nice paring of wine and cheese. I'd only nodded. I understood what she was saying.

This was all before Emma.

I couldn't care less what Emma and I would look like on paper. What little time I had with her was magic. And I ruined the whole thing.

"I don't know yet," I say in answer to my sister's suggestion.

Connor laughs. "And you won't know any better by the time it gets here."

I give him a look and he grins. We both know he's right.

"I'm just saying, this is exactly the kind of thing you're going to overthink. But if you pick someone tonight, the decision's done and Lizzy isn't stressing about it."

"I say we make him call whoever it is tonight so he can't get out of it," Corrine says, joining in on their game.

I could put a stop to this at any time. Or I could get it fucking over with like Connor says, because he's right. What difference does it make who I take?

"Fine."

"Really?" Lizzy asks.

"Why not. One less thing to worry about."

She does a little fist pump and silently mouths "score" to Whitney. Maybe she really has been worrying about it. Even though I only kept changing my mind for Connor's because they got married down in fucking Mexico and that was a whole lot of time to commit to spend with the same woman.

I begin my usual pick-a-date routine. Aside from Sarah, there's Kim. She's very sweet and probably the right kind of person to have at a family function, but her personality is so bland that she's best endured in small doses. Her father is William Morris, but she inherited none of his charisma. Lynda is fun because she's energetic, both in her public persona and in bed, so several hours with her wouldn't be so bad—though I've lost all interest in sleeping with her. But she's high-maintenance and a bit of a snob.

Of course, the thing that counts against all of them is the same thing. They aren't Emma.

"Where are you going?" Lizzy asks as I get off the couch.

"Getting a drink."

I head toward my office, and hear her call after me in a playful voice, "Don't think you're getting out of this tonight."

I take my time. In fact, I pour three fingers, drink half of it, then re-top off my glass before heading back out there. Corrine and Whitney have migrated to the kitchen island and started Corrine's favorite game, gin.

Lizzy looks at me expectantly. "Well?"

I don't know what answer to give her any better now than I did before. The only person I can think about is Emma. I don't want to take anybody else.

But regardless of what I want, I may as well suck it up and make a decision.

I'm tempted to tell Connor to pick a number between one and three and settle things that way, but if I'm going to be an asshole about it, I'd rather keep that to myself.

Corrine lays down an eight of spades.

All right. The next card she lays down makes the decision. Diamonds for Lynda, Clubs for Kim, and Spades for Sarah. I'll just go with whatever the cards decide. Connor's right. It's one fucking night. Who the hell cares?

Corrine slaps down another card.

The queen of hearts.

"Well, fuck," I say aloud.

# Chapter 21

## Emma

It's been two weeks since Rayce kissed me.

I put in the last week and a half of my contract, and he stayed away as promised. We did no more than communicate via text, and that was only to minimally coordinate our schedules. I'm back in banquet, though Alice thought sure the chef job would become permanent so she was only able to give me a few hours this week. Starting next week, I'll be full-time again. I've been working inside his resort for the past two days, and haven't seen him once.

I think it really is over. I think if he were going to try anything, he would have done it by now. But instead he's staying away, just like I told him to.

It's been two weeks, so it should be easier now. But it isn't. I'd like to say that I've moved on and am feeling better about things, but I don't. Each day that passes is more difficult than the last.

Alice hand delivered my check from the chef job, and I used that money to pay back Aaron and Pierce, over their many protests. I had just enough left to put down a deposit on a cheaply-furnished apartment. Next Friday, I'll be able to move in with the few belongings I have left. The apartment's on a bus line, which will be my new form of transportation until I have enough money to get something else.

I should be happy. I got out of what was an improper situation, I paid off my debt to my friends, and in less than a week I'll have a place to live that's my own.

In fact, I should be nothing but happy.

But I'm not. I'm torn up with wanting him.

Yesterday, I helped Pierce and Aaron load up a U-Haul with paintings and display panels and all the other stuff Pierce needed for an outdoor show he has in Northern

California this weekend. Aaron's going along to help. They'll be gone until Sunday night.

This massive apartment feels too big and too lonely. I have the day off, so I have way too much time on my hands. I put in a morning workout, cleaned the living areas of their apartment, went for a run, then got desperate enough that I started straightening up Pierce's area. I have no idea if he's going to mind. I've never gotten into his stuff. But I'm too pent-up with frustrated energy to care.

I straightened up his desk. I cleared off and put away the supplies on his big wooden framing table, then wiped down the top. I swept and mopped the floors.

I'm giving serious thought to cleaning the windows. That would take all damned weekend.

Instead, I decide I need to get out of the house. I get cleaned up, but when it comes time to get dressed I have no idea where I think I'm going to go.

"Fuck it."

I throw on my workout pants, a tank, and a loose-fitting tee. If a run along the beach doesn't tire me out, I don't know what will.

Minutes later, I'm on my way to the ocean, wondering why I didn't take the long way around so I wouldn't have to pass so near the resort. It's as I'm approaching Guido's, at the bottom of the hill, that I see Rayce's black Jag in the parking lot.

I grip the wheel and my heart pounds against my chest as I drive by, trying to get a glimpse of him through the windows of the building and wondering if he's in there.

But I know he is.

He's in there.

And I'm here.

I stop at a light. Adrenaline courses through my body as I look at Guido's in my rearview mirror. The light turns green, and I take a right, not in the direction of the ocean. As if my body is making its own decisions, I navigate a U-turn, pull into Guido's parking lot, and turn off the car.

The voices in my head that have argued with me ever since I first saw Mr. Rayce Rivers have gone silent.

There is no more thinking. There is just doing.

# Chapter 22

## Rayce

I'm sitting in my usual spot in the back and see her through the window before she comes in the door. Just like the first time I saw her I can't take my eyes off her, but it's so much worse this time. Because now I know her. And because I can't stop wanting her no matter how hard I try.

She told me to stay away and I have, only because of the hurt look she had on her face when she said it. She meant it. It's taken all the self-control I have not to go to her and persuade her to give us a chance.

I almost feel like... begging, if I'm honest. I don't think I've begged for anything since I was eight.

But when Emma walked out of my kitchen two weeks ago, she scooped a big hole out of my chest and took it with her. That hole isn't empty either. It's filled with wanting so strong I'm out of my mind half the time.

And now here she is, opening the door. The mere vision of her is torment.

She's wearing soft workout pants that ride low on her hips and a loose shirt that comes just to her waist. It has a wide neck and the strap of a sleeveless tank peeks out from underneath. This is the most I've seen of her neck ever, the smooth skin unmarked, and it's driving me crazy. How many times have I wished I could just gaze upon her body and take in the complete package, swirling tattoo and all, instead of these maddening pieces here and there.

When she comes inside, her eyes sweep the room as if she's looking for someone. She spots me and her searching halts. She holds my gaze. Her blonde hair is falling in loose waves to her shoulders.

It's physically painful, this wanting her.

She doesn't look away. She doesn't look surprised. She looks like she knew I was here already. She slowly approaches the counter, eyes still on me.

We don't break eye contact until Guido's son asks if he can help her. She glances at my plate, which is empty. This seems to decide something for her. She looks at me, heat flashing between us, then to Guido's son. "I'll just take a Sprite. Small."

She watches him as he goes to get it, crossing her forearms and resting them on the high counter. The hem of her shirt lifts slightly, revealing a slender slice of her stomach. That curling tattoo I saw on her thigh all those weeks ago isn't just on her thigh. That sliver of bare stomach is marked on one side by that same, thin, graceful design.

My entire body hardens with desire and the seat of my pants get uncomfortably tight. Right here in fucking Guido's. I need to look away, get myself under control. Instead I drink her in, from that sin-inducing waist to her sandaled feet and pink pearl toenails to the curve of her breasts and lower back to the graceful line of her neck.

Finally, most powerfully, to her delicate, heart-shaped face. Because this is more than wanting a woman's soft curves. It's wanting *this* woman, and everything she is. And everything she makes me feel.

She's been watching me. She *wants* me to watch her.

She pays for her drink with cash, tells him to keep the change, and heads for the door. I'm struck with a moment of panic. I want to hurry after her, but the last time I saw her was agony for both of us. Remembering that devastated look on her face when she begged me to stay away from her keeps me pinned in place.

Before she leaves, she glances around the restaurant, as if to be sure no one is watching. In the space of a heartbeat, I do the same.

There's an old couple in the corner, eating their pizza in silence, eyes on their food. A group of young men circle another table, laughing and talking too loudly. Guido's son is assembling a pizza behind the line, focused on laying out pepperoni slices in a fan that follows the curved line of the dough's edge.

No one's paying attention to either one of us.

My eyes swing back to her as she pushes open the door. She looks over her shoulder and gives me a meaningful glance. I straighten slightly, and this seems to satisfy her.

She exits the building and heads for the parking lot. Heart beating in my ears, I watch through the large, open windows until she disappears from my sight.

Am I imagining this? Does she want me to follow her?

I recall again her distraught expression the last time I saw her, the pain in her voice as she told me to leave her be. But the last five minutes seem to be undoing all that. Still unsure of her intentions, I at least make a decision about what to do next.

I've managed to keep my physical response to her controlled enough to be able to walk out of here without disgracing myself. I grab my plate and stand. I tap the counter as I pass by Guido's son. "Tell Guido I said goodbye."

"Will do. See ya, Rayce."

I toss my plate in the garbage and push through the door, wondering if maybe I've got it all wrong and she's gone. But no.

When I get to the parking lot, she's standing by her open car door, watching for me. She holds my eye for a second, then smoothly turns and gets in her car.

My blood is pumping thickly. I debate between going to her car or mine, but she's starting to pull out of her parking spot. I'm still not sure what's going on.

Keeping one eye on her, I go to my car and get in. I start the engine, but look over my shoulder to see what she's doing. She's stopped, waiting to exit the parking lot.

I watch her for a minute. Then two. I don't move. Neither does she, even though it seems there have been opportunities for her to pull out.

I back out of the space and pull in behind her. She lets a small opening go by, but when there's one big enough for two cars, she pulls out.

I follow.

And this is how it goes. One turn after another, she leads me through downtown and to an industrial section of town. She pulls up to a large, dark grey two-story building that's home to "Joey's Chop Shop." My mind is trying to work out what's happening and where the hell we are, but it's difficult with the dull roar of desire and hope fogging up my brain.

She pulls into the alleyway next to the building, then under a covered parking area with room for only two cars. The other space is occupied by a motorcycle I've seen once before. I find a spot farther down the alley.

By the time I do this and get out of the car, she's standing by a side door. She's holding the door open a few inches, and watching me. Meeting her eyes is like getting struck by something that makes it hard to breathe. Let alone think.

I start to head over and she disappears inside the building. The door swings shut. When I get to it and reach for the knob, the thought crosses my mind that it could be locked. But it pulls open easily. It leads not inside the back of the chop shop, as I'd expected, but to a stairwell rising to the second floor. I'm guessing there's an apartment up there.

Hers.

I stand at the open door, hand on the knob, looking up that stairwell and not moving. Not because I'm hesitating. Not because I don't know what to do, but because it takes me a moment to absorb the fact that she's trying to change the rules. And she has.

But whether she knows it or not, I'm the one in charge of this game.

I march up the stairs, unsurprised to find a door hanging open at the top. I swing it wide, revealing a massive space that must take up the entire second floor. I know immediately that there's no one else in it. I'm vaguely aware of easels, what looks like a ballet barre and mirror in a near corner, and a kitchen and living area at the far end. There's a wall of windows. High ceilings. Half-finished paintings damn near everywhere.

There's a million things I could look at, but in the middle of it all, in front of a large

work table not too far into the room... is
Emma.

Standing there.
Waiting for me.

# Chapter 23

## Emma

He's standing in the doorway, maybe twenty feet away, wearing the most intense expression I've yet seen on him. He's in slacks and a button-down maroon shirt, no tie, the top button undone. He looks worn, like he hasn't been sleeping well, but this does nothing to lessen the impact of his appearance.

He's striking. My body is lit up from his presence... and the fact that we're alone.

I can hardly think. It's been that way since I first turned my car around. I've been driven by something so deep inside me it defies reason. It drove me to walk into Guido's, get his attention, and keep it. He was at a back table, facing the door, and it seemed like he didn't want to take his eyes off me long enough to even blink.

I lured him out, led him here. It was all I could do to drive, hardly breathing as I kept checking my rear view mirror for him. All the while my pulse pounded in my ears and between my legs. Like it's doing now.

And now that he's here, I couldn't say what I want to happen next. I only know that I've been going crazy without him. I'm still going crazy, because even though he's here, he feels so far away.

I shuffle on my feet slightly, something I almost never do. "I wanted to talk to you." As if I had any sort of plan.

"Oh yeah?"

He flicks the door shut and it slams behind him as he takes one long stride after another toward me.

"What do you want to say?"

Then he's to me. I take one step to meet him and our mouths crash together. He's clutching my face. Claiming my mouth. Demanding entrance. Gripping my hair with both hands. I'm clinging to him. Moaning. Spinning. God, how I've needed this.

More, please more.

His mouth assaults my jaw with urgent kisses. He ravages my neck. When he gets to the tender base, my knees actually buckle. He tightens his grip, supporting me with solid arms as my mind and body are dazed with his touch and his presence. His masculine scent, unmarred by cologne, is making my uterus clench.

He wrenches the loose collar of my shirt over my shoulder. His hot breath warms my exposed skin. He runs his fingers over my neck, giving a groan—almost a growl—as if frustrated by something, but I can't stop to think what because now he's devastating my shoulder with his mouth. My legs are still too weak to do their job properly, a problem I've never experienced. What is he doing to me?

He grips my face and returns to my mouth, our tongues searching, warring, desperate for what we've been craving for weeks.

Then everything stops.

He pulls back slightly, still holding my face. The only sound is our hard pants, mingling together. His intense eyes are on mine. My mouth is partly open but I'm unable to speak. <u>Please, more.</u>

I want all of it. All of him. This. Us.

"Are you ready for this now?" His voice is low and controlled. He's always been in control.

I breathe more than speak. "Yes."

But he doesn't kiss me again like I wanted. He releases me, and the tiniest whimper of protest escapes me.

He steps out of my reach and my body sways after him, following his movement like a reed in the tide.

I'm confused for a moment, because in spite of his sudden departure, his eyes have lost none of their heated intensity.

He gives an authoritative nod in my direction. His voice is deep and steady. "Take your clothes off." His strong fingers began smoothly unbuttoning the sleeves of his shirt.

A rush of relief and anticipation falls through me. I am struck. Unable to command my body. My eyes flit between his face and this controlled unbuttoning. One cuff undone. Two. I still can't move.

When he starts on his top buttons, my eyes lock with his. His eyes sharpen, and the command repeats itself in my mind. Take your clothes off.

I hook my thumbs under the waistband of my pants, slip the material over my hips, and let them fall in a soft pile at my feet. I step out, then kick them away with one pointed toe. My movements are smooth like his. I don't need to see myself in a mirror to know that. But I'm trembling at my core, and wonder if he is as well.

His eyes have dropped to the curling mark on my thigh. He was not surprised to see it, which answers a question I'd wondered about before. He did see my tattoo beneath the dress I wore that night at the art show.

He's still unbuttoning his shirt. The material is gently gaping open, giving me a vision of his chest. Again, I am temporarily still. He releases the last button. The material hangs open and he slips it off his broad shoulders.

I gaze at him shamelessly. His chest is chiseled and firm, his trim waist taut and smooth. His movements are fluid and intentional.

He begins to undo his belt.

I smoothly lift my shirt over my head. I'm not wearing a bra underneath, just a black tank. In the gap between the tank and my black string panties, my mid-drift is slightly exposed. His eyes are on the section of the mark he can see there.

He wants to see how far this tattoo goes. I see it in his eyes. He looks more than hungry for it, he looks <u>starved.</u> I think I know what that groan was about when he exposed my shoulder. It was just bare skin, with no mark.

His eyes come smoothly to mine. He doesn't even need to say the words.

Keep. Going.

He wrenches his belt out of the loops with one even movement, the sound of it making my breath catch. He tosses it aside, the buckle clattering against the concrete floor.

I grab the hem of my tank. He pauses for the first time, his hands hovering at the top of this unbuttoned slacks. His eyes lock on my body and the mark it contains.

I slowly pull off the tank, baring my breasts, and let the material fall softly to the floor. As I let him look at me, my core turns molten. We're both still.

His eyes travel first over my tattoo, which curls in a smooth line up my thigh and side before cupping underneath a single breast. Then he takes in all of me, both marked and unmarked. Both body and soul. I've spent my whole life moving my body for other people to watch, but I've never felt so <u>seen.</u>

He slowly comes nearer, eyes holding mine. I don't move. My breath shallows as he comes close. He stops when he's within arm's reach and his gaze drops to my tattoo.

His fingertips gently brush the base of the swirling mark. Heat hums through me. His other hand comes to the same place on my other leg, then both hands slowly travel up my thighs. His hand follows the swirling mark—caressing, pressing, tracing—laying claim to even this, the one thing that is truly mine.

His warm hands travel over the curve of my hips, up my sides, moving in concert as they cup my breasts, the thumbs sweeping over the peaks. My breath hitches in my chest.

My hands go to his elbows and travel to his biceps, the hard knot of muscle under my thumbs. As his hands move smoothly up both sides of my neck, I lift slightly on tiptoe, lean closer, part my lips, needing him to satisfy this desire swirling deep in my core.

He answers with his mouth on mine, his hands in my hair, his bare chest pressed against me. Our kisses become urgent as he backs me up. He lifts me easily and I wrap my legs around his tapered waist. He carries me the rest of the way and sets me on the edge of the large, wooden framing table.

He goes back to claiming my jaw and neck. I prop myself with both hands, my head falling back, as he hungrily takes first one breast and then the other into his mouth. I'm clutching at his back, his hair, his shoulders.

I tighten my legs around him, bringing his hard chest against my throbbing center. The next happens in a heated whirlwind: he ditches his pants, sheathes himself in a condom, and literally tears off my damp panties. In one swift move I'm flat on the table and he's on top, angling over me like a predator.

"Ready?" he asks again.

I nod urgently, scooting down slightly, trying to get closer to him.

He enters me in a single, powerful stroke. I'm seized with a mix of pain and pleasure so strong I gasp and clutch his biceps.

"Whoa…"

He holds steady, allowing me to adjust to him. And *holy hell* is there a lot to adjust to. I breathe, my body heating up even more and my core softening as I expand to fit him.

"All right?" he checks, his voice low with desire, but I don't respond. My body is ready, back to wanting, but I am overwhelmed with our joining. He waits, keeping his eyes on me while I keep mine on his. Mr. Rayce Rivers is *in* me, in every sense of the word. I lace my fingers behind his neck, hanging on.

"Slow," I whisper.

My breath catches as he slowly strokes me again, then waits, testing my reaction. Our mouths are inches apart, our hot breaths swirling together.

My fingers slip into his hairline and I sink deeper into his arms, my legs curling around his hips, asking for more. He gives it, and I answer in movement against him. Again, harder. Again.

His mouth claims me. I tremble against his thrusts, gripped by unspeakable ecstasy edged with a hint of pain. We climb in passion and intensity. All the pent up frustration and desire that's been building since I first stepped into his office swells into a frenzied roar.

I am lit up by his groans, as if his sounds were a hot lick of flame at my center. My cries echo in the cavernous space. I don't recognize my own voice.

My head arches back sharply and I grip the table edge above me for support.

I'm stunned. Astonished. Quivering on the edge of a sexual height I've never experienced. "Almost…" I gasp. "Almost…"

"I know." His lips murmur against my neck. "I feel you."

That does it. I am careening over the edge, split at the seams, digging my fingernails into his back as I unravel into a pulsing, formless mass. His body hardens as he comes with me and I'm overwhelmed to experience him so raw.

It is a slow, hard descent back to the reality of this world. We each struggle to catch our breaths. My limbs are heavy, uncooperative in a new way now. I can barely move. My eyes are still shut and my heart is pounding painfully, trying to get back some semblance of control.

The energy that's been coursing through me starts to settle and wane. A weird mix of contentment and unease seeps into its place.

What was I thinking? If things go bad, as they did before, how will I ever recover?

I didn't mean to give him so much of myself.

I open my eyes to discover him watching me. My heart flutters thickly in my chest. He lifts some of his weight off me as our bodies soften. I'm just now aware of the hardness of the table beneath me. I didn't even notice it before.

Our breathing is quieter now, almost normal but not quite. I adjust slightly under him, my hips beginning to protest about the hard surface.

"Here," he says, pulling out and hopping down. "You can't be comfortable." He smoothly picks me up and sets me on my feet. I'm able to stand, but still unable to talk. I already miss his skin against mine. "I'll be right back," he says, gently nipping my chin between his fingers.

As he heads back to the bathroom to take care of things, my sense of unease grows, and now I know why. With Chad, once an evening progressed to sex, it was pretty much over. As bad as that was, I already know it will be so much worse with Rayce, because Chad never once made me feel the way Rayce just did.

I'm not only talking the sex either, though if 'sex' is the word used to describe what Chad did to me, there needs to be a completely different word for the mind-altering encounter Rayce and I just had.

But I was completely unprepared for what Rayce just did to <u>me</u>. My heart and my soul. I may not have consciously planned for this to happen, but I must have still had some sort of expectation of what it would be like to have sex with Rayce. I guess I thought if I gave in, it'd be mainly physical, like scratching an itch, terrible as that may sound.

Now, watching his lithe, naked body crossing the large space, going farther and farther away from me, I think I may have been lying to myself about what this really is for me. But it's too late to save my heart from pain now.

Because this is the part where he leaves.

# Chapter 24

## Emma

By the time he's coming out of the bathroom, I have my tank back on and I'm pulling my yoga pants over my hips. I'm going commando because my underwear is in shreds on the floor and I don't want him to see me get another pair out of the suitcase behind the chair.

Anyway, that's the least of my concerns. I'm just trying to steel myself so I don't look devastated when he bugs out of here.

It's probably not helping that I'm allowing myself to take in every inch of his body. Rayce Rivers is nothing but lean muscle mass and smooth confidence. He seems to have no qualms about being nude in front of me. And why should he? Even without an erection, his masculinity is impressive.

As he crosses back through the apartment, he's looking around. I see him putting two and two together. He knows I have roommates, there's only one bedroom, and a quick glance is all it would take to tell him who occupies it. The walls and dresser are full of pictures of Aaron and Pierce together.

His features darken as he looks first at the couch, then at me. "Where do you sleep, Emma?"

"Couch central," I confirm, pulling my shirt over my tank. "But not for long. I put down a deposit on an apartment this week."

"Good," he says with seemingly genuine relief as he scoops up his pants. He's wasting no time getting dressed. At least I beat him to the punch.

I lean back against Pierce's framing table, a swoop of longing descending through my core as I remember what we just did there. I cross my arms, trying to look nonchalant and needing to put my guard up.

"Where is it? Is it a safe neighborhood?" He's fastening his pants, naturally assuming his man-in-charge mode.

"Don't worry. I know how to handle myself."

This attempt to reassure him completely backfires. He looks flat alarmed. "Why? Where is it? What is there to handle?"

I have to admit, I find this little bit of protectiveness nice. "I don't mean I know how to handle the local muggers. I mean I know how to find myself a decent place to live, all right?"

He's still giving me that appraising look.

"Cross my heart." I make the little crisscross sign on my chest and can't help but smile at him, putting up my guard be damned.

He smiles back and wanders over to me, only in his pants and bare feet. You'd think my body would be satisfied enough to last for weeks, but no, no. My pulse ratchets up a notch or three.

"We'll see," he says easily.

"What, are you going to check it out and see if it passes muster?"

He doesn't answer. Instead he just continues with that confident gait, as if his investigation of my future home is none of my affair. "Where are your roommates?"

"Out of town at an art show. They get back Sunday night."

His smile widens and he comes right in front of me. He puts his strong hands on my biceps. The heat from his abs warms my still-crossed forearms. "So they wouldn't notice if you didn't sleep here tonight?"

So much for acting nonchalant. I blink at him stupidly. "What?"

"Come home, Emma."

"Home? Your home?" I know that's a stupid question. Of course he means his home. But the way he said it, like it's *our* home, hit me so strongly that the words were out of my mouth before I really thought them through. I'm also too busy being shocked that he wants me to go home with him and actually stay the night. I don't think I stayed the night with Chad once.

Maybe that's because he and Chad aren't anything alike.

But he's still my boss, and there's this whole side of things he knows nothing about. He might not be inviting me back to his home if he knew.

"Yes." He gently cups my face in his hands and gives me a soft kiss. "My home."

Oh, man, how I want to give into this. I mean really, really give all the way into this. No holding back, no worrying about whether it's wrong or a mistake. But I can't. Because whether this is wrong or a mistake or not, I don't know anymore, but I do know something he doesn't.

"We... actually do need to talk."

"All right." He softly brushes my hair away from my neck and rests his hands on my shoulders. "I'm listening."

"I don't want to tell you." As usual, I can't seem to stop myself from saying what I'm thinking.

His brows come together in concern. "What is it?"

But I can't. I can't tell him. It's going to change what he thinks of me, I know it. If all I did was sleep with my old boss, that would be bad enough, but it's so much more than that.

Starting to panic at the thought of telling him everything, I shake my head and step to the side out of his grasp. "Never mind. Forget it."

"Emma."

"No, I don't want to tell you."

"Then don't tell me," he says calmly.

I cross my arms again, examining his expression. He doesn't look... *amused* exactly. But he doesn't seem the least bit concerned either.

God, I don't know what to do. I should tell him right now. I should. Hell, I should've told him before, then he wouldn't have chased me so hard and we never would have kissed and I never would've lured him here and we wouldn't have gotten in any deeper.

But I didn't tell him and now here he is, and I can't say I regret it if I'm honest with myself. I do need to tell him. I do. But once I do, that will probably be that, and I'm not ready for this to be over yet.

His face softens and he comes close again. I let him pull me into his arms.

"You don't need to be afraid to talk to me, Emma."

"You don't even know what it is. You might think differently about me... once you know."

He brushes his fingertips lightly along my jaw. "You're afraid I won't want you anymore?"

My heart flutters in my chest, cherishing the thought that he wants me now. I shrug in answer. "I don't know."

"You don't need to worry. Whatever you have to say isn't going to change anything. I've been wanting you from the moment I first laid eyes on you."

"You didn't know me then," I argue, as if I couldn't say the same thing about him.

"I know you now."

"You don't know everything."

"It doesn't matter."

"Now you're just being stubborn."

He chuckles softly and pulls me more snug against him. I instinctively soften against him, our faces close. "I've missed this, Emma."

"I've missed this, too. Stop trying to distract me."

"I'm not distracting you from anything."

"I have to tell you something."

He kisses me, and lingers long enough to change the mood from playful to serious. He pulls back, keeping me in his arms. "I'm listening," he says again.

God, why does he have to be so perfect? Why does he have to make me want him so much? When he finds out the whole story, he might think I've been playing him and end the whole thing. I know I need to tell him, but it feels so good to be in his arms.

Still holding my eyes, he drops his forehead to mine. I sigh. We're already this far. Maybe it wouldn't be the worst thing to make it last just a bit longer?

"Tomorrow," I whisper. "I'll tell you tomorrow."

I mean it, too. Anything beyond that and I couldn't live with myself. I think he must know I'm serious too, because his expression matches mine.

He comes in closer, his lips hovering over mine. "Then we'd better make the most of things, between now and tomorrow."

*My thoughts exactly.* He kisses me and I allow myself to get lost in the slow heat of it. As I let him take charge, willing for now to go wherever he wants to take us, I realize something.

I trust him.

Trusting myself is another story.

# Chapter 25

## Rayce

After she packs a couple things into a beach bag with the blue sailboat on the front, we head down the stairs. I'm keeping her close, her hand in mine. I don't want her to escape again, nor am I prepared to simply say goodbye and go home without her. If there was an emptiness at my house before I met her, I didn't notice it. But over the past few weeks, home hasn't felt like home without Emma in it.

I'm still reveling in finally being with her. Little flashes pop into my mind: the way she clutched me to her when I first kissed her, that first taste of her skin, finally seeing all of her with nothing hidden from me. So goddamned lovely.

The first time I entered her, that moment when we paused so she could mold herself to me is a memory I will take to the grave. She yielded beneath me with such an intoxicating blend of trust and wanting. As we held each other's eyes in that moment, I thought, <u>This is why they call it becoming one.</u>

To go from that almost otherworldly sensation to such wildness and lust, then to such quiet tenderness after. The entire experience was a torrent of physical sensation and fluctuating emotions. Sex has never been like that for me. In fact, 'sex' doesn't seem to be the right word. What <u>is</u> the word for what we did? 'Making love' isn't the right way to describe it either. It was too primal for that. Whatever was, the emotional connection was overpowering.

This woman has been knocking me off balance since the day I first saw her.

Now here she is. By my side, right where she belongs. "Have you had dinner?" I ask.

"Just a Sprite." She gives me a mischievous grin.

"You were too busy seducing me to order a proper meal, huh?"

"I didn't seduce you." But she's still grinning like she knows exactly what she did.

We get to the base of the stairs and I back her against the wall, my arms bracketing her head. Her expression morphs from surprise to heated longing so fast I wonder if I'm not the only one being thrown off balance here. I like this new version of Emma, the one that doesn't fight this anymore but instead responds to every touch. "You seduced the fuck out of me," I say deeply.

Her smile widens, pleased with this compliment. Her hands trace a line from my lower back to my shoulder blades. "Well, you've been trying to seduce me from the start."

"That's right." I lightly brush my lips along her jaw and to the tender spot under her ear. Her body softens, her head leaning back, but her hips angle closer to me and she grips my shoulders. "Don't you ever forget that my response to you has always been *yes*."

I gently suck on her neck, pulling the soft skin between my teeth as I snake my hand into her hair and cup the curve of her ass. She moans softly, her hand going into my hair, too. The seat of my pants is getting uncomfortably tight. I'm tempted to carry her back upstairs and give that damned couch she's sleeping on a proper send off. But I want to get her home first, where she'll have room to get comfortable and enjoy things.

Next time, I intend on going slow and savoring every inch.

I step back, pulling her off the wall and supporting her by the elbow as she catches her balance. The word *swoon* comes to mind. I've always thought that was a ridiculous word, harking back to corseted women with lace handkerchiefs, but I rather like the thought of Emma swooning over me.

She slowly breathes out of her mouth. "You are so good at that."

I cup her face and give her a kiss. "I'm not the only one." I lightly tug on her hand and lead us to the side door. I've always prided myself on my ability to please a woman, but pleasing *this* woman is a whole different experience.

I put my hand on the knob, then halt.

My heart beats <u>one, two, three.</u>

"Um…"

I'm not typically one for "ums" but too many thoughts just assaulted my brain to come up with anything else.

I'm about to go out in public with Emma's hand in mine. All right, the back alley of this out-of-the-way chop shop isn't exactly "in public", but there's a funny side-effect to appearing in the local gossip rag when least expected. I've developed the sensation of being watched any time I step out my front door.

At the same time I'm calculating the risk of the wrong people seeing us together, I'm resentful that I should even have to care. I'm not ashamed of Emma or my feelings for her, but it's never that fucking simple, is it?

No. I have to constantly think about how everything I do affects the resort's brand, the reputation behind the Rivers family name, and the well-being of my siblings and employees. It's never just about what I want.

Not to mention, a photo of Emma and I together would only fan the flames of whatever Taylor Norrell has cooking. I'm up to three emails from her now, the last one only a few days ago. I keep thinking I need to take this to our lawyer, but she's being so vague about what she intends to do, or what she might want from me, that I don't know what to even tell him. For all I know these emails are nothing but rants.

And really, what's really bothering me about those emails is the idea that word might get out about what happened between us, so why would I tell our lawyer? I don't want him to know either.

On top of all this, my mind is running through the various ways we can get back to my place unseen, or if maybe we should just stay here, though my car could be spotted, or maybe already has been. It all seems ridiculous and annoying, which are not uncommon emotions for me to have whenever I start to resent the whole "prominent member of the community" thing. Like a pouting child.

Which brings me to the last part. One side of me wants to tell the world to fuck off and not care what anyone thinks, and the other side of me thinks I need to man the fuck up. This is the culture we live in. Right or wrong, image matters. Period. It wouldn't be fair to everyone who counts on me if I went around screwing things up for them for my own selfish reasons.

So yeah, "um" about sums things up.

"What's wrong?" Emma asks.

"We can't be seen together."

"Yes. I know. You want me to wait and follow you in my car or something?"

She sounds a little perturbed and I don't blame her. I'm not happy either. "No." I don't want her thinking she has to sneak around like she's my mistress. "Let's go in my car."

"Together?"

I'm not worried about anyone seeing us in the car because my windows are tinted enough to prevent a problem. Technically, they're darker than allowed by state law but if I ever get pulled over for it (no one hardly ever does) I'll just pay the damned ticket. If people want to judge me for it, *they* can spend their entire adult life hounded by the papers and then come talk to me.

I open the door and gesture to indicate she should go through first, which she does. "Wouldn't you rather we be together? I'll bring you back whenever you're ready."

"Well…"

I lead us past her car and she follows. I guess it's settled then.

As we cross the alley way and head down to my car, I can't help but check to see if anybody's around. It kills me to see the look on her face when she catches me doing this. I try to give her a reassuring smile, but I don't take her hand—just in case—and she doesn't smile back.

Dammit. Why does she have to be my employee? It shouldn't be like this with us.

I open the door for her and give one last look around as she gets in. I shut the door, relieved we've seemed to manage this without detection and grateful that we're in such an unobtrusive part of town, but still feeling terrible.

I get in but don't start the car right away. We sit there for a moment in silence.

"I'm sorry," I say. "We'll get this figured out."

"Let's don't worry about that yet. It doesn't matter." I get the feeling she's referring to this mysterious confession she feels she needs to share. I refuse to worry about that, especially now.

I take her hand and she lets me. "Tell me what you'd like for dinner. You can have anything you want."

"As long as we order in, right?"

Dammit.

"Emma—"

She lifts her free hand. "No, it's okay. I understand. I don't want to trot this out in front of everybody either. I don't know why I'm acting like this."

I squeeze her hand. "Because you understand but it still sucks?" I offer.

She nods and brushes the back of my hand with her fingertips. "I wish we met at the art show instead."

"Me too." I lean in slowly, testing the waters. She lets me give her a tender, reassuring kiss. I'm not used to kissing a woman like this, with so much emotion. I like it. I pull back to discover a soft smile on her face and that trusting look in her eyes. I told her I would find a way to fix this, and I will. This is far too good to keep hidden.

We settle back and I start the car. "If I'd known you were about to escape that night," I say playfully, "I would've shoved all kinds of people out of the way to get to you."

"Uh huh," she says playfully back. "Because <u>that </u>wouldn't have ruined your reputation at all."

If only my reputation were the only one to worry about.

Because otherwise, I'm not sure I'd care.

# Chapter 26

## Rayce

So much for taking my time. We didn't order dinner or even *make it up the stairs* before we indulged in each other right on the living room floor. It was as heated and intense as before, as if the last time had been <u>days and days</u> ago, instead of an hour.

Afterward, I ordered her something to eat. She finally got to try Guido's—agreeing the man knows how to make a damned good pie—while I got the address of her new apartment and investigated it online. It's passable, and definitely better than the couch, but not near good enough for her, as far as I'm concerned. When she teasingly asked if I approved I said yes, but I'm secretly making other plans. If that's where she's going to live, it's going to be up to snuff.

Then I suggested we go swimming, but somehow we ended up in my bed instead. I guess I took my time. There was no part of her body I didn't touch or taste. I wanted to experience it all, and I intended to draw out her pleasure from every nook and curve, every dip and fold. She moaned and writhed under my ministrations. Layer by layer, she yielded more fully until she lost all semblance of control.

I took more time, yes, but every caress, every taste, every movement was powered by a driving need to claim her. Even once I'd settled my attention to the sweet folds between her legs, I did not allow a hurried climb.

I would swipe my tongue softly up the center, rock it firmly back and forth over the hardened tip of her clit, and slide my fingers inside her moist core until she started to tighten and tremble. Then I'd ease off just enough to let her come slightly back down before bringing her to an even higher peak that I yet again wouldn't let her tip over.

When I finally edged her to a screaming orgasm, her hands an iron grip in my hair and her body clenching around my fingers, my taut cock throbbed against the mattress. I was delirious with wanting her.

Even then, I took the time to build her up again so that when my pent-up intensity and desire finally released and I came fiercely inside her, she was squeezing me with her own climax.

So yes, you could say I took my time, but it wasn't the indulgent scenic tours of past conquests. It was laced with depth and urgency and the need to make her mine.

Mine.

"What's the story with this?" We're back in my bed after spending the evening in the pool, sprawled out on our sides without a stitch on, and I'm trailing my fingers along the long, smooth lines of her tattoo.

She's still and relaxed, allowing me to touch her as I please. Her hands are tucked under her cheek. "What do you mean?"

Leisurely tracing the soft dip of her stomach, then the curve of her hip, I answer, "You don't strike me as the kind of person to get something like this just because it's beautiful. It means something to you."

She smiles. "Do you think it's beautiful?"

How have I not told her this yet? "Very."

"You don't strike me as the type of man to enjoy tattoos," she says, echoing my words back to me.

"I'm not. This one's different. What does it mean?"

"Hmmm," she says slowly. "That's kind of a long story."

She rearranges herself so she sitting cross-legged facing me, pulling the sheet loosely around her body. I sit up too, leaning against the headboard and resting my arm on one raised knee, the sheet a tent over my lower half.

She breathes out a short exhalation, as if preparing to say something difficult. "I used to be prima for the LA Ballet Troupe."

My eyebrows raise. Jesus, that's one of the most respected ballet companies in the country. "That explains a lot."

"It does?"

"You move like a cat."

She smiles, pleased. "I move like a dancer."

"But you don't dance anymore?" Her features darken, which gives me my answer. "Why not?"

"Well, I loved it. Really loved it, especially once I went pro because between class and performances, you're dancing practically all day."

Still processing this new revelation about her, I watch with wonder as her face takes on a nostalgic glow.

"I loved practicing for hours until I got my body to do exactly what I wanted. God, it was so fun. And it paid off, too. I advanced so quickly, people either admired or resented me. But no one was neutral about it."

I have no trouble envisioning her on stage, poised and in command. I can completely see it. I'm a little awestruck. A prima ballerina, right here in my bed.

With a tattoo a mile long.

She's watching me carefully. "Does this change how you see me?"

"Yes. I'm impressed as fuck."

I can't tell if this pleases her or not. She seems to absorb my statement as common fact. There's no arrogance there, but I get the sense that she's used to people being impressed with her, and I guess if she was good enough to be prima in the LA Ballet Troupe, she would've had a lot of practice.

But there's something else going on behind those eyes. Something I can't quite sort out. She drops her gaze and lightly scratches the back of her neck. "There's a lot of emphasis on perfection in ballet, especially physical perfection."

She gives me a significant look. I'm not sure I catch her meaning.

"No matter how thin you were," she clarifies, "it was always better to be just a little bit thinner."

A chill drops into the pit of my stomach. "Ah." My eyes pass over her body in a way they haven't before, searching for any signs of unwellness. But there are no jutting collarbones or protruding ribs. I've explored her body pretty thoroughly by now, and it is a picture of good health.

"My entire professional career, food was a constant battle. I managed not to do my body harm. I wasn't binging and purging. I made sure my calorie intake never went below medical guidelines. But I was still far too preoccupied with the whole thing. I knew exactly how much I was taking in. I knew exactly how many calories I was burning. And if I had anything extra… a cookie, a bite of cake, anything… I made damn sure to burn it off with extra strength training. I've seen some ballerinas eat an apple and call it lunch," she says flatly. "And there were too many times I was far, far too tempted to do the same."

I sit up cross-legged too and rest my elbows on my knees, absorbed by what she's telling me. I hurt for her, too. A profession so beautiful shouldn't be marred by something so ugly.

"I lived in constant awareness of every, tiny imperfection. How do you *not* think about your body when you're literally analyzing every inch of it in front of a mirror all day long? Is my leg extended at the exact right angle? Is the line from my shoulder to my fingertips correct? Should I rotate my wrist another quarter inch to the left? Everything. Absolutely everything must be visually perfect. Flawless. And that's just the baseline. If you want to go from the back row to prima, you have to be even better."

Her face is awash with longing and joy mixed with sorrowful restraint. It's a look I've seen before; it's how she used to look at me before she finally gave in.

"You have to use your body to make the audience <u>feel</u> something," she continues, "to give them an experience. It's transcendent, for you and for them. Except they're swept away while you're the one in control. This arm here. That leg there. Making these crazy huge leaps but landing <u>just so.</u>"

For these last two words, she softens her voice and makes a delicate gesture in the air with her hand, bringing to mind the lighter-than-air landing of a ballerina.

"You can't do *any* of that, without knowing every inch of your body. So it was this never-ending war with myself. I *knew* these ideals of beauty in the ballet world are too extreme. But that didn't change how I *felt*. It became such a chore to give my body what I logically knew it needed, but really wished it didn't. Does that make sense?"

I nod.

"For the last, I don't know, year or so that I was in the company, I knew I couldn't go on like that. Something had to give or I would break. I just..."

She stops, for the first time since she got going, really. She's frowning and looking down, squeezing my hand a little tighter. I squeeze back, trying to give her the courage to say whatever words are scaring her.

She takes another deep breath, then says slowly and deliberately. "I was afraid that if I stayed in ballet I would eventually give in to the pressure. I didn't trust myself. But I didn't want to leave either."

She swallows hard. Her eyes glisten for a moment as she fights tears. It's a minute before she speaks again, and when she does, there's a slight tremble in her voice.

"I knew I had to leave, but I just… loved it so much."

I squeeze her hand again. I know what that beautiful, swirling mark flowing down one side of her body makes me think of now. Graceful movement, like a dancer. "You still love it." I say quietly.

"That doesn't <u>matter!</u>" she says, her voice ringing through the room. Regretting her sharpness, she pinches her eyes shut. "I'm sorry."

"Don't be."

"It's just that…" She drops her forehead into her hands. Resting her elbows on her knees and still holding her head, she says, "Do you have any idea how many times I've heard people tell me I need to go back and I never should've left?"

"I wasn't going to say that."

Though I wish I could. God, the whole thing is such a damned shame.

"It took me a year." She's still speaking to her lap. "A whole year of trying to work up the courage to walk away." She lifts her head and looks at me. "You know what finally woke me up?"

I shake my head.

"A dancer I knew from school was at her sister's house one day, sitting on the couch watching her niece run around the living room, and her heart gave out." Her eyes glisten with tears again. I cradle her hand inside both of mine. "Just like that. One moment, she was fine, and the next she was slumped over in her seat. Gone."

"God, Emma." I rub her arm and shoulder as she wipes away the tear that's running down her cheek. "I'm so sorry."

"I'm sorry, too. For her and for her family. But I'm not sorry for me. It gave me the courage to do what I thought I couldn't. I left and never went back. Jean-Claude did everything to try to get me to change my mind. He yelled at me. Threatened me. Tried to talk sense into me."

She puts air quotes around the words 'talk sense.'

"He said I was throwing my life away and that I'd regret it. He even begged and let me tell you what. Ballet masters don't beg. *We* beg them, not the other way around. *They* call the shots, not us. But I was done with that. I was done with all of it, because I was not going to be dead at twenty-six just because I feared the gap between my thighs was too small."

She looks away, catching her breath and trying to settle her emotions. I'm still trying to process this new layer she's revealed of herself.

"Wanna know the irony? The way he fought me to come back made me realize that all the extra weight I thought I had wasn't going to jeopardize my career. He would keep me around anyway, just like he had all along. But it was too late, because by then I'd figured out that wasn't the problem. It was *me*. I knew I couldn't stop seeing the flaws as long as I spent every day looking in the same mirror as the girl who was a quarter-inch taller but twenty-two pounds lighter."

She shakes her head firmly, her face reflecting that stubborn determination I already know so well.

"There was only one way out and that was to *get out.* The idea for this tattoo had been in the back of my mind for probably six months or so. I went to one of the best artists in town, paid him extra to fit me in and that was that. Once I was on that table and he had the outline done, it finally all felt final. Smaller companies might work around something like that, but not the LA Ballet Troupe, that's for damned sure."

I'm gaining a new appreciation for Emma's iron will.

"I actually… it was a little embarrassing. I started laughing and kind of crying all at the same time. Just for a second. But I couldn't help it, because I was finally free from that battle I'd been fighting for <u>so long.</u> I finally knew I was going to be okay."

I let out a long exhalation. I don't think I've been hardly breathing at all. "Wow, Emma."

She finally gives a small smile.

"Are you okay now? Do you still find it difficult to eat?"

She shakes her head. "No. I'm much better now."

Is she though? I'm relieved to know she's kept herself healthy, and I'm glad she got out of a bad situation. But that look she had when she was describing her passion for dancing was so striking. Is she really okay not having that in her life anymore?

"This tattoo was my way of saying my body belongs to <u>me</u>. No one else. It means, <u>My body is mine. I do what I want with it. I accept it as it is.</u> It gave me courage and freedom all at once. And it reminds me that I'm more than just a reflection in the mirror."

I shake my head slightly, in awe of her. I scoot closer, cup her face in my hands, and hold her eyes. "You amaze me more and more all the time. I'm so proud of you, Emma. I'm proud of you for working so hard to accomplish something so incredible, and for having the courage to do what you did to take care of yourself."

She softens as she smiles at me.

"Thank you for telling me."

"Thank you for listening."

"Of course. You can tell me anything."

A flash of concern crosses her face.

"Was that the thing we needed to talk about?"

She presses her lips together and shakes her head.

"Are you ready to tell me? It's tomorrow now."

It's just past midnight.

"No. I've been talking too much already. Besides, it's not tomorrow until we go to sleep."

"Are you sure?"

"I have all day. Don't rush me."

I hold her hand and rub along her forearm. "I'm not rushing you. You don't need to tell me at all."

I want to know what's bothering her, but I don't want her to tell me unless she really wants to. I have no fear that anything she has to confess will change how I feel about her. Whatever this is between us, it's far bigger than that.

"Yes I do. And why is it that you don't even look the tiniest bit worried?"

"Because I'm not. Why should I be?"

"Because you don't know what it is. I could be an ax murderer."

I blink at her. <u>An axe murderer?</u> Then I laugh out loud. Oh my god, she's too much. An axe murderer.

"I'm serious," she says, but she starting to laugh, too. It lifts my mood even more to see a smile on her face.

"You could *not* be an ax murderer." Still laughing, I lie back to get settled under the sheets.

She follows suit. "You don't know. I could be."

"All right, come here, you dangerous woman, you." I pull her into my arms and she snuggles in, tucking her head into the crook between my shoulder and chin.

As I wrap my arms around her, our legs scissor together. I've held women before, sure, but never like this. This is so much more intimate. It's like we can't get close enough to each other. I'm surprised how much I like it.

She's quiet long enough that I think the topic is over, but then she says quietly, "I'm telling you tomorrow. Before sunset." I hear the same determination as when she said it in her apartment, like she has to be firm with herself or she won't do it.

I consider teasing her about the logic of today not being over until we go to sleep even though it's past midnight, but tomorrow being over at sunset. Instead, I kiss the top of her head. She's right that I don't know what it is, but there's one thing I need her to understand.

"Whatever's in your past belongs to you. You don't have to—"

"You need to know."

"All right. That's fine. I'll trust you about that. But remember Emma," I tuck my finger under her chin and turn her to face me, "you're safe with me."

We should be sleeping. It's pushing two in the morning. Instead we're floating in the languid aftereffects of the fifth round of sex inside of seven hours. I can't get enough of her, and she seems to feel the same.

The lights are out, but there's enough moonlight coming through the windows to cast a pale blue light on her lovely face. I lightly draw one finger along the curve of her cheek. She gives me a sleepy smile, and blinks with heavy lids. Maybe we'll finally go to sleep now. Maybe not.

I once had sex with a woman four times in one evening. And what did I think then? I thought, <u>This is the best one night stand I've ever had.</u>

That's how it felt. Transient. With Emma, every time we come together it further solidifies what I've felt about her all along. <u>This means something.</u>

Of all the women I've been with, even the ones I enjoyed enough to actually date for a while, they never felt like more than someone who was just passing through.

I used to wonder why this was. Some of them were accomplished, beautiful, good women. I eventually came to the conclusion that it wasn't them, it was me. I thought I wasn't the kind of guy who can let other people in enough to really love them.

Other than family, of course. Because other people? I don't even <u>want</u> them close.

But lying in my bed, the very picture of strength and grace and loveliness, is the one exception. I don't believe in fate or signs or grandstanding from the universe at large, but I'm starting to think the problem wasn't me after all.

It's as if my soul knew she was coming, and couldn't be bothered to invest in anybody else.

# Chapter 27

## Emma

It was close to noon by the time I was slowly waking up, stretching and luxuriating in the soft sheets on his king-sized bed. Not to mention feeling a bit *raw*. I guess that's what happens when you do it six times in one day.

My previous record was one. One time in one day. That seems kind of pathetic now. I didn't even know I could come six times in one day. Well, more than that actually because twice he got me to come with his tongue, then immediately followed it up by making me come with his cock. When Mr. Rayce Rivers decides I'm going to have an orgasm, he doesn't screw around.

We tried to go to sleep over and over again. But after a while our lazy, almost sweet post-sex caresses would turn into suggestive, teasing touches, and then that would turn into rolling around and every manner of indecency. Then I'd think we were done and finally ready to fall asleep, but we'd end up talking quietly in the dark and eventually I'd feel the stirring and pulsing of desire. <u>Again.</u>

He wasn't in the bed when I woke up, but I heard noise down in the kitchen so I wasn't worried that he'd gone too far. Not long after, he appeared at the door carrying a tray that not only had a legitimate breakfast on it but a glass of juice and a cup of coffee. He made French toast—actually made it himself—and sprinkled it with powdered sugar and topped it with some berries. There was even a tiny pitcher of syrup to the side, just like they have in restaurants.

It was damned impressive and he was adorably proud of himself. He did a good job, too. The toast was perfectly cooked, soft in the middle, firm at the edges, and tasted incredible. When I teasingly expressed my surprise that he'd actually cooked something, he said, "It's the one breakfast I actually know how to make. I might be playing my cards a little early, but I didn't want to bring you Fruity Pebbles on our first morning together."

My heart lifted at that, like he considered it our first morning among many. But maybe I was reading too much into things and he didn't mean it that way.

I'm having to really watch myself. I keep getting caught up in the fantasy of being with Rayce Rivers. Not just now, here, in this house and frequently in his arms, but for a long, long time to come. I have to remind myself who he is and who I am and all the reasons why this could be over by sundown.

After breakfast, I wasn't sure if I'd be heading home or what, but he invited me to stay and enjoy the pool again. I agreed, amazed not just because he hadn't had his fill yet but because I hadn't either. I've never spent so many hours in a row with a guy before. Usually by the time a date is wrapping up, I'm ready to be home so I can relax and absorb everything. But I don't feel that way now. I could easily spend the whole day here.

I feel so at home, even more than at Aaron and Pierce's apartment. Of course, that's probably because that's not really my own place.

Well, then again, neither is this.

But I'm not questioning it. I took to heart what he said, that we may as well make the most of things before I let the cat out of the bag. And damn if I'm not trying.

It took us a while to actually make it down to the pool. Before changing into our suits, we got cleaned up in his massive rainfall shower and I discovered I wasn't too raw for him to take me from behind while I braced myself against the tile wall.

Just thinking about it now gets me tingling in all the right places. I've never been with a man who turns me on *all the time*. He's not even here and I'm turned on thinking about him.

He had to make some calls in his den first, so I'm waiting for him outside, on one of the comfy couches under the gazebo. I'm lying on my stomach in my neon string bikini. The sound of ocean waves hitting the shoreline far below the cliff's edge and the smell of fresh sea air both soothe and rejuvenate me. It's a nice counterbalance to the other thing I'm doing: reading the latest article about my dad on my phone.

I have what is probably an unhealthy habit of Googling my dad's name to see if there's anything new. I get updates from my mother, of course, so I already know what's going on, but I can't seem to resist reading what the papers are saying.

In spite of their diligent use of the word "allegedly," the tone of these articles suggest guilt on his part. The commenters on the articles aren't shy about saying it outright.

When you embezzle enough money to put a company out of business, all to support your secret gambling addiction, the hundreds of workers who lost their jobs thanks to you don't tend to be too forgiving.

And by secret, I mean secret. Apparently my dad had been wasting money on horse races for years. He handled the family accounts, so Mom had no idea the extent of their debt. First the arrest, then the discovery that they were on the verge of bankruptcy themselves. It's been a shit storm ever since.

My half-brother has said that my mom should, "divorce his ass," but she says she loves him and wants to help him with his gambling addiction, which he in turn says he's committed to beating. I can't decide who's right, my dad's wife or his son. Part of me has compassion for my dad, and thinks if he's able to overcome this, it's good that Mom is standing by him. The other part of me thinks I'm too trusting and forgiving and she should cut her losses and get while the getting's good.

"Hi, gorgeous."

I roll onto my side to see Rayce stepping onto the patio. He's wearing a navy blue swimsuit and nothing else. His arm muscles flex as he closes the door with the same hand that's holding his phone. Since I'm allowed to shamelessly ogle him now, I roll all the way onto my back and enjoy the show. His chest is firm and defined, his abs taut. The defined V on his inner hips dip beneath the waistband of his suit.

He's striding over with a smooth gait, his eyes sweeping up and down my body. From my breasts to my stomach to my long legs, he seems delighted by every inch and I can't help but enjoy it.

He crawls up and tosses his phone on the cushion next to mine before settling on his side next to me. Cupping my jaw and giving me a kiss, he says, "Have I told you how sexy you are?"

I grin. "Yes. But you can tell me again."

He starts to gently caress my side and hip, watching his hand as he slowly travels down one thigh then back up to my side and onto my stomach. "You are without doubt the sexiest woman I've ever known."

He might just be the boss giving his little employee a line, but he doesn't make me feel that way. And besides, I want to believe it. He has said he likes my tattoo, and he does seem to, but it's so contrary to what I would expect from him that I have to wonder what it's really about.

Maybe it is sexy, and a little edgy. Maybe guys are bound to like that. But Rayce is a powerful, respected man. Even if we didn't have to hide things, would he really want me to be the woman on his arm when he's out schmoozing the Swan Pointe elite?

I'm not incapable of holding my own. I've been to gatherings with high-profile people and know how to behave. But I also know how people like that can get. They're always looking for reasons to judge you.

Admiring my body is one thing when he's in the privacy of his own backyard, but would he want to be on a public beach with me where the papers could take photos of him and his tattooed girlfriend? Doubtful. And no *way* would he ever make me his wife.

My chest aches as I consider the reality of things, but I tell myself yet again to keep what's going on here in perspective. It's not like I didn't know this going in: an affair with the boss is not going to end well.

The fact that he makes me feel so amazing is irrelevant. Isn't it?

He points his chin toward my phone. "What were you reading?"

"Um…" I hand him my phone. "It's an article about my dad. He's facing trial for embezzlement." He lifts his eyebrows toward me, searching my expression. "Yeah. It sucks. But it is what it is. Go ahead, you can read it."

He scans the article and I examine his profile, looking for clues in his serious expression. Clues to what, I'm not sure.

About halfway through the article, he asks a question and I end up filling him in on the rest, giving the abridged version. Strangely, this is a far easier story to tell than the one about my tattoo.

Still, he can't want to know all this garbage about me. It has to be too much. But I just keep *telling* him stuff. He's always been easy to talk to, but before we slept together, if he edged too close to topics I wanted to avoid, I could back away and it was fine. Now it's like I can't help but open right up. Want to hear about my tattoo? Let me talk your ear off for half an hour. Want to know more about my family? Let me tell you about the great disappointment that is my father, which seems even worse in comparison to his fairy tale family.

My heart thumps painfully, nervous about just how much I still have left to tell him. Eventually, anyway. But do I have to do it now? The topic of my dad does make for the perfect segue. But God, I'm not ready for this to be over yet.

How is he going to look at me when he realizes I'm not the amazing woman he keeps saying I am?

"Wow, Emma," he says when I wrap things up. "That's terrible. How are you?"

"Okay, I guess. I mean, I'm fine. I'm just so mad at him."

He nods. "That makes sense."

"I can't look at him or even think about him without being so ashamed of him. He's not the man I thought he was."

See? All it takes is one thing for someone's opinion of you to change.

"I'm sure."

"That didn't stop me from bailing him out when he got arrested though."

"How much was bail?"

I hesitate. "Thirty grand."

Rayce's focus sharpens on me in a new way. He gives me a probing look, like he's trying to put puzzle pieces together again. "You had thirty grand for bail?"

Uh…

"Well, my mom was able to get a couple grand from a credit card, but they were maxed out everywhere else."

Tell him the rest. Just tell him.

But I don't. Instead I say, "Anyway, that's why I don't have a car right now."

Well it's <u>kind of</u> why don't have a car.

"I had to sell it."

He shakes his head, and I'm just waiting for that look to appear. It's the look that says, <u>You shouldn't have done that.</u> My brother told me not to hurt myself financially just to bail Dad out. Even Mom told me not to.

"I know I was being stupid. He's probably going to end up in prison anyway. But I couldn't stand the thought of my dad in jail."

"I didn't say you were stupid."

That's true. And I haven't seen that you-shouldn't-have look, or really any disapproval.

Maybe I'm the one judging myself. I wouldn't go back and change it, but I still don't know if it was the right thing to do. "But it was stupid," I say quietly. "Right?"

He takes a thoughtful breath, watching me. "I think you did what you thought you had to do for your dad." He squeezes my hand. "He's family. I understand that. And if you're willing to go without a car and your own couch to sleep on for a while, that's for you to decide."

"Except it affected Aaron and Pierce, too."

He frowns. "Are they giving you a hard time about it?"

"No. Not at all. They've been really great."

His face relaxes. "Well, then, no long-term damage done. You'll recover. You're getting your own place. Will you be able to get a car soon?"

I smile, reassured by his easy practicality of things. He's the first one who hasn't made me feel like a complete idiot about it. True, he doesn't know all the details, but I don't care right now. It's nice to have someone understand why I did it. "That depends on your definition of 'soon'. But you're right. Things are getting better."

"Right." He gives my chin a gentle nip with his fingers. "Eventually this will all be in the past."

He returns to the article and I let him finish reading. I close my eyes and take a deep, satisfying breath. See? He just makes me feel so relaxed.

When he's finished with the article, we finally head to the pool.

"Is <u>this</u> what we needed to talk about?" he asks.

"No."

Because I'm a great, big chicken.

"Jesus, Emma. How many secrets do you have?"

"Just one more." But it's a big one.

And time is running out.

# Chapter 28

## Emma

We're in the hot tub talking about the most random stuff. I've learned things like the fact that he's been to seven different countries but that he's got nothing on Connor. His Grandma Rivers had a cat named Moses, so named because if you filled the sink with water he would jump right in and splash around like he was trying to part the Red Sea.

I learn he's never broken a bone, but holds himself personally responsible for his baby brother's first broken bone, which he got cliff diving when they were kids.

"I knew I should've grabbed that scrawny little arm and stopped him from jumping," he said.

He loves Mars bars and isn't a fan of Snickers, but I'm the other way around. We both have pretty intense exercise regimens (mine are left over from my dancing days), and we've half-heartedly said we should try to get a short workout in later. Right now, though, we're enjoying the hot tub far too much.

Our playful flirtations have escalated to dead-serious. He's come in front of me, hitching my legs around his hips as he delivers the most expert, toe-curling kisses. The warm water jumps around us as we get more and more heated. Our chests press together, the feel of his bare skin against mine electrifying my body.

He cups my ass and brings me closer to him, pressing his erection against my core. I throb and squirm against it. I'm getting too worked up and hot to stay in the water, but just in time he smoothly lifts me onto the edge. Staying in the water himself, he leans over me, scandalizing my mouth. I sink back, trusting him to support us both. With the way his tongue is assaulting mine I can hardly manage anything more.

He rocks his hard length against me and I groan. I need him to pull my suit to the side, satisfy my need for him, fill and stretch me. If there's a limit to how many times a person can have sex within twenty-four hours, we haven't found it yet.

He slips my top down, exposing my breasts, cupping them both before taking one hard peak into his mouth. I arch to meet him, vaguely aware of his phone ringing on the table.

His tongue does devilish things to my body and I writhe shamelessly. I don't know where he learned to do this, but I would marry this man based on his skills with my nipples alone.

The phone rings again. He switches to the other side, giving it equal treatment and causing me to make far, far too much noise. The neighbors can't see us, but if they're outside they can damn sure hear me. I can't help it. I lose all control with him. The way his tongue swirls and flicks, circles and—

He freezes. Comes off me. A breeze cools my wet nipple.

Dazed, I give him a questioning look. He's looking over my shoulder toward the gazebo with a dazed expression of his own. The phone is still ringing, and he seems to have just now realized it.

Then everything changes.

"Shit." He abruptly releases me and hops out of the tub.

He hurries to the phone, water streaming off his body and onto the sun-drenched concrete. My body feels like it's been hit with a blast of arctic air.

He picks up his phone. "Hello?" He pulls it back and scowls at the screen. "Dammit."

So not only did he leave me in the middle of all that, but he's calling back whoever it was? As I tuck myself back into my top, I'm trying to keep my cool. Maybe he has a good reason. Maybe he does. But I'm burning. I guess I know my place.

I climb out of the hot tub. The phone is back to his ear, and whoever he's trying to get a hold of has his full attention because he doesn't so much as look at me crossing the patio to the opposite gazebo. No, his attention is on the call and nothing else.

As I snatch up a towel, I hear him mumble, "Pick up."

I plop down on a couch and start drying off, my cheeks on fire. I don't want to be angry. I don't want to be hurt. But I am. It doesn't help that my body's still worked up from what he was doing to me. But is he such a workaholic that even if he gets a call in the middle of sex, that's going to take priority?

I try to settle my emotions. I don't need to feel slighted. This isn't a real relationship anyway. What he does is none of my business. I don't even know what's going on. He could have a perfectly reasonable explanation. I just need to calm down.

"Hey," he says to whoever's answered the phone. "Are you okay?"

My ears perk, wondering why he would lead with that kind of question. I really look at his face for the first time since he jumped out of the hot tub. It's tense with concern.

Okay, maybe there really is something going on.

"Oh." He closes his eyes and lets out a silent breath of palpable relief. The in-control man I've been so used to makes a reappearance. "Yes. That's no problem."

He looks at me now, finally, an apology in his eyes.

He comes over, continuing his conversation. "Let's make it tomorrow evening." Sitting next to me, he places a warm hand on my knee. "Do you want to bring your stuff here or do you want me to go over there?" He squeezes my knee, holding my eyes. "Sure." Now he smiles at whoever he's talking to. "That sounds great. See you then."

Once he's off the phone, he immediately turns his attention to me. "Emma, I am so sorry."

"Who was that?" I don't sound jealous, right? I didn't mean to.

"Corrine."

"Your cousin?"

He nods. "She has questions about some investments she's handling."

"Oh."

"I've been teaching her how to evaluate her numbers. She's still learning."

"I see."

I feel weird. This isn't what I was expecting. It turns out there wasn't a previously-known problem that he needed to rush over and handle. I really am just low on his list of priorities.

Well, what did I expect? Why do I keep making situations like this more than what they are? Do I just suck at men?

"I owe you an explanation."

I try to keep my voice casual. That's what this is, right? Casual? No problem.

"No, you don't." I start to get off the couch. "You don't owe me anything."

Yeah, okay. That totally didn't sound casual.

He grabs my wrist to stop me from leaving. "Sit down. Please. I want you to understand this."

I sit back down, hopeful in spite of myself. My constant inner dialogue, the one that's been telling myself to keep this relationship in perspective, totally isn't working. It's not my fault. I blame Rayce this time. He looks way too vulnerable right now for my heart not to open up as well.

He holds my hand. "I always answer when family calls. Always."

"Okay," I say slowly, still feeling like I'm missing something. I get wanting to answer for family, but even in the middle of sex?

"It's because..."

He stops, apparently struggling to say whatever it is.

He sighs and pinches the bridge of his nose, resting his elbow on his knee. "I don't usually talk about this."

I soften. Whatever it is, this is a big deal to him. But he's been understanding about the thing I'm struggling to tell him. I can do the same, even though I'd really like to know what just happened.

"Listen," I say softly, "it's all right. I'm not mad. You don't have to talk about anything you don't want to talk about."

He straightens and drops his hand. "I know I don't." Our eyes meet and I feel that connection I've felt so many times in the last twelve hours. "I want to. It's just... not easy. For me."

I scoot closer, our thighs, hips and shoulders touching. I tuck his hand inside both of mine. "Then tell me later. If you want to."

He slowly laces our fingers together. My heart pinches at this gentle intimacy. "The last thing I want is for you to think I wasn't into that and would rather take a phone call then be with you." He holds my eyes and shakes his head. "Because I wouldn't."

I squeeze his hand, believing him.

He takes a resolute breath. "The reason I answer the phone when it's family is because the day our parents died, my mother called me from the boat." He swallows hard. "And I didn't answer."

"Oh, Rayce. I'm so sorry." How horrible to think there could've been one more chance to hear their voices. But I see something else on his face. "You're not blaming yourself are you?"

"I did," he confirms. "But that led to nothing but trouble."

Now I feel like an ass. I shake my head. "I'm sure. Feeling responsible for something like that could really screw a person up."

He nods. "It kind of did. For a long time, I—" he stops, his eyes searching my face.

This can't be easy to talk about, and I don't blame him. But I want him to know he's safe with me, the way he's made me feel safe with him.

"I'm listening."

He nods slowly, his eyes still searching my face. It seems like he's weighing his words.

"I wasn't myself," he says carefully. "After they died." He stops himself again, then shakes his head. "I felt…" He looks out to the ocean.

I wait in the silence, wanting him to confide in me. "You felt what?"

"I just felt…really…" His eyes go soft on the horizon. "… lost."

My heart aches for him. As mad as I've been at my father, I'd be devastated to lose him so early in life.

"I wasn't myself," he says again. What does he mean by that?

"How so?"

He frowns slightly, then sits back, holding my hand more loosely. "I don't know. Things were just more difficult than they needed to be because I thought I could've stopped it." He seems to have changed course.

I get the feeling there was something he was going to say that he decided not to say. I'm disappointed, wishing he would trust me with whatever it was.

"Maybe that was just wishful thinking on my part," he continues. "What do they call that stage of the grief process? Bargaining? Anyway, I finally talked the whole thing over with Connor and the truth is, even if I'd answered the phone, it probably wouldn't have mattered. The autopsies indicated they died from blunt force trauma, not drowning. We think they were injured by the boom when their boat capsized. But..." His eyes hold mine. "I am always, always going to wonder. And I will never miss a call from family again."

Yeah. I get it now. "That's why you keep your phone with you all the time." I didn't realize how much I'd been noticing that.

He nods. "My family has a different ring tone so I know it's them."

"And here I thought you were just a workaholic."

He smiles, and it warms my heart to see it. I hate him being in pain, and I'm glad this isn't such a painful topic that he can't smile right now. "Well, according to my family I am a workaholic, but no. That's not what it was. I'm perfectly fine ignoring work under the right circumstances."

He wraps his arm around my shoulders and pulls me against his warm chest. "I want to make sure you didn't think I wasn't into it. If you'd left me for a random call I would've been annoyed as hell, too."

"I wasn't annoyed." I'm such a liar.

He chuckles. "What word do you want to use then? You were definitely something."

"I was…" I don't want to say. Because I was annoyed.

Giving me a heated, mischievous look, he rubs his hand along my outer thigh and says in a playful voice. "Hurt? Frustrated? Still horny as hell?"

His hand travels up the curve of my side, and my nipples peak beneath my damp swimsuit. I grin. "'Horny' is such a crass word."

"What word do you prefer?"

"I refuse to say."

He laughs and I join him. I love these games we play.

"Then I'll say it." He nudges his nose along my jaw, then brushes his lips lightly on the side of my neck. "You make me horny as hell." He's slowly lying us back, settling on top of me. "Over and over and over again."

He presses an impressive erection alongside my seam and I instantly react to it. I angle back against him, more than ready to pick up where we left off.

"But if I'm the only one horny here," he teases, starting to lift himself up.

I tighten my grip around his waist to keep him in place. "Don't you dare leave."

He grins, eyes on mine. "I won't." He settles his weight on me, his cock just to the left of my hardening bud. "I won't," he says again, still holding my eyes.

He cups my jaw with one hand, and we descend into a deep, heated kiss. He makes it so damned hard to keep my head screwed on straight. In spite of my better judgment, I've let him draw me in, one inch at a time. I've told myself I didn't want this, but it's exactly what I wanted.

I've been wanting to fall into Mr. Rayce Rivers from the start.

So I do. For a brief, blissful time, the guilt and worrying and wondering disappears. In the warm California sun, on his luxury patio, I wrap my legs around his waist as he ravages my neck and my mouth and my breasts. Keeping in each other's arms, we work out of our clothes and join together again. I've lost count of how many times. I don't even care.

I just need him. He's slick with my need for him. I'm still surprised at how much he fills me, in every way. My body responds to his, yes. I'm almost delirious with the pleasure he draws out of me. My head arches back and my fingers dig into his shoulders as he lifts me in a swell of ecstasy I've only ever experienced with him.

But the rest of him fills me, too. He fills me in all the places I didn't know were empty, and brings light to all the places that had been in shadow.

I won't let myself think the L-word, though it's tried to surface more than once. It only shows how out of my mind I am. Plus it's not love if you're hiding things, not the best version of it anyway.

As we build together, he starts to lose control, too. Diving as deep as I can take him, he clutches me to him, grips the back of my hair, groans deep and low. This. This is what I love. I'm not alone in my hunger for this.

He thrusts deep and hard, commanding an orgasm from my body and getting it. I'm a shuddering mass of splintering light. His body hardens as he comes with me. The edges of our bodies blur into one.

After, when we're trying to catch our breath and my body is humming with the aftereffects of being with him, that's the part I mentally return to, and the part that scares me: just how much he joins with me.

Every time we've been together, afterwards I have to try to bring myself back to reality. Because no matter how he makes me feel, I have to remember that for him, I'm probably just another woman he'll be able to say he had once. A weekend romp. The thought of him holding someone else like he has me, of being so tender and gentle makes me wonder, but… well… he's had lots of women so he probably knows how to treat them.

No matter how he makes me feel, I have to remember, this is the boss having a fling and no more.

A little voice in the back of my head whispers, This is different. This isn't a fling. It means something to him, too.

But I don't trust that little voice. Why should I? I said I would never sleep with my boss again, and not even two months later, here I am. This is exactly why I'm supposed to keep a distance between myself and the things I know are bad for me.

But I just… don't know…

He pulls up on one elbow, looking down at me and giving me that tender smile that makes me feel so cherished and special.

Is this bad for me?

Or is he the best thing that's ever happened?

I wish I knew how to tell.

We had breakfast so late and snacked by the pool so much that by the time we're ready for a genuine meal it's practically dinner time. I thought sure he'd insist on ordering in, but it wasn't hard to persuade him that we could make something simple instead.

Rayce pulls a box of pasta out of the pantry, then holds up a can of tomato sauce. "One can or two?"

"Two. This sauce freezes well, so then you'll have it." He brings the items over to the counter next to me. I pull out a deep pan and set it on the stove.

"What else do we need?"

"Onions and garlic, if you have them."

As he heads to the fridge, I'm drawn to the way the colors of the sunset are playing on the white walls in his living room. Almost the entire, massive space is reflecting orange, yellow, and the slightest tint of pink. God, that's beautiful.

"Onions, no. Garlic, yes," he says, setting a bulb on the counter.

I don't respond, because I've realized something. It's sunset.

Sunset.

He grabs the cans and takes them to the counter behind me. I hear the whirring of the electric can opener. "Is this lunch or dinner?" he asks, in a playful tone.

But all I can think about is the fact that it's sunset and I still haven't told him what I said I would. He won't make me, either. I know perfectly well that he won't ask or push and I could just go on not telling him.

A little longer. I could have this fantasy for a little longer.

"We'll call it linner," he says.

But if I don't tell him now, I'm not sure I ever will. I sense that if I justify waiting, then I'll just keep on waiting, and why? So I can try to keep him in spite of the fact that he probably doesn't want me beyond a fling anyway. And even if he does, he won't want me once he knows. How is that fair to him?

"Why does 'linner' seem like such a little kid word," he says, "while 'brunch' is so grown up?"

My body is buzzing with dread. I don't want this to be over.

He sets the opened cans on the counter next to me. "What else, babe?"

Babe. I can't do this to him.

I turn toward him and spit it out. "I slept with my boss."

He gets this self-satisfied look and starts to grin, as if to say, <u>Damn right, you did.</u>

"Not you."

His grin falls and he blinks at me. "What?"

"At my last job. I slept with my boss there, too."

His expression darkens. My stomach drops because I know this is going be a deal breaker. But I just keep going because if I'm going to spill it, I'm going to spill all of it.

"It didn't feel like it has with you but I did sleep with him and we had an affair for two weeks and I knew it was stupid but I did it anyway—" I can't stand the look on his face so I walk away and run my hands into my hair, grabbing at the roots and pinching my eyes shut and I just keep talking. "—and then when I broke it off with him, he fired me and accused me of stealing from him but I swear I didn't. It was a loan and he said I could pay it back when I could but when I ended it he said I had to pay it all right then or it was theft—"

I'm on the other side of the island from him now, pacing and rambling like an idiot and he's just watching me with this dumbfounded expression like he can't believe I'm saying any of this and I *knew* this was going to change his opinion of me, I just *knew* it. I have to get out of here but I can't shut up.

"Then I found out he was married and I think he was afraid I'd tell, but I said I wouldn't and who was going to believe me anyway because he was this great, adored man, just like you."

I gesture in his direction and he flinches slightly, still looking stunned.

"He came from another location to cover for my boss because she was on maternity leave and everyone thought he was so fucking great and I did too because I thought he wanted to help me, but no. So I had to sell my car and almost everything I had to pay him back and he made me promise to keep quiet about everything or he'd still come after me for it, and I don't know if he would have but fuck him because I paid him back anyway. And then Aaron and Pierce had to come down to rescue me because I had nowhere to go and no job and no money and no car —"

My voice cracks over the lump in my throat, but I swallow that down hard because I will *not* cry about this like a broken little bird, even though that's exactly what I am.

"—and Aaron *told* me not to take the job with you and he was right, because the whole thing before was my own stupid fault. I shouldn't have borrowed money from him to start with and I shouldn't have slept with my boss and now I've fucking done it again! And on top of it all I've been lying to Aaron and Pierce to cover up what's been going on with you and it was all for nothing because we both know this isn't going anywhere anyway so let's just—"

I throw my hands up and look around the kitchen as if I'm going to find the answers there.

"—forget the whole thing!"

And now I'm out. I rush to the counter, snatch up my purse, and somehow manage not to run down the hall. Once I'm out the side door, I do run across the darkening driveway. As the shaft of light from the open door narrows and disappears, I run through the opening in the hedges. Here, at last, I come to a full stop.

Aaron's car isn't there. There's no car. No nothing.

Because I came here with Rayce.

I gape… then pitch my purse across the lot. "Mother<u>fucker.</u>"

# Chapter 29

## Emma

It takes a few seconds to reign in my panic and come up with plan B. Thank god I have money in my account and thank god for Uber.

I march across the lot and retrieve my purse from under the hedges.

"Emma?" Rayce's strong voice carries across the still, night air. I startle, my heart thumping. I can't see the door, but it sounds like that's where he's standing, and the light's cutting across the driveway again.

No. I can't talk to him. I can't do this. What's the fucking point anyway?

And I can't read anything from his tone so I have no idea what he's thinking, which irritates me even further.

I don't answer. I just start beating the dirt off my purse.

"Emma." In that commanding tone.

"What!"

Calm as ever, he says, "Get back in here."

I stand there. The shaft of light slowly thins until I'm left in the dark.

I do want to go back in there. I want to go back in there and have everything be all right.

God, why can't I get my head screwed on straight about this? It's like my heart has no sense at all. Not at all.

But I do go back to the house like he told me to. I drift down the hall holding my hands in front of me and feeling so damned hopeful my chest feels like it's being torn in two.

He's not in the kitchen. He's on one of the beautiful white chairs in the living room, under a soaring ceiling, in front of a sweeping Pacific view. He is the master of every inch of this space and apparently the master of me.

"Come here."

I do. I am silent and afraid and hopeful, and studying his somber expression as he watches me approach.

I walk to the chair next to him and before I can sit down he puts out his hand, palm up. I give him my hand instinctively and he takes hold, bringing me to him. By the time he pulls me onto his lap, I am swallowing past a lump in my throat and blinking back tears. I'm squeezing my hands together on my lap, but I long to curl up inside his arms and tuck my head under his chin.

With one arm wrapped around my waist and one hand resting gently on my thigh, he holds my eyes, forbidding me from looking away.

"Emma…"

"I'm sorry," I whisper.

He cups my cheek in his warm, strong hand. "Listen. I would like to understand better what happened to you if you care to share it with me, but there's one thing I'm clear on, and you're about to be clear on it, too. It wasn't your fault."

The lump at the base of my throat hardens and I drop my eyes to my clasped hands. I nod slightly. "Yes, it was."

He lifts my chin until I'm looking at him again. "No. It wasn't."

How is he making me feel so reassured, when I know he's wrong?

"I shouldn't have slept with my boss."

"Maybe. Maybe not. But there are worse crimes. Like a married man having an affair, sleeping with his employee, then manipulating and threatening her to hide his sins."

I shake my head. "He's an ass, but—"

"He's an ass period."

"I shouldn't have been in that mess to start with. I shouldn't have borrowed money from him."

"Is that how you bailed out your dad?"

I nod. "It was stupid."

He sighs. "Emma, you're thinking about this all wrong."

I shake my head.

"Yes. Now pay attention. Why did you run from me?"

His tone suggests he knows the answer and is just asking to get me to say it. Like a teacher patiently asking a question that really leads to another answer.

"Because..." I press my fingers against my eyes, because I'm embarrassed to say why I ran. I'm embarrassed that I did it at all. But here he is being so careful and gentle with me. He's trying to tell me I can trust him with all of this. I can at least give him an honest answer.

I drop my hands and meet his eyes. "I ran because I'm afraid of what you'll think of me. I'm afraid you'll think I was an idiot for getting myself into that mess and then doing the same thing all over again. I'm afraid that... this is just nothing to you and you'll think I'm stupid because it's not nothing to me."

He opens his mouth to say something reassuring, I can see it, but I have to finish now that I've started.

"And I was afraid that even if this wasn't nothing to you either that you won't see me as this amazing woman anymore and you'll be done with me."

"Emma," he says, shaking his head. "I told you. You don't need to be afraid to tell me things. I don't think any less of you." I soften slightly in his arms. "I understand you better now. I understand better what's been holding you back. I'm sorry this has been so painful."

"This whole thing with you has been so confusing. On the surface, it seems like another mistake. You're my boss. We're sneaking around. I should know better. But inside, it feels…"

I swallow hard.

He puts his hand over mine. "Different."

Yes. Exactly. I nod.

He slowly takes my hand, and laces our fingers together. Watching this, something inside of me shifts. He may be my boss, like Chad was, but that's where the similarities end.

"I'm sorry for comparing you to him. You're not the same caliber of man at all. You'd never do what he did."

He looks down at our hands, frowning slightly. "I'm not perfect, Emma."

"But you wouldn't do what he did. You wouldn't take away my job or threaten to tell people I'm a thief."

"No, I fucking wouldn't," he says, his voice hard.

"And if you were married, I bet you wouldn't cheat on your wife, either."

"No." He holds my eyes again. "I wouldn't. But I'm not perfect either, Emma."

"But this is different," I say. "With us. Isn't it?"

He cups my face again. "Yes. This is different. This is unlike anything I've ever experienced. And you are unlike any woman I've ever met."

"It really doesn't make you think less of me?"

He cups my face with both hands. "Sweetheart." He gives me a tender, reassuring kiss. "If that's the worst you've got, you are golden and I will never, ever be worthy of you."

Something inside of me shifts. Something dark and heavy lifts off and just flies away.

For the first time, since this whole thing started, I'm not afraid.

I don't know how we go forward from here, but I trust this. I trust that he'll try to work it out like he's said he will, and I trust that he cares for me like he says he does, and maybe I can trust myself enough to just know that this situation really, truly is different and doesn't have to end the same way.

I'm going to stop comparing this to what happened with Chad because it's not the same.

It's different.

And I'm all in.

# Chapter 30

## Rayce

Emma isn't the only one with a confession to make now, is she?

I'm not someone who thinks you have to lay out every little thing about your past when you're dating, especially not when it's so new. But this is a detail she's going to care about.

While I don't understand why she was afraid I would think any less of her—she wasn't the one in the wrong—the same cannot be said of me. Maybe I wasn't the kind of asshole her boss was. I would never pull that kind of shit. But I was still an asshole.

I was already not proud of how I behaved back then, but the thought of telling Emma about it… it pains me to think of how she might look at me. Is she going to see me as the kind of guy to prey on his employees, the way her old boss preyed on her?

What if she thinks that's what I'm doing now?

Even if I try to explain what was going on with me at the time, it sounds like I'm just trying to give myself a pass. Still, I'll have to tell her at some point. But telling her now? That's out of the question.

She's finally trusting this, I can see it. But it's so fragile. If I told her about my past indiscretions with employees now, I don't think there'd be any coming back from that.

I have to get her ready to hear it first. I need to show her how special she is so she knows this is something she can trust. Because it is. I also need to get this relationship out in the open as soon as possible, so there's no fear on her end that she's just a cheap, closeted affair.

But both of those things are going to take time. Tonight, all I want is for her to feel better.

Still holding her and stroking her soft face, I ask, "Are you hungry?"

She nods.

"Let's forget cooking." I pull my phone out of my pocket, already having a plan.

She puts her hand on top of mine, pushing the phone onto my thigh. "This first." She puts her hands on my cheeks and leans in, her blonde hair falling in a sheet over her shoulder. Her presence surrounds me. Nothing else exists.

When she kisses me, I literally have the sensation of falling. It's a little alarming. Our kiss deepens and she sinks into me and I am still falling.

I clutch her to me.

Emma, Emma, Emma...

So <u>this</u> is what it is to fall in love. I thought I knew what it was, but I didn't. I had no idea.

I would give up my kingdom and all that I have... for this.

It took me all the way until noon on Monday to realize I'd been getting a lot of strange looks at work all morning. Not strange like I had something stuck in my teeth, but strange like people were pleasantly puzzled by me.

I didn't give it much thought. All I can seem to think about is Emma and the amazing weekend we had. I've never spent that much time with someone I wasn't related to (or ever wanted to). But when it was time for her to go home on Sunday, it was hard to say goodbye. In fact, we texted through the evening, much to the chagrin of her roommates.

They were back from the art show earlier than planned, and saw me dropping her off at the apartment. It was too late. The damage had been done. Apparently they gave her an earful about what a slime ball I must be, but promised her they wouldn't say anything to anybody.

Maybe I should be worried about that, but she says they're good for it.

I don't figure out what all the strange looks are about until I'm wrapping up the afternoon meeting with my siblings.

"So are you going to tell us what you're smiling about all the time or what?" Connor asks.

Huh. Have I been?

Actually, I'm smiling right now. I smile wider. I guess Emma makes me happier than I realize.

"Nothing in particular," I answer.

He's giving me a disbelieving look.

I shrug. "Life is good."

"What's so good about it?" Lizzy prompts, a happy smile on her own face, much less suspicious than Connor.

"What isn't good? The resort's doing well." I tap my fingers on the latest financial report we just finished reviewing. "You're happy and settled," I gesture to Connor. "My little sister is getting married to the man of her dreams. What's not to smile about?"

"Awww," Lizzy says sweetly, placing her hand on her heart.

"Uh huh," Connor says, still giving me a suspicious look.

I stand, bringing the meeting to an official end. "Aren't I allowed to be happy?"

"Of course you are," she says, lightly slapping Connor on the leg before they stand themselves. "Stop harassing him."

"I'm not harassing him."

They head for the door and I retrieve my suit coat from the stand in the corner. I slide it onto my shoulders and turn in time to see Connor shutting the door after Lizzy exits, leaving just the two of us in the room. He faces me with a conspiratorial grin, hand still on the knob. "So what's really going on?"

Maybe I do need to watch how I'm acting if he's this serious about finding out the cause. I drop my smile and button my coat. "You're acting weird."

This throws him a bit and his smile fades. "There's really nothing?"

"You know, I'm not sure what it says about my life that a smile on my face should be so noteworthy."

He throws his hands up. "No, hey. I'm sorry. You're fine."

I clap him on the shoulder as he opens the door, and put my business persona back in place. "Let me know what Robert says about our proposal. I'll be back right after my session." I'm headed to our on-site spa for my weekly massage appointment, a habit our father instilled in us as essential mental health insurance.

Connor nods, back to business himself. "All right."

Yes, I definitely need to watch myself. Yet, a few minutes later as I pop my head into the spa manager's office to let her know I am there, I realize I've done it again. Dee Ann cocks her head and gives a perplexing grin to the smile on my face.

Well, what's a man do? It's not my fault Emma just sent me the cutest text ever: <u>You give me butterflies and you're not even here.</u>

Adorable, right?

I text her back once I'm in the room and on the table: I'm thinking about you, too. I may or may not have been accused of excessive smiling today.

Emma: See? Just like that.

Me: I'm looking forward to seeing you tonight.

Dee Ann comes in and I settle in. We exchange a bit of small talk as she gets to work on a knot between my left shoulder blade and my spine. She's been doing this for me for so long, she doesn't even need to ask what I need. My chronic sore spot has actually been bugging me a lot less today. Maybe it was all the relaxing I did over the weekend. I hardly touched my computer or phone at all.

"I wanted to ask you about my vacation next month," she says.

"All right." She'll be gone two weeks. She deserves it, but will be missed. She keeps everybody in line over here, for sure.

"Should I schedule one of the girls to work on your back while I'm gone?"

"No, I'll wait," I say automatically.

Though… I realize… not for the reason I normally would.

It used to be I'd take whichever girl was available on the schedule, but things got out of hand one day, back when I was living in that black cloud. It wasn't the first time an employee had hinted she might want something more from me, but it was the first time I followed an opening like that all the way to its conclusion. It was the first, and just the beginning.

After I made that promise to Connor to keep my nose clean, I wanted to avoid any opportunity for temptation and that's how I ended up with a standing appointment with Dee Ann. She's a beautiful woman, yes, but she's worked here since I was a kid, is happily married, and is the same age as my mother.

She's safe.

Not to mention one of the many people around here it'd kill me to disappoint.

But when I told her I didn't want to take a session with someone else, it wasn't because of me. It was because of Emma. I don't have any idea if Emma would care who gives me a massage, but... well, I don't know. I guess I don't want her to ever have to wonder if she's the only girl in my life.

My phone dings with another text from her.

And I smile.

# Chapter 31

## Emma

Pierce and Aaron are definitely not happy with me. They're convinced Rayce is just using me, and the fact that he wants to keep our relationship a secret is only proof. I can't bring myself to tell them he's letting me borrow a car he just purchased. They just think I got a killer deal on a loan.

Rayce already had a garage full of cars, but he bought another saying he was going to get it anyway. I know he did it for me. No way was he going to buy a six-year old Acura to park in that garage full of luxury cars. But I couldn't exactly drive one of them without raising questions, and since it's not a car he already owned, anyone seeing me in it wouldn't connect it to him. I'll be able to get my own car in another month or two anyway, and hell, I didn't want a long commute on public transit any more than Rayce wanted it.

"That's <u>our</u> time," he told me.

I can just imagine what Aaron and Pierce would have to say about it. They have enough to say already. I'm trying not to let their constant nagging get into my head, but I have to admit, I'll feel better once everything's out the open.

But we can't do that until I find another job, which is going to take some time, especially since Rayce doesn't want me to apply for anything that would mean a cut in pay or loss of benefits.

That doesn't leave a whole lot. Not many places can compete with what the resort has to offer. My work history doesn't help matters much, either. That, according to Aaron and Pierce, is exactly why I shouldn't be risking my newfound stability by sleeping with the boss.

But this is a risk that's making me so damned <u>happy.</u>

Like right now, for example.

I spent the night at Rayce's for the third night in a row, and we were up far too late. Too late for him, that is. I don't go into work until three, and he's told me I'm welcome to stay in bed as long as I'd like, but he has an early morning meeting.

When I heard him rummaging around in the kitchen downstairs, I got up long enough to take a pee and brush my teeth, but then I slipped back into his bed, moaning with satisfaction. His is the most comfortable bed I've ever slept in. The mattress is so soft and the pillows are so fluffy. The comforter is so thick it's like being hugged by a cloud. I could stay in this bed all day.

When he comes back upstairs, in only his boxers, he sees that I'm up and comes over to sit on the edge of the bed. "I thought I heard you. Did I wake you?"

I shake my head, still feeling languid and drowsy.

"Good." He gives me a soft kiss. "Sleep in as long as you want. I'm going to take a shower."

Poor guy. We've only had something like four hours of sleep. He gives me another kiss then disappears into the bathroom. I'm tired enough that I think I'm going to drift off, but I'm too aware of him. He's awake and I want to be, too. I don't want to miss anything.

From inside this cozy cocoon, I end up watching him get ready for work. It's arousing as hell. From the way he comes out of the bathroom with a towel wrapped around his waist and a hint of dampness across his bare chest, to the way he fastens his pants and buttons up his white shirt. My eyes follow his strong, confident movements like I'm partaking in a dream.

In between everything he does, his eyes find mine and he gives me a soft smile. He's being quiet, as if trying not to wake me too much, but my body is becoming more and more alert by the minute. He disappears into his massive, walk-in closet and reappears with a tie in hand.

He turns his collar up, and I watch him, my breath shallowing and my heart fluttering against my chest. I slowly start to sit up. This simple movement draws him to me. He drapes his tie around his neck and lets it hang.

I'm in nothing but my panties and one of his undershirts. It's soft and worn and carries his scent. I settle cross legged, covering my bare legs with his fluffy, fluffy comforter.

"Aren't you going to sleep more?"

My entire body is bathed in whatever it is that's making my heart beat fast. It isn't just that I'm turned on—because I definitely am. If he gets any closer I'll be positively squirming.

But it's more than that. So much more.

"I don't know," I answer.

He sits on the end of the bed so he can kiss me again. As our lips meet, I slowly bring my body against his. His tongue sweeps over mine, and our kiss deepens, slow and molten.

His hand brushes down the line of my neck, sweeps over the fullness of my breast, and follows the curve of my hips. The slow burn that's been smoldering all morning morphs into brisk fire.

His fingers slide under the front of my panties. He slips into my folds, and my head falls back. I moan softly.

"Mmmmm." He hums against the crook of my jaw. "You're so wet."

"I've been wanting you for so long."

"For so long?" His fingers swirl over my clit. My hips mimic the circular motion. I don't know if he realizes how close I am or how crazy he's making me. The thought of him leaving right now is almost painful.

"All morning. What time is your meeting?"

"Two minutes after I get there."

"It wouldn't take long," I plead. I'm throbbing against his hand already.

"Is that so?"

He works his way down the curve of my neck, nipping and sucking. He lays me back and my legs unfold. His fingers increase their speed and pressure. I bloom against him, slowly arching off the mattress.

His hand slips under my upper back as his mouth moves from my collarbone to the fullness of my breast. Maybe he would have kept going but I'll never know because I'm quivering with a powerful release of ecstasy. He responds immediately, clutching me to him as he sucks hard on my nipple and firmly strums me with his fingers.

I pulse and throb, shudder and shriek, until at last I'm a puddle on top of his comfy, comfy bed, panting and grinning like a lunatic. The fluffy comforter is in a disheveled heap at my feet.

He sits up slowly, looking like he just conquered an entire nation. "You were right," he says, slowly licking my juices off the end of his finger. "That *was* fast."

I groan and cover my face. "I know. It's embarrassing."

There's that low chuckle. My chest thumps hard, not because of what he did with this hand but because of what he does to my heart.

"Don't be embarrassed." He leans in and presses his lips just below my earlobe, making me curl around him, grinning. "You make me feel like a god."

You are a god, I think, as he gives me one last, lingering kiss. A god I'm falling in love with.

Those are the words that cross my mind. This tiny, sane part of me wonders how that can possibly be. How can I be in love with him?

But really, it isn't my love for him that surprises me. I think I've known all along that I was going to fall in love with this man. I just didn't know it would be so fast.

When he leaves, he leaves me with a smile on my face and so many questions in my heart, and more joy than I knew it was possible to feel anywhere but on the stage.

# Chapter 32

## Emma

We're on day one of a four-day conference for one of the resort's biggest clients, and I just fucked it up. Big time.

Maybe it all happened because I'm a little distracted by the fact that I've spent the last few weeks dating The Boss and enjoying it too much to even care that we're having to keep the whole thing under wraps? I don't know.

We're in the middle of dinner service for over 400 guests, one of whom is a man who Rose and I have dubbed Mr. Obnoxious because he's been loudly complaining to anyone who will listen about his recent demotion within the organization. Rose thought she saw him pull a flask out of his suit coat. I don't doubt it because I caught a whiff of vodka as I was serving his plate. Even his poor tablemates seem sick of him.

The whole thing happens so fast I'm not even sure exactly <u>what</u> happened.

Rose and I are walking along the outer edge of the room, heading for the cluster of tables we're each giving service to on the far side, getting closer and closer to the booming voice of Mr. Obnoxious. I'm carrying a tray with a pitcher of water, a few glasses of iced tea, and a carafe of hot coffee. Rose is ahead of me, carrying a tray of her own.

In front of me, Rose suddenly backs up, quickly correcting to keep her tray steady and I come to an abrupt stop to prevent running into her. I barely register that someone must have stood up right in front of her, but I'm not sure because my attention is drawn to my left.

Mr. Obnoxious, who is right by me, makes a sweeping gesture with his arm and upsets the tray I'm carrying from underneath. I grab it, managing to keep it from being upended, but several items on the tray are tipping over, including two glasses of tea and the hot carafe of coffee, all headed directly for Mr. Obnoxious' lap.

Miraculously steadying the tray with one hand, I manage to grab the coffee with the other, then watch in horror as two full glasses of tea spill over the poor man's shoulder and down the front of his white button-down shirt, drenching his plate and splattering the crisp, white tablecloth for good measure.

He gasps and his big-bodied frame bolts upright, knocking the entire tray out of my grasp. Glasses, tray, water pitcher and all fly against the back wall where a cacophony of shattering glass brings the entire room to a halt.

Dread pulses through me as I stare open-mouthed, first at the wreckage that used to be my neatly organized tray, then at the man whose tea-drenched self is the center of everyone's attention. I'm still holding the carafe of hot coffee. I'm grateful he didn't get burned, but oh my god, what a mess!

"Sir, I'm so sor—"

He spins on me, his face a dangerous shade of red. "You idiot!"

I flinch, heat blooming on my face too. "I'm so terribly sorry."

"Why don't you watch where the hell you're going?"

His tablemates are bringing their napkins into service, mopping up tea on the table before it goes any farther or offering him the ones on their lap—his is drenched. Rose and other nearby servers are scuttling over to help.

I try to retrieve his plate—his food is swimming in tea—but he'll have none of it. "No, thank you!" He thrusts his chest in my direction and I step back. "You've done enough!"

"Walter," the woman to his right snaps, "it was an accident."

"Accident? She ran right into me!"

Another server steps in to take the plate—which he permits—and I back up as Alice zooms over and steps in, trying to get a handle on the situation.

He continues to bluster at her. Not knowing what else to do, I join my coworkers in trying to clean up the mess on the floor. Which is substantial. Broken cups.

363

A shattered pitcher. Bits of glass everywhere. There's even a huge dripping tea stain on the wall. A man who I gather is the president of the group has come over as well. It just gets worse and worse. My cheeks are flaming hot.

Rose leans in to another server and whispers wide-eyed, "Mr. Rivers is here."

I spin and sure enough, here comes Rayce. Wearing a suit and approaching us with long, purposeful strides, he takes in the situation with one sweeping glance—three of us kneeling down cleaning up the glittering shards of glass, Alice and the other guests trying to calm down Mr. Obnoxious, who's pointing at me and shouting at his tablemate, "No, she bumped into me!"

God, it's mortifying.

Rayce glances at me. Our eyes lock for a split second before he returns his attention to the man and steps forward. Rayce is such a powerful presence that even in the midst of the chaos we all stop for a moment to see what will happen next.

"Excuse me, Mr. Stewart," Rayce says with that way he has of garnering someone's attention. I guess I shouldn't be surprised he knows this man's name, if he used to be a leader in the group and they're long-standing clients.

Mr. Stewart turns toward Rayce but is still preoccupied with the front of his shirt. "Look at this!"

The president speaks up. "They already said they would replace—"

"This is a $300 shirt!"

I squint at it. I've seen $300 shirts before and if that's what he paid, I do believe he paid too much.

"We'll take care of it," Rayce confirms. "We can send someone to—"

"And <u>what</u>," Mr. Stewart says, shocking me because I don't think I've ever seen anyone dare to interrupt Rayce when he's in command of a room as he is now, "—do you plan on doing about <u>her?</u>" He points a finger at me.

Rayce glances in our direction and we jolt back into action. I pick at a shard of glass with shaking hands. My heart is thumping in my ears. God, I can't believe this happened. What a disaster!

"Let's get you taken care of first," Rayce says firmly. "Then I'll speak with my employees."

Fuck.

"Well, I trust she won't have a job after this!"

"It was an <u>accident</u>, Walter," the woman at the table hisses at him. "Be reasonable."

"Oh excuse me, I didn't know they made a habit of hiring—" and here he turns to glare at me, "—such incompetent morons."

"Enough," Rayce says in a frightening tone that brings the room to silence once more. He's still as poised as ever, but those blue eyes of his have turned to flint.

Mr. Stewart blinks, finally speechless. He looks like he still wants to rage at someone but is now thinking better about doing it to the man standing in front of him.

"I will not stand for the abuse of my staff, Mr. Stewart."

Mr. Stewart blinks again. He glances around as if finally realizing the extent of the scene he's caused. "No," he says, looking contrite. "No, of course not. I apologize."

Rayce does not move or respond. I instinctively know what he's waiting for, and I guess the man does, too.

He turns to me and says in the softest tone I've heard out of him all day. "I'm sorry."

I nod, wanting to apologize again myself but sensing I'd better keep my mouth shut. In the next minute Alice has ushered Mr. Stewart out of the room to arrange getting him a replacement shirt and the room has slowly spun back into motion, the sound of conversations rising in hesitant waves throughout the massive ballroom.

My cohorts and I go back to cleaning up the last of the glass as quickly and quietly as we can. Rayce approaches us. "Meet me in the staging area when you're done," he says quietly to the three of us, then walks away.

The other two exchange ominous glances, but I keep my burning cheeks aimed at the floor. Someone shows up with a small vacuum, an additional disruption to the dinner but it can't be helped given all the little pieces glittering in the carpet.

"I'll do it," I say, grabbing the one unbroken iced tea glass left on the floor to put it on the tray. It must've been cracked though, which I didn't notice. At the slightest pressure, it collapses in my grip and the sharp edge slices hot across my palm.

I drop it on the tray and ball my hand into a fist, wincing. God, what next?

"Are you okay?" Rose asks.

"I'm fine." I open my hand to examine it. It's smeared with blood.

"Oh geez," someone says.

Rose stands with the tray and I stand with her. "Let someone else handle the vacuuming. Go take care of that."

I really have no choice. I go back into the staging area and to a little sink we use just for handwashing, more and more angry with myself all the time.

Rayce must've come into the room shortly after me, because just as I start to run the water, I hear Rose say, "I'm sorry, Mr. Rivers. It was my fault. I almost backed into Emma's tray and—"

"I shouldn't have been following so closely," I say curtly, not even bothering to turn around.

"You weren't that close."

"It was the perfect storm," Alice says. I have no idea when she joined the conversation. "I saw it." She starts to explain what happened, but doesn't get very far before Rayce cuts her off.

He's at my side, his hand touching my shoulder for just a moment. "Emma, what happened?"

"It's just a cut." A cut that hurts like hell and is making short work of bleeding all over the place. I hope the running water is making it look worse than it is.

He takes my hand. "Let me see."

I'm trying to act like it's just any old boss holding my hand, instead of Rayce. I hope he remembers there are witnesses too, because I can see the worry all over his face.

"I'm okay." But I let him examine my hand, leaning over the open slice at the base of my thumb. It's the first good look I've had of it myself. I'm relieved to see it hurts worse than it looks.

"Go to first-aid," he says, meaning the resort's first-aid station not far from the main pool.

"It's not that bad. I'll just get a couple Band-Aids."

He grabs a couple paper towels, folds them, and puts them over the wound. "I want someone to look at this in case you need stitches."

All right, maybe it's bad enough to need better bandaging than a couple Band-Aids, but it doesn't need stitches.

"No. I just—"

"Don't argue with me."

Now *I'm* being given the boss look. I shut my mouth and clench my teeth managing not to give him a look right back. At least, I think I do. "Fine." I hold the paper towels against the cut and march toward the door.

On my way out, I notice Alice looking at her boss like something isn't quite right but she can't figure out what.

Great.

When I get back from first aid with a butterfly bandage on my hand, they've moved into clean up. As if I didn't feel badly enough about the accident, it's even worse knowing they had to carry on with one less person when we needed all the hands we could get.

I'm eager to dive in and make myself useful. I head into the vacated dining room to help clear off the tables and reset the room for tomorrow. Rose gestures me over. She's lifting off a floral centerpiece and placing it on a wheeled cart with the others. "Mr. Rivers said for you to find him when you got back."

I scowl and start pulling off the tablecloth. "All right." I toss it onto a nearby pile of dirty linens and head for the next table. She follows me, the wheels on the cart squeaking behind her.

"He said to go as soon as you got back."

My cheeks start to burn. I've been nothing but mad ever since the whole thing started. Between making such a horrific mess and being called an <u>incompetent moron</u> and

371

getting put in my place by Rayce right in front of everyone and leaving my coworkers in a bind, I'm in no mood to go talk to anybody.

I grab the next centerpiece and set it on the cart. "I'm not going to ditch out on you guys again."

Rose gives me a strange look. "But he's asking for you."

"Emma," Alice calls from a table behind me. I didn't realize she was there. She's giving me a shrewd look that I don't like. "Mr. Rivers has asked for you. Do not keep him waiting."

Crap. I was worried about Rayce giving things away when he was leaning over my hand with so much concern. I didn't even think about my stubbornness doing the same thing. Would I have argued with him before, or delayed following his instructions now, if I weren't in a relationship with him?

"Yes, ma'am. Sorry. I just wanted to help first."

She doesn't reply, because she doesn't need to. I read her look loud and clear, and head off to find Rayce.

When I appear in the open doorway of his office, he jumps up the moment he sees me and comes over and shuts the door behind me. It's late and there's no one else in the executive offices, so I'm not worried about anyone seeing us.

"How's your hand?" he asks, taking my hand gently in his and looking over the bandage.

"It's okay."

"You didn't need stitches?"

"No."

"Thank god." He kisses the bandage tenderly, and that's all it takes for the anger I've been feeling about this evening to finally start dissipating. "Do you hurt?"

"It stings a little. I'm okay." Then we both say at the same time, "I'm sorry."

"What are you sorry for?" he asks.

"For making such a huge mess. They're such big clients, too. And—"

He tucks my chin between two fingers. "It was an accident according to everyone who saw it. Even our clients. They all know Walter is a childish blowhard and that's what

I'm sorry for. I wanted to kick his ass for the way he was talking to you."

I smile. God, I'm such a sucker for this man.

# Chapter 33

## Rayce

"Are you sure you're okay?" I ask again, leading her away from the door and farther into my office. I don't know which I'm more concerned about, the fact that some asshole had the balls to treat her like that or the fact that she got hurt. Both give me far too much anxiety over her.

The unhappiness and stress that's been on her face tonight is finally starting to soften though. This is why I called her to my office. Not to review the incident with her as I did with everyone else, and as I led everyone to believe this meeting with her was about. I want to lift the weight of tonight's events off her shoulders.

"I'm okay, but…" She leans back on my desk, sitting slightly. "I'm worried people might be picking up on things between us."

My heart knocks against my chest. We can't let our relationship get out the wrong way. "Why? Someone said something to you?"

"No. But it was pretty obvious you were worried about me."

Of course I was worried about her. She was bleeding all over the place. "Well, I would've been concerned about anyone."

She shrugs. "Yes, but the way you were acting. I don't know. Alice was giving you a funny look, and then…" She scrunches up her face, looking slightly embarrassed, "I don't think I helped matters either by arguing with you. I think people are too used to everyone obeying your every command." She gives me a playful smile.

"Well, I don't see what the problem is," I say smiling too and pulling her into my arms. "You still did what I told you to do."

"Don't rub it in." She wraps her arms around my waist and runs her hands up my back.

I chuckle and give her a kiss, then bring her snug against me, her head tucked under my chin and resting against my chest. Her body softens, and I stroke her hair, determined to hold her until she decides to let go.

"I should probably get back to work," she says. But she doesn't move or lesson her grip on me.

"No rush."

"People will wonder if I'm gone too long."

I want to say, 'Let them wonder. I don't give a fuck.' But I don't get to magically decide image doesn't matter just because it's inconvenient for me. Though, when has it ever been convenient? "I'm tired of hiding you."

"Yeah. Maybe I'll find something else soon."

I know she'll find another job eventually, but we're definitely running up against some obstacles. I'm not going to let her take anything that hurts her financially. She needs to be making the same pay or better, and not lose any benefits. Unfortunately, too many places around town are run by cheap bastards. To get benefits she'll probably need some sort of supervisory position, but her job history is going to make that tough unless I can convince her to let me help.

I pull back slightly so I can look at her. "Let me make some calls for you."

She gets that stubborn look on her face again and shakes her head firmly. "No. I can't be taking favors from you." She puts her hand on my chest reassuringly. "I know you're not him," she says, not for the first time because we've had this conversation before. "I just can't do it. I have to find something on my own."

"People find jobs through networking all the time. That's how it's done."

"This is different and you know it."

I groan slightly but cup her sweet face in my hands and give her another kiss. Stubborn little thing. But I don't push, because I know how strongly she feels about this and why. Still, I'm getting impatient. I'm tired of our entire relationship being behind closed doors.

Then I get an idea.

"Let's get away together."

She smiles. "Yeah?"

"Yes. Somewhere we won't have to worry about being seen."

She makes a face. "Well, that sounds great, but by the time I have a weekend off I may have another job and then it won't matter."

She's right about that. We have conferences booked the next several weeks and chances are good she'll be scheduled on the weekends to help out. I hate that she should have to do it at all. I wish we could just fast-forward our relationship so I could take care of her and she wouldn't have to do anything she didn't want to do. If she works, I want it to be for passion, not rent money.

"We'll go midweek then. You have Monday and Tuesday off, right?"

She straightens slightly. "Don't you have to work?"

"I'll take it off. One of the many advantages of being the boss."

She looks a little surprised that I would make this kind of time for her. She still has no idea how special she is. It makes my heart hurt.

"You'd really do that?"

"Of course. How about we leave Sunday night after you get off work?"

She grins and bounces a bit on her tip toes. "Where will we go?"

Now *that's* the kind of joy I've wanted to see on her face tonight. "Let me take care of it. It'll be a surprise."

Feeling my objective has finally been met, I give her another kiss, but this time I linger. Her body softens, molding against mine as we open to one another and slide into a kiss that slowly gets more and more heated. As usual when I'm around her, the seat of my pants is way too tight.

Our hands begin to wander and my lips do, too. When I suck on the tender skin on the side of her neck, she moans softly and her fingers snake into my hair. Suddenly I want to be very, very naughty with a certain Emma Swanson.

I lift her, wrapping her legs around my waist and depositing her sexy ass on top of my desk. Taking her mouth with more passion now, she gives it right back to me. It's exhilarating how much she wants me, too.

I thrust my fully-erect cock against her heat and she clutches my ass, pulling me harder against her.

Oh, we're definitely doing this now. Our mouths still working together, hungry for each other, I start unfastening the buttons on her shirt. They open smoothly, in quick succession, <u>one, two, three.</u>

"We shouldn't," she says half-heartedly.

I stop long enough to get a good look at the desire written all over her face. "We shouldn't as in 'no' or we shouldn't as in 'bend me over this desk and fuck me like a boss'?"

She exhales heatedly and starts clutching at the back of my shirt, hurriedly untucking it. "Two," she whispers. "Option two."

In a frenzy of movement and loosened clothes, I do exactly what I said I would. With my pants around my thighs and my cock stretched tight, I bend Emma over my desk and dive deep. For the first time I'm aroused not just by her but by the forbidden nature of what we're doing. Fucking an employee on my desk is erotic.

She's arching her bare ass up and back against me, opening up for more. I'm gripping her hair so hard that her head is pulled back and her lovely neck exposed and all she has to say about it is, *yes, yes, yes.* When I reach around to work her clit, she's so slick it's a challenge to keep the flat of my fingers over her bud where they belong.

She clamps around me and starts to pulse, crying out loud. "Shhh baby," I manage to get out, but I'm careening out of control, too. God, this woman undoes me. I grip her shoulder, holding her body hard against mine as we climax together.

I feel not a whiff of shame or desperation or darkness.

There's no question in my mind that there's only one woman I want like this, whether it's sweet and tender or dirty as fuck. I don't truly know if this woman belongs to me yet like I want her to, but that doesn't change one fundamental fact.

I definitely belong to her.

First thing Friday morning, I talk to our executive assistant and have him clear my schedule for Monday, Tuesday, and most of Wednesday. Emma doesn't come in until three that day so I won't check into the office until the afternoon either.

That only leaves telling Lizzy and Connor, which I do during our morning meet up. "Just so you know, I won't be here the first part of next week."

Lizzy cocks her head at me. "Why?" They're sitting across my desk from me, each balancing a small stack of files that we've just finished reviewing. Connor is still making notes on the Anderson project.

"No reason. I just wanted a few days off."

Connor's pen freezes and he slowly raises his head to look at me. They're both giving me puzzled looks, which they turn toward one another before turning back at me.

"A few days off?" Lizzy parrots back.

"Is that a problem?"

"Uh, no." She sits back and spins her pen in her hands. "No. It's just so unlike you."

"Well, even I need a break from work every now and then."

They're still giving me looks like they don't quite believe this is happening. Maybe I should've made up some sort of business trip as an excuse, but that would've meant a more involved lie than I care for. Sure, I'm not usually one to take off during the week, but is it really <u>that</u> noteworthy?

"What's the problem? Connor's taking next Friday off to go rock-climbing with Whitney."

"Hey, I'll be here Saturday for the IEA Conference."

"So will I. I work all the time. Can't I take a couple of days without catching grief for it?"

"Of course, you can." Lizzy gives me a sweet smile. "I think you work too hard anyway."

I do not. I love my work. But there are a few things I love more than work. Two of them are sitting across this desk from me.

One of them is an amazing woman who I think I might love even more.

"Enjoy," Connor says. He's giving me a knowing look. He knows I'm hiding something. Sometimes this kid is too damn observant.

Honestly, I'd love to just tell them. This isn't like before, and I think I could make Connor understand that. But there's still the matter of resort policy, harassing emails from a certain Taylor Norrell, and the potential fallout if people find out I'm dating an employee.

No. Better to get things arranged the way we want them first.

# Chapter 34

## Emma

I've been home from work maybe five minutes and have barely started packing for my trip away with Rayce when I get a text from him. <u>There's a driver out front. Take your time getting ready. His job is to wait for you.</u>

I go to the window and peek through the blinds and sure enough, a shiny black town car is parked out front. Nothing could look more out of place than a car like that in an apartment complex like this. Although, this apartment turned out to be a better living situation than I thought I was going to have. Right before I moved in they started remodeling, conveniently beginning with the third floor where I'm at. The place is still small and the neighborhood isn't fantastic, but the apartment itself is nice and inviting now that everything's new. Not that I'm hardly ever here.

As I head to my closet to get my clothes, I take a deep breath, still feeling frustrated from a conversation I had with Aaron earlier. He and Pierce keep trying to get in my head about what's really happening with Rayce, insisting that even a trip away proves nothing as he's still keeping me a secret. They're both convinced he's the asshole boss having a fling.

I know they're just protective of me, and I understand why they're worried. I do. Still. I wish they would just stop. I don't need them feeding old doubts.

Packing serves as a decent distraction, even though it doesn't take me long. My wardrobe is a little sparse these days so it's not like I had a whole lot of options. But I have no idea where we're going or how nice I'll need to dress. He told me not to worry about it and to just make sure I bring a swimsuit. That, at least, is something I know he likes me in.

I change into some cute olive green capris, a soft white halter top that ties behind my neck, and some strappy brown wedges. Fifteen minutes later I'm being driven through the heart of Swan Pointe in a town car so luxurious I determine it would be pretty easy for a person to get used to town cars.

Eventually we arrive at the Swan Pointe Regional Airport, drive straight onto the tarmac, and come to a stop alongside a sleek private jet. The stairs are down and at the base is a young man in a trim steward uniform, apparently waiting for me.

As the driver retrieves my suitcase out of the back, the steward smiles and gestures upward. "Right this way, Miss Swanson."

Wow. Rayce sure knows how to treat a woman right. No surprise there.

Holding onto the metal guardrail, I ascend the stairs, wondering if he's going to be inside or if we're meeting at whatever mysterious location he has planned for us. But as soon as I enter the cabin with its luxuriously-appointed seating, I spot him near the rear, his laptop open on a little table.

He spots me too, and immediately gets to his feet, coming toward me with a broad, handsome smile. "Hello, beautiful."

"Hi, handsome." He's still in his dress clothes from work, but his top button is undone, his sleeves are rolled up just enough to showcase his sexy forearms, and his suit coat and tie are nowhere to be seen.

He pulls me into his arms, the familiar scent of his aftershave still lingering on his skin. He gives me first a kiss on the lips, then on my cheek, before pulling me into a firm hug.

I sink into it, the remnants of my conversation with Aaron falling away. He just doesn't understand how Rayce makes me feel. I smile up at him. "This is already the best vacation I've ever had."

"We haven't even started yet."

"We're together. That's all I need."

He rewards me with another kiss and leads me to our seats. As soon as we're settled in, the cabin is secured, and we're told to prepare for departure.

As we're taxing toward the runway, he stows his laptop away, but tells me it will be temporary. "I'm sorry. I still have a few loose ends to tie up. Another half hour max, then I'll be yours."

"That's fine." I still can't believe he's taking time off in the middle the week for this. It's not going to bother me if he has to keep tabs on things a little. Besides, I'm too busy being distracted by this beautiful jet, and the fact that we're the only ones on it.

"Is this yours?"

He takes my hand and settles back as we turn onto the runway and the engines start to rev. "Technically, Lizzy and I own it with Connor, but Connor uses it more than any of us. Those itchy feet of his. I wasn't that interested in buying a plane, but if that's what he needed to stay in Swan Pointe, that was fine by me."

I love how far he's willing to go for his brother, and the fact that he had the resources to do it is impressive. I wonder, not for the first time, how they manage the lifestyles they do from owning just one resort.

We start accelerating down the runway, and turn our attention to the view out the window. My hand is still in his, and my cheek resting on his shoulder, as the city gets smaller and smaller beneath us.

Soon the climb evens out enough for the steward to ask what we'd like to drink: white zin for me and brandy for Rayce. After he brings our drinks, he tells us that he'll be in the cockpit and to buzz him if we need anything else. I'm grateful to know we'll have the privacy.

"You know, I didn't think the resort business was this profitable." I don't realize how tactless a thing that was to say until it's too late and already out of my mouth. I really need to work on the whole tell-him-whatever-crosses-your-mind thing. But he doesn't seem bothered.

"Profitable, yes. This profitable, no. The majority of our income comes from other investments."

"If most of your money doesn't come from the resort, why not hire someone to do your job?" He's clearly smart about money, and the people who are *really* smart about money know when to hire out.

"Because it's not a job. It's..." he rubs his bottom lip like he's looking for the right words. "All right, so Mom and Dad. This was their thing. He was in real estate and she was in the hotel business. He found this beat up old resort and decided that was his passion. He sacrificed literally every penny he had, and a few he didn't, in order to take this run-down old property and make it so incredible people would cross continents to get to it. And they do. On any given day, no small percentage of our guests are from somewhere overseas."

I smile at the pride I see on his face.

"Once they got it up and running, they were able to rebuild with other real estate and portfolios, but they still went in to work every day because there's no passion in portfolios. At least, there wasn't for Mom and Dad. And there isn't for me either. I mean, I enjoy that, too. I kind of have a gift for numbers. I can get lost in the right kind of spreadsheet for hours."

"I literally have no idea what that feels like."

He laughs. "Well, take my word for it. It's enjoyable. But enjoyable is not the same thing as *passion*. Which is why…"

He stops abruptly and gets a troubled look on his face.

"What?"

He's looking at his hand resting on my knee, thinking. "Well, I do enjoy working at the resort, in part because it's always been about family. We all grew up in it. I never did understand how Connor was able to walk away from it. He was raised by the same people, but he's so different. He has such a wild streak in him. But Whitney's been good for that." He shakes his head slightly. "God bless Whitney. If it weren't for her, I have no doubt Connor would be long gone by now and we'd be lucky to see him every couple of years."

My heart warms at this little speech. I love how important his family is to him. You wouldn't think he was the type, this sturdy alpha male. But he has a huge soft spot for the people he loves.

My chest lifts with the idea that maybe one day I could be one of the people fortunate enough to be loved by him.

He's gotten off track though, and I want to know what he was thinking. "But you said 'Which is why.' Which is why what?"

He nods and takes a sip of brandy. "Right. Well. I do enjoy the work and don't mind bringing it home even though I could delegate more. I like it. But…"

He's hesitating again. This is so unlike him. I'm doubly intrigued to wonder what could have this confident man hesitating.

"But?"

"But… I think the Rivers Paradise Resort could be so much more."

"More how?" He and his siblings already run a world-class resort. And they've already made some impressive expansions and improvements since their parents passed away. What more could it be?

"More of a brand. Like The Ritz-Carlton or Four Seasons. Couldn't you see Rivers Paradise Resorts all over the world?"

His voice takes on a different quality, and I recognize it right away. <u>This</u> he's passionate about.

"We could have locations in Hawaii and the Caribbean. Europe. Asia. Everywhere. God." He shakes his head, his voice tinged with a rare emotion. "I'd love to be the one to blow this thing up." He takes my hand and laces our fingers together. "Our kids wouldn't inherit a resort. They'd inherit a worldwide empire."

Our kids?

Empire?

Maybe he didn't mean it that way. Maybe I'm just being presumptuous, but it sure seems like he's included me in the picture he's drawing. And wow. What a picture it is. He's already such an impressive, powerful man. What sort of man would he be if he created an *empire?*

Does he really see me as a worthy partner to walk that road with him?

"But…" and now his voice takes on a more practical tone. "Building something like that would mean a lot of travel and working elsewhere."

I spot the difficulty for him immediately. "Leaving your family."

He nods.

"Maybe they would build it with you."

He nods again. "Maybe."

"You don't think so?"

"I don't know."

"Why not find out?"

He takes a while to answer, softly stroking the back of my hand and looking thoughtful. "Because I know myself." He holds my eyes. "If I put it out there, I'll go for it. Whether they join me or not. And that's a lot to give up."

I'll be with you, I want to say. You won't be alone.

But I stop myself. Just the thought of saying that gets me all confused. How can I already know I want join my entire life with his? Isn't it too soon?

I squeeze his hand. "I'm sure whatever you decide, it'll be the right thing and it'll be amazing."

He cups my cheek and gives me a soft kiss. He holds my gaze, his eyes going soft. He looks like he wants to say something, but the moment passes and he kisses me again before leaning back in his seat and exhaling. "I suppose I should get my work over with so we can get on with our trip."

"Go right ahead. I'll just sit here enjoying this magnificent wine." I take a sip to prove my point.

He smiles and gives me another kiss, then retrieves his laptop. I do try to be patient. I watch the sunset through the windows, listening to the soft clicks of the touchpad on his laptop. But his thigh is pressed against mine, and I can smell his amazing smell, and I'm eyeing the long couch on the other side of the aisle from us.

"I'm curious," I say slowly, turning and looking up at him. "Are you in the Mile High Club?"

His hand hovers over the keyboard and he looks at me. "Are you?"

I shake my head, giving him a slow smile.

He snaps his laptop shut. "Well, we'd better take care of that right now."

# Chapter 35

## Emma

As always, Rayce is a man of contrasts. We took a private jet to San Diego where a rented Mercedes-Benz was waiting for us, because this man does like his luxury vehicles. From there he drove us to a street taco stand near the beach. We sat on a rickety wooden park bench devouring the best street tacos I've ever had, laughing and talking about certain food joints he's encountered on his travels that he craves when he's at home. This taco stand is one of them.

I love this simple, human side of him. I love that he knows how to wear the hell out of a suit and can command the attention of an entire room with just the tone of his voice, while still enjoying the simple pleasures of life and indulging in the occasional bowl of Fruity Pebbles.

After dinner we take a short walk on the beach, reveling in the freedom to be in public together without any worries. I'm surprised to learn he's just as affectionate in public as he is in private, always either holding my hand or tucking me under his arm and making me feel so special and adored.

This is what Aaron and Pierce don't understand. If they saw us together, maybe they'd see he's not the slime ball they fear he is.

However, once we reach our hotel, some of my own doubts start to come to the surface.

He's brought us to a luxury resort adorned with marble floors and soaring ceilings and intricately carved solid wood furniture. While the bellboy takes our luggage up to our room, Rayce and I give ourselves a tour.

We descend a curving marble staircase that lets out onto a gorgeous restaurant complete with candlelit lanterns on the tables and a central gleaming wooden dance floor. From here we exit onto the patio, the immaculately landscaped garden dotted with tiny ground lights.

As we go, he talks about what he thinks they're doing well here and what he has strived to improve upon at his own resort, because even amidst this five-star luxury there are things that aren't quite up to his standards.

It's the first glimpse I've really had of how his mind works as a businessman, and I am simultaneously impressed with his brilliance and wondering if I truly live up to standards myself. He inhabits this beautiful world so naturally. More than inhabits it. He is the master of this domain.

I've been exposed to this kind of wealth enough myself to know how to navigate it. But there's still that nagging, little doubt.

Holding hands, we walk alongside one of the pools, the soft tinkling from the water features lending a soothing quality to the air. The pool is lit under the water and glowing turquoise against the black evening night.

"It's so beautiful," I say, trying to push my insecurities away.

"It is," he agrees, rubbing the back of my hand with his thumb. "I don't know if you're more of a pool girl or a beach girl, but we probably have time for both."

Me in a bikini, in a place like this.

I'm not ashamed of my body, or my tattoo, but I know Rayce. He has to think about how things look to the outside world, or at least believes he has to. How does he think I'm going to look to the outside world?

I feel a gentle tug on my hand and I look up to find him examining my expression. "Is something wrong?"

Geez, I didn't mean to let my fears come out like this. I put on a smile and shake my head.

He doesn't buy it though, because he's starting to know me too well. "What is it?"

I shrug. "I was just being silly."

"Oh yeah?" He brings us to a stop pulls me snugly into his arms. "Silly about what?"

I exhale. God, this man is so sweet. I should keep my mouth shut, but that's never worked around him. "I'm just... you know, this is a really nice place and of course anyone looking at you wouldn't be surprised to learn that you run something just like it. You look like you fit in. But I'm…"

His brows pinch together and he watches me with concern. "You're what?"

I spit it out. "Probably not the kind of woman you're used to."

"Thank god for that."

I don't think he understands what I'm saying. "Just… think about it. You, me. In our swimsuits. You're not the kind of guy who's usually seen with someone like me."

"'Someone like you?' You mean someone beautiful and interesting and kind and strong enough to be her own person?" His voice has that firm don't-even-think-about-arguing-with-me tone. "How about someone who's head and shoulders above every other woman out there, and *especially* above anyone petty enough to judge her about a tattoo. A tattoo that's absolutely beautiful, by the way."

Through his firm admonition I've softened in his arms. "Really?"

"Emma," he says softly, cupping my face in his hands. "I can't *wait* to show you off to everyone I know."

And that's how Rayce takes my fears and doubts and blows them into the wind like dandelion puffs. I do trust the things Rayce says. In fact, I don't think I've ever trusted anyone as I trust him. This reinforced trust of him has been the best part of this entire trip so far, and the trip has been pretty amazing.

Even though we were up late last night, seemingly unable to satisfy our craving for each other, we were out and about at a reasonable hour this morning. I think we've done so much hanging out indoors and in bedrooms that we were both eager to do something different. Not that we haven't been enjoying our time in the bedroom as much as we always do. But we both keep talking about how fun it is to be out together.

We started with an amazing brunch at the resort's patio café, then came to a beautiful upscale outdoor shopping plaza near the resort to explore. Neither one of us seem to be much in the mood for buying anything. The halfhearted window shopping we've done has been more of an accessory to the main attraction, which has been strolling along and enjoying each other's company and the beautiful SoCal weather.

Though, there is one purchase I wish I could have made if it weren't so obviously out of my price range: an absolutely stunning red brocade dress I spotted in a window display.

The elaborate bodice fit snug through the breasts and hips, and the skirt flared out from the thighs in thick, luxurious layers of red satin and black lace. The hem in the front was high enough to reveal an equally beautiful pair of black strappy heals, but the fabric in the rear was long enough to sweep the ground.

I didn't even bother to go in. Just gave it a wistful glance as we walked by. Well, maybe "glance" isn't the right word. It was somewhere between "glancing" and "drooling over."

But oh, was it beautiful.

After a delicious lunch of enchiladas and margaritas at the Blue Iguana, we continue our browsing. As we pass a Build-A-Bear store, I examine the colorful displays of outfits and different kinds of stuffed animals, everything from bears to monkeys to frogs.

"Did you want to go in?" Rayce asks.

"Well..." I hesitate. I kind of do, but... "Isn't that more for kids?"

"You remember the video games, right?"

I laugh. "Okay, yes. I want to go in."

Then I'm not quite sure how it happens, but we both end up with stuffed bears, trying to outdo one another in the outrageous outfit department.

Rayce's is wearing a little black suit which he declares is, "dashing against his brown fur," along with a black superhero mask and purple white-trimmed cape fit for a king.

Mine is a white bear sporting a tiny pair of overalls, a bold feathered hat, and a purple faux pearl necklace. I thought I was done until I found the tutus. I'm currently working stiff pink tulle over his chubby bear body.

"Yours needs one, too," I tell him.

"My bear is a boy."

"It doesn't sound like he's very comfortable with his masculinity."

Rayce laughs. "Okay, fine. But at least make it a purple tutu."

"No, no, he likes pink." I grab a second one out of the bin. "Don't you want pink?" I ask the bear, then grab its furry little head and make him nod.

"This is my bear," Rayce says, pulling him out of my reach. "You have your own."

Soon were scuffling over the bear and giggling like a bunch of rowdy teenagers. And just like a bunch rowdy teenagers, we draw yet another disapproving glare from the woman behind the counter.

"You are <u>trouble,</u>" Rayce says, that adorable, playful grin on his face. He grabs my ass, pulls me up against his side, and starts marching us up to the register. "We need to pay for these and go before you get us kicked out of here."

"Are we actually getting them?"

He looks me in surprise. "Didn't you want to?"

"Well…" An adult is supposed to say that they don't want something like this. But I look at my tutu-ed farmer bear with his granny hat and pearls and I want him. I grin up at Rayce. "Yes."

"Me too."

"I love that you're so crazy sometimes," I say.

"And I love you."

We both stop and I look at him in shock. He's looking shocked right back. My heart is pumping against my chest like I just finished a 400-meter sprint.

"I didn't mean to say that out loud."

So it was just an accident. I can't tell if I'm relieved or not. I mean, it's probably too soon for us to start making declarations of love. No matter how I actually feel. But still, hearing those words is doing something to me. My entire system is revving up, and I feel a little unsteady on my own two feet.

How does he keep <u>doing</u> that to me?

I need to save him from what has to be an embarrassing moment, though. I laugh, trying to lighten the mood. "It's okay. I understand. One time I ended a call with an insurance agent by saying 'I love you.'"

I laugh again, because I can't read the expression on his face. The shocked look is gone, at least.

"I have no idea why," I continue. "It's funny how things can slip out sometimes even when we don't mean it."

"I didn't say I didn't mean it. I said I didn't mean to say it out loud."

My heart starts in with the pounding again.

Then he says with the same confidence with which he says everything, "Don't worry. I don't expect you to say it back. No pressure. Pretend the bear said it."

He holds his bear in front of his face. "I love you, Emma," he says in a fake, deep bear voice, then he pokes the bear's furry nose against my cheeks over and over again while making kissy sounds.

I start laughing so hard I'm getting tears in my eyes. "Oh my God, you <u>are</u> crazy."

"But you love that about me, right?" he says with a wink. He gets us walking again and I peek up at him, not sure whether he was serious or not. <u>Did</u> he mean what he said but he's playing it off to spare himself, or was he just playing in general? I'm not sure now.

Still, as he pays for our bears with their silly outfits, all I can think about is how long he's going to make me wait before I get to hear those words again.

We spend the rest of the afternoon at the pool, and between the way he looks at me and the way he treats me, I feel like a goddess the entire time. This is definitely something I could get used to.

As it gets close to dinner time, we debate where to go to eat. He suggests the resort's restaurant at the bottom of the marble stairs, but I didn't bring anything nice enough to wear at a place like that. Too bad, too, because that place looked amazing.

But I don't care where we eat as long as we get to eat together, and tell him so. We head back to our suite to clean up and change. As soon as we come into the bedroom, I spot something on top of the bed. It's a large, white garment box with an elegant store logo embossed on the top.

I recognize it immediately.

I look at him. He's leaning against the door frame, arms crossed and smiling at me. He didn't.

I return my attention to the box, slowly lifting the lid. I pull back thick sheets of tissue paper to reveal the red brocade dress. I press my fingertips to my lips, then lift the heavy dress from the box. It looks to be exactly my size.

"You shouldn't have," I whisper, but I can't stop myself from running my fingers over the fine needlework on the bodice and the silky material of the skirt. "When did you even do this?"

"I called them when you went to the restroom during lunch."

I look at him. He's giving me that soft smile again.

"We also have reservations downstairs in thirty-five minutes."

410

"Rayce…" I carefully lay the dress on the bed, keeping my eyes on him.

Part of me wants to tell him I can't accept it. This dress has to be at least a couple thousand dollars. But I sense it would be tactless to do so. He looks so pleased. Even though that's a hell of a lot of money for me to spend on a dress, I know the same is not true for him. He can probably purchase a dress like this as easily as he can buy a couple of bears that epitomize the phrase "fashion faux pas," and I didn't argue with him about buying those.

I walk up to him and slide my hands around his neck. He wraps his arms around my waist and I lean against his warm chest. "Thank you. Thank you so much. It's beautiful."

He gently rubs the back of his fingers down my cheek. "You are a woman of grace and class, Emma Swanson. That dress is almost worthy of you."

# Chapter 36

## Rayce

I did not know it was possible to feel this happy. This woman lifts my heart, brightens the entire world, and makes me feel like the best possible version of myself. And this version cannot stop smiling. At least, not at her.

I came down to the restaurant without her, since she wasn't quite ready when it was time for our reservation. I told her not to rush, that'd I'd hold our table.

This has turned out to be a fortune of fate.

I'm sitting at a table near the far side of the dance floor, watching Emma descend the marble staircase. The dress hugs her curves and flares just below her hips. The hem is angled from front to back, revealing her calves and black high-heeled feet but sweeping down the steps behind her.

One delicate hand glides over the marble banister while the other rests confidently at her side. Her hair is swept up in a gentle knot, the tips of loose strands brushing the base of her neck. God, that woman's neck.

The room disappears. The other diners, the few couples on the dance floor, the sweeping waltz they're playing: it all seems to go still.

Emma is the very picture of elegance and beauty.

And I am struck.

Just like the first time I ever saw her, it's all I can do just to breathe.

As she nears the bottom, her eyes sweep the restaurant, seeking me. I get to my feet and start in her direction. Her eyes leap to mine and immediately a smile blooms on her face.

Oh, the way she smiles for me. It literally makes my heart hurt. But it's a good kind of hurt. It's the kind of hurt that says, <u>I can't live without this.</u>

We cross the room toward one another and meet in the middle of the dance floor. I pull her into my arms, the soft floral notes of her perfume pinching my heart. I frame my body, hold her hand and waist, and start to lead her in a dance.

She follows effortlessly, her hand resting on my shoulder. Her brows are raised though, and she's smiling. "You know how to waltz!"

"Are you surprised?"

I spin her gently, the fabric of her skirt flaring out. I bring her back in and she answers. "Yes. Though I don't know why. You know how to do everything else."

"Not true. But you don't get to be the child of Grant and Sharon Rivers without knowing how to dance."

"What other dances do you know?"

"Foxtrot. Salsa. West Coast." I keep going down the list, and with each dance I name, her smile widens and her eyes light up a little more.

"You've been holding out on me. We have to do all of them. Tonight."

I chuckle. "Anything you want."

Literally. Anything she wants.

We circle around the edge of the dance floor, and I'm grateful my parents taught me how to showcase a woman like this. She's a stunning beauty, drawing the eyes everyone we pass. She has no idea the attention she captures, or the admiration she inspires. That's part of what I love about her. She's confident without being cocky, appreciative of fine things without demanding them, down-to-earth without being afraid to rise up.

As we finish the dance, I pull her into my arms, nuzzle against her ear, and whisper, "You look amazing."

It's not what I want to say, but I'm not going to alarm her with the L-word again.

I feel her smile against my cheek. "So do you. I thought you looked good in a suit, but in a tux?"

She makes a cute little growling sound and I pull back, laughing. I lead her toward our table, and give her ass a little slap. "You saucy woman, you."

She's laughing, too. "Is that what you love about me?"

"I love everything about you."

Ah well. I tried.

She blushes and gives me a tentative smile. I wink and start telling her the highlights on the menu, wanting to take the pressure off her. I see that same wondering on her face I saw before. She doesn't know if I'm teasing. I'll let her know I'm dead serious when I'm ready to take that chance. But I have never in my life said those words without meaning them, and never once to anyone I'm not related to by blood or marriage.

I never imagined something like this could happen so quickly, or that the words could come so effortlessly. I've felt sort of close to being in love once or twice before, I hoped anyway, but it was never enough to tip me over the edge. With Emma, I've gone careening over.

I only pray she catches up to me, and doesn't let me crash on the bottom.

When we get to our seats, I spot my phone lying on the table and my heart jumps into my throat. I manage not to dive for it. I pull out Emma's chair and get her comfortable first, but there's a slight tremor in my hand when I reach for it. I can't help it. I'm never away from my phone this long. I just wasn't thinking about it.

"Sorry," I say as calmly as I can. I glance at Emma before entering in my unlock code. She's giving me an understanding smile. Guess I haven't fooled her at all.

My home page comes up and I scan the icons. No voice mails. No missed calls. Two text messages.

I touch the icon and force myself to breathe. My blood pressure starts to drop the second I see who they're from. There's one from Taylor Norrell and one from Lynda, who I completely forgot I asked to be my date for Lizzy's wedding.

When I'd asked her, she said she wouldn't know for a while if she was free due to a pending work commitment. I was more than happy to delay wrapping up that particular detail, then promptly forgot all about it. Now she's telling me she's free and "delighted" to accompany me.

"Well, *that's* not happening." I'll have to call her and cancel.

"Everything okay at home?"

"Home? Oh, yes. Yes, these are..." I can't resist the urge to tap on Taylor's latest message so I can give it a quick scan. She's only ever sent emails. Did I even give her my private number?

Taylor: Since you're ignoring my emails. Last chance.

Last chance for what? She's never even asked for anything. True, I haven't responded, or even consulted with our lawyer, which I maybe need to man up and do. But I'm starting to think this woman is seriously unhinged. As I recall I got a weird vibe off of her when we were "together", too.

I look at Emma, her expectant face waiting for me to finish my sentence. She's so trusting. And though I've shared a lot with her, I'm reminded that there's something I'm hiding.

Something Emma will care about.

A nervous vibration settles into my chest. How much is she going to care? When I finally tell her, will I be able to make her understand that that man was not the best version of me? Will she take me as who I am now, or will her own past make that impossible once she knows?

I can't think about that right now. Instead, I tell her about the second text. "This is from a woman who I had asked to go to Lizzy's wedding with me."

Emma's eyebrows slowly raise and she straightens, her hands drifting to her lap. "I see."

"This was before we got together. It was after, um…"

She raises her lovely eyebrows further.

"After I first kissed you and you told me to get lost."

"Ah."

"The next day at the family dinner, the topic of came up and I told Lizzy I'd make a decision and Lynda's card came up."

"Her card?"

I give her a sheepish grin and scratch the back of my neck. "I thought I blew it with you, but I didn't want to go with anyone else either. So I took three options, assigned them a suit, and let the next card my cousin drew in gin make the decision."

I wait in silence as she blinks at me with big doe eyes. Maybe I don't have to tell her about my past transgressions to give her a reason to walk. This could've done it all by itself.

But she throws her head back and laughs. "Seriously? Oh, poor Rayce. So many women to choose from."

"Laugh all you want, but it wasn't funny. You think I want to spend all evening with Miss…" I gesture at my phone impatiently, "Too Good for the Universe?"

"Hmmm," she says, still smiling and opening the menu. "I'm sure it'll be torture."

I watch her for a minute. Does she really think I'm still going through with it? Would she be all right with it if I did? She's acting like it's amusing her, but if what's happening between us means this little to her, I'm in trouble.

I need this woman to care.

I examine her closer. Her eyes are on the menu. Her posture is poised and in control. But I spot that little vein at the base of her neck fluttering in agitation. I exhale and unclench.

"Emma." There's no humor in my voice and her eyes fly to mine immediately. Such beautiful clear, blue eyes.

So open and vulnerable. Thank god she cares.

"It's not happening."

Her face relaxes slightly, but she's still watching me expectantly.

"Honestly, I forgot all about her." I lean forward slightly. "You've been a little all-consuming."

A smile tugs at the corner of her mouth. "Yeah?"

I nod slowly, still holding her eyes. "You're the one I want to go with."

Her cheeks turn a pleased shade of pink. "Really?"

"Of course."

"When is it?"

"Three weeks."

"Well, how are we going to do that? What if I don't have another job by then?"

"We'll figure something out. Or if worse comes to worst I'll just go stag. But I'm not going with anyone else, that's for sure."

She smiles, relaxing even more. "So, I'm not going to be the Paris wife?"

I cock my head at her. "The Paris wife? As in Benjamin Franklin?"

"Right," she nods, slipping into playful mode. "Like, the respectable wife is the one you take to family affairs and the Paris wife is the one you have on the side."

This again? No, no, no. Job or no, I clearly need to get our relationship out in the open as soon as possible so this precious woman has no reason to doubt where she stands with me. "Emma, if you talk about yourself like that one more time, I swear to god I'm going to bend you over my lap and spank you."

Her eyebrows fly upward and her mouth goes slack.

Oh, the things I want her to do with that mouth.

She slowly smiles and pulls her bottom lip between her teeth. "That hardly seems like a punishment, Mr. Rivers."

# Chapter 37

## Emma

It's past midnight, and we're still awake. We're lounging on the bed in the most luxurious hotel bedroom I've ever been in. Our suite has a living room and another bedroom as well, but we've spent most of our time in this room.

Rayce is propped up against the headboard, in nothing but his boxers, and I'm leaning against his chest. I'm in panties and one of his white button-down shirts. It's big and comforting and carries his smell. I want to take it home with me.

His tablet is balanced on his lap and he's pulled up YouTube so he can watch a clip of the LA Ballet Troupe's performance of <u>The Firebird.</u>

Back when I was prima.

It's always a little surreal, watching myself on a screen, especially now. I can see how thin I was, for one thing. Far too thin, really. I remember how badly I wanted the line that kind of body created, and it's a desire that seems so distant from me now that it'd be a struggle to summon it up again.

Aside from that, watching myself on a tiny screen is a different experience than the actual performance. Of course. But as I'm watching, memories of performing this particular dance pop up in little bursts. A flash of stage lights here. A vision of the ensemble surrounding me there. Spinning again and again, spotting Aaron's face as I turn.

Yes, he's in it, too. Those were the days. Back before he left it all for the love of his life and started over again in Swan Pointe.

And just what would I do for the love of my life?

I pull my eyes from the screen and watch Rayce's profile. He's completely engrossed. I've seen it before. That's the look we dancers strive to inspire in the audience:

complete awe. He's even breathing shallowly, too taken to remember to really breathe.

My heart pulses with pride unlike any I've experienced before. I'm no stranger to pride. I know I was good and I'd be lying if I tried to claim otherwise. I worked damn hard for years and years to learn how to captivate an audience like that.

But to captivate him?

It's otherworldly.

When the clip ends he stares at it for a minute, then recaptures his breath and exhales slowly. "Damn," he whispers.

I smile.

He looks at me with, I do believe, new eyes. "Damn, Emma," he says again.

I reach up and give him a kiss. "Thank you."

He groans and settles in deeper, looking at the screen with longing. "And to think, I missed my chance to see you live."

A familiar energy flows through my body.

Now I'm the one holding my breath. I can't believe I'm going to do this.

On the exhale, I pop up, climbing over his legs, padding across the thick carpet and heading for the large, open area between the bed and the terrace. Only in a place like this does such a large space exist for its own sake.

On the wall opposite the bed, there's a massive mirror inside an intricately-carved wooden frame that we've joked is there to give the visually-inclined a little extra pizazz during their love making sessions.

At least, it's been a source of extra pizazz for ours. The sight of myself on my knees, his hands on the back of my head with his own thrown back. Yeah, it wasn't too fucking bad.

But now it strikes me that this mirror, which extends almost to the floor, is the perfect size for checking body, position, lines.

I allow myself to really see my own reflection. His white shirt comes to my upper thighs, and the sleeves are rolled up to my forearms. My legs are tanner than they used to be, thanks to some actual time in the sun, but they are still strong thanks to my workouts.

As if I've still been training.

But what really strikes me is my face. I'm glowing.

I've only ever seen that kind of glow on other people. I didn't know it was possible to see it on myself. I know exactly what it's from.

It's from him. And the prospect of dancing for him, for however brief a time. It's from the two things I love most coming together in this one moment.

I turn to face him. I am going to dance for him. I am going to show him my body and my heart and share it with him openly and truly.

"Start the music."

# Chapter 38

## Rayce

I thought I knew what it was like to watch Emma move.

I didn't.

The video did not prepare me for this. She is in control of every inch of her body. From her muscular legs and strong body all the way to the length of her fingers and the tips of her toes. There is not one millimeter of her body that is not a perfectly controlled expression of movement and wonder.

I have no idea if her choreography matches what's happening on the screen. I'm not watching it. I'm vaguely aware of the fact that she has to be adapting to the space and the surface and to the fact that she's dancing alone.

But she is a vision of fluidity, grace, and wonder. I'm leaning forward, drawn to her. She keeps her eyes on mine, and dances for me in such a way that I do not feel like an observer. I am a participant. And she's drawing me into her.

She leaps and lands softly, and my heart leaps with her. She spins and I am dizzy with it.

I cannot take my eyes off her.

I don't know how long it goes on, but I don't move an inch and barely breathe the entire time. When the music stops, she ends with a pose that is at once delicate and sensual. She's partially turned from me, but looking at me over her shoulder.

She holds my eyes in an intense gaze, her lips turning up at the corners. It is a smoldering gaze that draws me in.

I'm off the bed.

She drops the pose and turns toward me, the ballerina gone but the astounding woman still there.

"You were stunning," I say, cupping her face and bringing my mouth to hers. She responds to me instantly, her arms coming around my bare waist and her amazing body curving inward against mine. All I can think about is how lucky I am that I should be privileged enough to hold this incredible woman.

"That was so fantastic."

Words. There are no words.

I was just going to give her a kiss. I didn't intend to pounce on her. But as usual, we're feeding into each other. She's pressing into me, her mouth softening and yielding beneath mine, her embrace tightening. I'm still swirling with the effects of watching her perform, of seeing the true core of her soul.

I hadn't seen it all of it before now.

I sweep my tongue over hers, clutch her body against me, inhale the heady scent of floral and citrus. I'm almost painfully erect, my body yearning to connect with her as much as my heart is.

We're soon tumbling to the floor, her long legs wrapped around me as we take each other in pulsing gasps.

"That was the most amazing thing I've ever seen," I say, tasting her jaw, her neck, her shoulder. She softens beneath me, her head tilting back, her fingers clutching my bare back.

I slide my hand up her soft side, slipping underneath the ballooning fabric of my shirt. I cup her breast and she exhales a hot breath in my ear.

"You're so amazing. I love you so goddamned much, you're making me crazy."

She exhales again, her warm breath against my neck. "I love you, too."

I pull back, my heart thumping painfully against my chest. "You do?" I didn't mean to sound so vulnerable, but she is the one thing in the world I need. I need her to need me, too. This can't end. Not ever.

She runs one gentle hand down my cheek. "So much it scares me."

I clutch the side of her face. "Say it again."

Her soft blue eyes look directly in mine. "I love you. I do. I don't care if it's crazy."

"It's not crazy," I say, resting my forehead against hers. "It's magic."

We meld together again, our tongues exploring softer now. Every move I make is to tell her how precious she is to me. Every move of her body and caressing touch delivers the same in return.

When I enter her, we're floating somewhere in space, one unit of sensation and pleasure and adoration.

Her rapid, short breaths warm my ear and I cradle the back of her head. "So good," she whispers, her core tightening around me. "You feel so good."

I suck on the sweet nectar of her neck, making her tremble and arch beneath me. "So do you, sweetheart." She feels more than good.

She feels like a drug. Like nirvana. Like the purpose of life.

# Chapter 39

## Emma

I'm melting right into the floor. The only thing keeping me in solid form is the feel of Rayce's firm body heavy on mine, his strong hand cupping my head, and the intensity in his voice.

"I'm so in love with you," he says, almost desperate. "What do I do?"

"Make me yours."

But he already owns me, inside and out. There's no emerging from this without him, not intact.

He brings me more firmly into his embrace and everything else disappears. It is only he and I, in each other's arms, in this moment of shared ecstasy. Forever.

I'm rising and rising, my body a quivering mass of pleasure and he's rising with me. I feel it. I feel him. Then it's a joint release that lifts me to a plane of existence I didn't know was possible.

He really loves me.

We grasp each other in shuddering tenderness.

He is my future.

It goes on and on, then when we finally start to come down from the high, my body turns to uncooperative mush. Both trying to catch our breath, Rayce lifts off me and settles to my side, pulling me next to him, back to front. I'm cocooned in his arms, my head on his bicep, our hearts pounding thickly and slowly settling down. The mirror is in front of us, so I have a complete view of us.

There was a time when I would've been mortified by these extra curves, worried about what that could mean for my career. But now I don't see a problem. I see a healthy body. And it doesn't feel like something that's trying to work against me anymore. I've always been the master of my body, but I wasn't always comfortable with all its bits and pieces. But now my contentedness seeps down into my bones.

I watch Rayce's hand as his fingertips lightly brush up my outer thigh, my hips, and down to the curve of my stomach. He pulls me more snugly against him, and his nose nestles into the hairline behind my ear. Our eyes meet in the mirror. Holding my eyes, he gently kisses below my ear. His hand softly cups my stomach, and I rest my hand on his. We lie there, eyes on one another, our naked bodies still and close. The mirror shows me all of it. I have no desire to look away. I love what I see. Him. Me. Us.

I slowly roll over, staying wrapped in his arms. Our faces are close and I brush my fingertips along his jaw, and look into his eyes. His arms are around my bare back, and his hand in my hair, fingers gently caressing the back of my neck. I am awash with him, buoyant with the love I see on his face and the love I feel in return.

His nearness is even more exhilarating than executing the perfect **grand jeté** in front of two thousand breathless people. It's astonishing.

Then it occurs to me.

He props himself up on his elbows, smiling down at me. "If I hadn't left dance," I say, still astonished, "I never would have met you."

He smiles and hmmms, all warm and rumbly. "Yes, that's true. But sweetheart..." he plants a gentle kiss on my forehead, "you didn't leave dance. You only left the stage."

# Chapter 40

## Rayce

It's time.

It's past time.

I have to tell her, before this goes any further. This is getting so much deeper than I knew was possible. She has to know.

But we go to sleep that night, and I don't tell her.

We go through the entire next day, and I don't tell her then either.

We fly home on Wednesday and put in our obligatory late hours at work and I verbally tuck her in on her phone after her shift before she goes to bed—in her own apartment because she works so early tomorrow morning—and I still don't tell her.

I'm in my office, staring at my phone, dozens of emails vying for my attention as I attempt to clear out my inbox. I know I can't let this go on.

And I'm terrified.

There are other notable times in my life when I've been terrified: when my twelve-year-old brother jumped from the cliff's edge, seemingly heading for disaster on the rocks in the ocean below.

When I had to lift a cool, white sheet off of two bodies in the Swan Pointe morgue, praying, praying, praying I wouldn't discover my parents' faces underneath.

When the realization sank in that I'd have to face the rest of my life without them.

Confessing my past to Emma measures up against all those times in my life. Selfishly, if I could hide this from her forever I would. But she deserves to know, and I can't let her continue down this path with me until she does.

I know I will chicken out again the next time I see her. I have to do this right now.

I pick up the phone and press her number.

My pulse pounds in my throat as I try to think how I'm going to tell her this. Maybe I'll just spit it out, the way she did.

But it goes to voice mail. She must be asleep.

The tone beeps. I open my mouth, wishing I were just there with her.

"Hi. I just… wanted to say goodnight one last time."

When I hang up, I make a promise to myself that this time I know I'll keep. I'm going to tell her.

Tomorrow.

Less than twelve hours later, I know I've made a grave error. If I'd just manned up and told her before, I wouldn't be wondering how in the hell I'm going to untangle the mess I'm in now.

It's a quarter after noon. I'm standing at the counter of Guido's, waiting for my slice of veggie pizza and Coke. The latest copy of <u>The Voice</u> is crinkling in my grasp.

Rita Becker is at it again.

Mr. Rayce Rivers, who co-owns Swan Pointe's internationally-known Rivers Paradise Resort with his two siblings, is the defendant of a lawsuit citing wrongful termination. Plaintiff Taylor Norrell worked for the resort for less than six months before abruptly losing her livelihood in June of last year. The claim is that she and the illustrious Rayce Rivers had been involved in an illicit affair, and when things went sideways, she lost not only the relationship but her job as well.

As previously reported in this column, Mr. Rivers (the elder) is known to have had more than one relationship with resort employees, a serious no-no according to their own handbook. Apparently the rules don't apply to the boss.

While Mr. Rivers has apparently denied these rumors to those who know him, there is little doubt Miss Norrell was one of many of Mr. Rivers' inappropriate conquests on his own property.

Though the charges are for wrongful termination, an anonymous source suggests it could be more than that. Will there be more lawsuits forthcoming? Or charges added to this one? Time will tell. But this columnist anticipates plenty to discuss in the coming weeks and will, as always, keep you informed.

So this is what Taylor Norrell has been hinting at this entire time? Taking a story to that damned Rita Becker so she can smear my reputation all over town? Why they went so far as to invent a sham lawsuit is beyond me. Neither one of them are my concern.

My concern is Emma. I was already dreading her reaction. This makes things far, far worse.

"I don't know why you read that drivel," Guido says, setting a paper plate with my slice of pizza on the counter, followed by my Coke. "The stuff they make up about you isn't going to upset you if you don't know about it to start with."

This is the other part that kills me. For the most part, people assume these sorts of rumors about me are lies. What kind of charlatan does that make me?

But Guido's question reminds me where I am. I've been gripping this paper like I want to strangle it, in a public place where anyone can see my reaction. That won't help matters any.

I force myself to take on a more collected composure. Before I get a chance to make a dismissive comment, blowing it off, someone taps me on the shoulder. I turn toward the person standing behind me, an older gentleman in a worn San Francisco Giants cap and a T-shirt that reads 'Duke's Waikiki'.

"Oh, wow," he says with a wide grin. "You're Rayce Rivers, aren't you? Owner of that resort?"

Impatient to get out of here so I can call Emma, but not wanting to be rude, I nod. "Yes, I am. Are you staying with us?"

Nodding and grinning, he offers his hand to shake mine, but when I reach for it, he slips a large manila envelope I hadn't noticed he was holding into my hand. I grab it instinctively. He drops both his hand and his smile.

"Congratulations. You've just been served."

Then that crafty bastard laughs and heads for the door. The long-dormant adolescent in me wants to bolt after him, knock his fucking Giants hat off his head, and plant my fist into that cheeky smile. Instead I remember who I am— always, always remembering who I am—and tear open the envelope, trying to ignore Guido watching me curiously.

I pull the papers out and curse under my breath.

Turns out the lawsuit wasn't a sham after all.

# Chapter 41

## Rayce

I call Emma, but it goes straight to voicemail. I don't leave a message but I send a text.

We need to talk. Come to my office.

There's no response. I tell myself that her phone is probably just put away because she's on shift, or it's off, or her battery is dead. None of this is helpful. She's at work, and if this has hit the grapevine on property, she'll hear about it.

I get into my car and head up the hill to the resort. A million scenarios run through my head—all of which can be summed up with one general idea: she knows and she's never speaking to me again.

I'm panicked. I can't lose her.

I pull up her number to dial again when I'm interrupted by an incoming call.

It's our lawyer, George Hollister.

"Hi George."

He gets right to the point. "Is there something you should be telling me or is this just Rita Becker flapping her gums again?"

"No. I was just served. Can I come by later this afternoon?"

"I'll have my secretary clear a slot and give you a call." He's always so calm, no matter what's happening.

"Thank you."

"Rayce, this _is_ just wrongful termination, right? Nothing else?"

I sigh. "Let's just talk about it when I get there."

There's silence on the other end as I reach the top of the hill, our parents' magnificent resort up ahead. What the fuck have I done? How much is this going to cost us? Why the fuck didn't I just handle this before?

Even George has been knocked into uncharacteristic silence by my stupidity.

I'm glad I don't have to face him right in this moment. I'm embarrassed enough. It's made worse by the fact that I like George. He and Dad were friends long before we kids were born, and handles not just any legal questions we have on behalf of the resort but is the trustee for Mom and Dad's estate.

I trust him implicitly and like him and he's just the first in what's probably going to be a long line of people I'm letting down.

He's never going to think of me the same way again.

"I see," he says. "Well, we'll handle whatever it is."

I rub my forehead with my fingers. "Thanks, George."

As soon as we get off the phone I try Emma again. Again no answer. Is she busy with work, or purposely avoiding me?

In the time it takes to park and head up to the executive offices, I try two more times. I know I'm losing it. It's taking a lot of fucking willpower not to go looking for her.

I enter the executive offices with the same purposeful steps I always have, and I don't look around at the faces in the center cluster of cubicles or at the ones behind the desks in the offices I pass. I act normal. Because if this hasn't hit the rumor mill, I'm certainly not going to do anything to help it along. And if it has, well then my demeanor matters now more than ever.

I pass Connor's office and see him sitting at his desk out of the corner of my eye.

I don't slow.

I enter my office, close the door behind me, and pull up Emma's number on my phone.

Before I hit dial, my door opens. Without anyone knocking. I stop just short of my chair and turn to see Connor coming in and closing the door behind him. He's got that look on his face. It's the same look he had when he asked me about an affair before and immediately understood my answer for the lie it was.

Fuck. I can't do this right now. I need to talk to Emma.

"Have you seen the paper?" he asks.

I grunt and head around to my chair. I plop into my seat and set my briefcase on my desk. "Yes."

His jaw tightens and his eyes flash with irritation. "And?"

I pull out the papers and hold them up to him.

His eyes dart to the papers, then back to me, then back to the papers. He steps forward and grabs them.

While he's reading, I lean back and stare at my briefcase.

After a minute, he holds the stack up and our eyes meet. He spits out, "Is this the only one or not?"

"The only lawsuit or the only girl?"

He slams the papers on my desk. "Fuck, Rayce. Are there two different answers?"

I rub my forehead with my fingertips, pinching my eyes shut. All right, I need to come all the way clean, but we're not doing it like this. "Sit down, Connor."

It takes a minute of him standing there while my blood thumps through my veins, but he sits. Before I can say anything, there's a knock at my door. Not that I'm answering it. Whoever it is can just go away.

Then we hear, "It's Lizzy."

"Jesus," I mutter. She must've seen Connor come in and knows we're the only two in here, or she wouldn't have called like that. "May as well tell you both at once."

Connor just glares at me and answers Lizzy himself. "Come in."

My sister slips in, a guileless smile on her pretty face, and pushes the door closed behind her. With a lightness in her walk, she heads for the chair next to Connor.

"Hey, I just had to see if you guys—" Her steps slow as she notices our expressions. She stops. "What is it?"

"Have a seat," Connor says, eyes still on me. "Rayce has something to tell us."

She slowly comes over and sinks to the edge of her chair, examining Connor. It's not too often he gets his feathers ruffled like this, so she has to be wondering what's up.

"You didn't happen to see Rita's column today, did you?" I ask.

Her green eyes come to mine. God, this is almost as bad as having to tell Emma.

Almost. But at least with Emma, I sort of had a chance to mentally prepare. I never, ever thought I'd have to tell my sister what I'm going to tell her now.

She notices the papers on my desk and picks them up. I watch her silently reading them, watch as her face starts to relax.

"So that *is* all it is, then." She tosses the papers back onto my desk dismissively. "She's got nothing on us. We have a paper trail on her a mile long." She leans back in her chair. "She was lucky we didn't fire her sooner."

Connor and I exchange glances. Of course, Lizzy is giving me the benefit of the doubt. Does it even occur to her to wonder if the rest of Rita's column is true?

Well, if it didn't, she must see it on my face now. Her expression slowly starts to change. My chest tightens and my stomach drops. Connor was bad enough. This is so much worse.

I look between the two of them and steel myself. "We had an affair."

Lizzy shakes her head just slightly and blinks her eyes several times, as if trying to undo the words I just said.

"And there were two others."

Her mouth drops into a mortified 'O'. She takes me in without blinking. It happens right in front of my eyes: my downfall in the eyes of my little sister.

Connor, meanwhile, is still glaring at me.

I keep going. "That's not including Emma. We've been seeing each other for a few weeks, but she's—"

"Emma?" Lizzy repeats, like she still can't believe what she's hearing. "Emma Swanson. Our employee in banquet?"

"Goddammit, Rayce. You promised you would stop that shit."

"I did. It's not like that with her."

Lizzy throws both hands in the air, palms toward each of us. She turns to Connor, her eyes dark slits. "You knew?"

"I knew about *one*."

Lizzy leaps to her feet and we instinctively follow. "What the hell! Are you kidding me?"

"Keep your voice down," Connor says.

But Lizzy's found a safer target for her anger. "Don't tell me what to do! You knew and what? Figured you'd just go along with it?"

"Don't take this out on him," I say flatly. "It's me you're angry with."

She spins on me, her anger wavering and hurt welling up in its place. "You don't get to tell me what I am right now. God," she turns away, her hands in the air. "I can't even look at you."

"Lizzy, please sit down. I'm sorry. Let me explain this to both of you. It was after Mom and Dad died and—"

"This has *nothing* to do with them," she spits out, "you..." But she stops before she says what I am.

She's marching to the door.

"Lizzy."

She grabs the knob.

"I love her."

She freezes, her back to me and her hand on the handle. Connor's mouth falls open. For the first time since he walked in here, he doesn't look ready to pound me.

"I'm sorry, but I'm in love with her."

Lizzy doesn't turn around or respond. She quietly leaves, closing the door behind her.

I turn and brace my hands on my desk, my head falling between my arms. My entire life is blowing up around me. And I *still* haven't heard back from Emma. Does she even know yet?

"Rayce," I hear Connor say. There's no anger in his voice anymore. If anything, there's a tinge of the distress I'm overwhelmed by. "What's going on?"

I take a resolute breath, drop into the seat next to him, and tell him everything.

# Chapter 42

## Emma

My shift is dragging today. The six hours I've been here feels like six days. Alice wants an inventory of our dishes so I'm going through cupboard after cupboard, tallying dinner plates, dessert plates, saucers, cups, water glasses, red wine glasses, white wine glasses, and on and on. I'm not opposed to menial tasks, but this one is driving me batty. I'm beyond ready to go home.

But, actually, that might be because of the message I got from Rayce last night. Mostly, it was crazy sweet. He wanted to say goodnight one more time, as if we hadn't just spent all that time on the phone saying goodnight, over and over before we finally found it within ourselves to hang up.

God, the way that man melts my heart.

I texted him this morning, no doubt while he was still asleep, and told him how much I loved waking up to the sound of his voice and that I couldn't wait to see him tonight.

I really can't, for all the normal reasons, but something in the tone of his voice has been nagging at me. He sounded… worried, which makes me worry every time I think about it. I'm trying not to, but counting salad plates isn't the most engaging task in the world so it's hard not to dwell on it.

Probably nothing's wrong and I'm fussing over nothing. It was late so he was probably just tired. But I'll feel better after I talk to him anyway.

One of my fellow banquet workers, a leggy brunette who I tend to avoid due to her penchant for gossip and drama, comes into the room and leans her hip against the counter.

"Crazy day, huh?" she asks.

Her tone feels like gossip bait, which is doubly likely since she has no reason to be in here. She's supposed to be taking inventory of the linens. I don't want to encourage her, so I stay focused on bringing the next few stacks of salad plates down from the cupboard. "Yeah, nothing crazier than counting plates."

"So you didn't hear then, did you?"

Yep. Called it.

Before I can stop her from going any further, she says, "Mr. Rivers is getting sued."

I turn toward her, forgetting my plan to not take her bait. "Which one? Not Rayce."

She nods.

What? How would I not know about this? And what on earth would he be getting sued for? She's gotta be full of crap.

"Huh," I say, reaching for the next stack. I'm hoping she'll take the hint that I don't want to talk to her, but she just keeps going.

"The paper said it's for wrongful termination. He was having an affair with an employee and fired her when he was done with her."

I tried to carefully set the plates on the counter, but I must not be as steady as I thought because there's a jarring clatter. Chills crawl down the back of my legs. I tell myself not to pay any attention to her gossip, but *what in the hell?* This can't be right.

I glance at her sideways and her face lights up, pleased to have my attention now. "But that's not the worst of it. Apparently it might be more." She leans in and lowers her voice. "Sexual harassment."

I start shaking my head. No. He wouldn't do that.

"Can you believe that?"

"No," I say flatly. But in spite of myself, my mind is turning on all gears, trying to sort out exactly what she's said. "Wait, did it say he's getting sued for sexual harassment or not?"

"Just for wrongful termination, but she hinted there might be more."

"Who's 'she'?" Then a ripple of relief breaks up the tightness in my chest. "Is this that stupid gossip columnist? Because if it is, it probably isn't even true."

She shrugs. "Some of the stuff in there is true and I know that for fact."

Sure she does.

"So it is the gossip columnist."

She confirms with a nod.

"Then we don't know if it's true and we shouldn't be spreading rumors," I say pointedly.

She straightens and frowns at me, her feathers ruffled. "I'm not spreading rumors. This is in the paper. And I'm not saying he did it. I mean, how do I know? But people can surprise you and there *have* been rumors about him. Though, I have to say, he's never done anything like that to me." She gives me a shrewd look. "Has he ever done anything like that to you?"

Why do I get the feeling she knows something? Then I remember how obvious he was acting when I got cut and wonder if I'm part of the rumors flying around right now.

"No," I answer firmly, so as not to leave any doubt in her mind. Yes, we've been sleeping together, but it wasn't sexual harassment so it's not what she's asking about.

Right?

"Yeah, me either," she says again, unnecessarily. "He's always super professional. Like, aloof. Even when I've tried flirting with him."

"You've <u>flirted</u> with him?"

She waves a hand in dismissal. "Not that seriously. And everyone flirts with him a little. Who can help it?" She nudges me with her elbow and gives me an annoying smile. "I'll bet you have too, even if you won't admit it."

My cheeks start to burn.

"But, you know, a year or two ago, I can't remember how long, there were *a lot* of rumors about him then. Not for sexual harassment, but that he was sleeping with some employees here, including that Taylor girl who worked in banquet. She's the one suing him. I didn't really know her that well, but I have to say, she was always screwing up and then looking to blame somebody else. I wasn't surprised when she was let go."

She gives a self-important *tisk,* then goes on.

"But she wasn't the only one. There was talk about him and a girl who used to work in housekeeping. Oh and another one about someone from the spa. So maybe the wrongful termination part is right because <u>none</u> of those girls work here anymore."

I blink at this astonishing report. I shouldn't be talking to her about any of this, but I can't stop now. "You really think he'd do something like that?"

"You never know about these things, right? Maybe he was taking advantage. Couldn't be hard. I mean, look at him. He's a <u>god.</u> What woman doesn't want to drop her panties just at the sight of him? A man like that can have anyone he wants, and if he ever decided he wanted an employee, well he probably got it."

A familiar dread settles over my shoulders, just like before.

But no. Rayce isn't Chad. He hasn't been sleeping with employees then tossing them out when he was finished. He couldn't.

"And you know what else?"

But I've heard enough. "Look, none of this is my business. I just want to do my job, okay?"

I lean closer to the plates and tick my finger on the edge of each one, working up the pile. As if I have the wherewithal to actually be able to count anything right now.

I ignore the huff she tosses in my direction and straighten when she leaves the room, not seeing the plates or anything else that's in front of me.

I press my palms to my eyes.

The dread that's been draped over my skin starts to settle deeper into my body. Every objection Aaron and Pierce have had about him echo through my head. 'Men who hide their relationships cannot be trusted,' Pierce has said.

But he doesn't know Rayce.

But... do I? There have been rumors about him for years.

What if I've been played again? What if this whole time I thought I was something different, but I really wasn't?

I shake my head firmly and try to get a hold of myself.

"This is ridiculous," I say aloud.

The whole thing is probably just made up. Gossip rag trash passed on by a gossipy bitch.

Leaving my unfinished work behind, I march toward the door. I'm not giving thought to one more word of this until I talk to Rayce myself.

I grab my phone out of my locker before I head down and see I've missed several calls from him, as well as a text. <u>We need to talk. Come to my office.</u> This does not help.

I tell myself it's nothing. All lies. He doesn't make a habit of sleeping with employees. He wouldn't. I just need to calm down. But in spite of all my stern self-talk, dread is churning in my stomach the whole way down to his office.

It doesn't help matters any when, as I'm approaching his open door, Ms. Rivers comes out of her office and stops abruptly when she sees me. We've only crossed paths a few times but I was impressed when she remembered my name the second time; other employees have since remarked on her incredible memory for names.

She blinks at me, then tosses a scowl in the direction of Rayce's office and walks on. Okay, this is starting to feel bad. Very, very bad.

I slowly approach his doorway, not sure what to think or what to do. I'm not sure I want to know what comes next. If it's bad, I really really really really really don't want to know.

Why am I letting a stupid rumor scare me so much?

Because this is way too similar to last time, and Rayce is supposed to be different.

He's behind his desk, looking like he hasn't slept in days. In fact, he looks like hell, and as soon as I see him, the dread I've been feeling is gone.

I'm numb. The expression on his face says everything. Something horrible is definitely going on.

Please God, not him, too.

He spots me and rises to his feet immediately. "Emma," he says, but quietly, so no one in the outer offices can hear.

Because we're a secret.

As he hurries over, I drift out of the way toward the credenza so he can shut the door behind me.

"I've been trying to get a hold of you," he says, still unnaturally quiet. He comes toward me. I take a quick step back, my rear bumping into the wooden edge.

He stops, looking as surprised as I feel about what I just did. But he looks apologetic too, like he knows full well I have a reason to back up and he has a reason to be sorry.

I shake my head.

No. No. No. No. No. This was supposed to be different.

"Tell me it isn't true."

He takes a breath. "Tell me what you've heard."

"Oh my God."

"Emma—"

"It *is* true."

"It was not wrongful termination."

"But you did have sex with another employee? Multiple employees?"

This accusation doesn't even seem to surprise him. What in the fuck?

"Honey, please keep your voice down." He comes toward me again but I'm on the move, going around the back of his desk. He sees I'm backing away so he doesn't follow, but he keeps talking. "People will hear."

Is that what he cares about? That people will hear?

The numbness is gone and now horror is pulsing through my body. I run my hands into my hair and clutch at the roots.

He tentatively reaches toward me. "Emma, listen. Come here. I was going to tell you."

I drop my hands and narrow my eyes at him. "Yeah, once you got sued."

"No, I was going to talk to you last night."

Last night.

This is the thing. This is what it was. Suddenly I realize something. He didn't say he wanted to say goodnight one *more* time. He said one *last* time. Was that because this whole thing is over?

I sway a little on my feet. "Oh my God."

The whole disaster with Chad runs through my mind. I honestly wasn't shocked when that relationship, or whatever it was, went nowhere. But I *was* shocked when I found out he was married and I was shocked when he went after me with such cold venom. I never fell in love with Chad, but I also never would've imagined him capable of being so heartless until it was too late.

And of course nothing shocked and hurt me more than finding out my own father stole and gambled away enough money to put the company he worked for out of business.

Except this. This is beyond shocking. Beyond horrifying. I don't even know what this is.

But if I know anything, it's that sometimes people are not what they seem. And now it's happening all over again, but this time with Rayce.

Rayce.

A dark knot clutches at my heart and I run my hands into my hair again, grabbing the roots. I pinch my eyes shut, already cringing at the answer to a question I haven't even asked yet. "How many of us were there?"

There's the briefest hesitation. "Four."

My eyes fly open, somehow still shocked to hear him say that number even though I already knew it. Because sometimes rumors and papers have it exactly right. *"Four?"*

He glances at the door, no doubt worried about the people outside hearing because I'm not keeping my voice down *at all* and god forbid anything happens to tarnish his precious image. Why isn't it *me* he's worried about? Why isn't he worried about us?

Maybe because there's been no us. There's been a secret, and a player, and a gullible, foolish woman, and that's it.

"Oh my God." It really is happening all over again. I press my fingertips against my temples, pacing away from him again. "Oh my God."

"Emma, let's talk somewhere else. Let's meet at—"

"Oh my God." My pulse is pounding in my ears. I can hardly breathe. I think I'm going into a full-blown panic attack. How could he do this to me?

"Emma—"

Something in me snaps. I spin on him. "Four? You fucked four different employees?"

This time he doesn't shush me. "It hasn't been like that with—"

"Don't you do that." I jab a finger in his direction. "Don't you dare lie to me."

"I'm n—"

"No!" I can't believe this is happening. I never should've opened myself up to him. "No, I'm done believing your bullshit! You stay the fuck away from me!"

I dart past him, throw open his door, and storm through it. The sound of his door slamming against the wall draws the attention of a few people nearby, their heads popping up from their desks to stare in our direction.

I don't care.

I stop on my heels and spin. Mr. Rayce Rivers looks like he has no clue what kind of damage control to do next and I don't fucking care.

"By the way," I spit out. "I quit."

# Chapter 43

## Emma

"I thought he was different," I say, grabbing yet another tissue out of the box. If I keep crying like this I'll need to buy stock in Kleenex.

"Well, he's not," Pierce says.

A fresh stream of hot tears make their way down my cheeks. I blot them with the tissue.

He and Aaron have come over to commiserate with me. Aaron and I are on the couch and Pierce is perched on the folding chair. One day I'll have to thank them for not saying "I told you so," but I'll have to stop crying first. Poor Aaron's shirt is soaked.

I feel so gutted. And shocked. And shocked that I'm shocked. Why the hell should I be surprised that it turned out exactly the way I knew it would from the get go?

This is what I get. With Chad I could chalk it up to my own naiveté, but with Rayce? I walked into this with my eyes wide open. I should've known better, but instead I let him make me feel special when the truth is, I was just like all the other girls.

It kills me that there were other girls. A long fucking line of them and I was just one more.

It kills me that he's been lying to me this whole time.

God, and that crap about wanting to protect the resort's image? Sure. He cared so much about it that he was willing to risk it over and over again for whichever employee he fancied at the time. What bullshit! He just wanted his secret flings and that's it. He never intended to bring us into the light.

He's just another selfish bastard after all.

This thought just makes me cry even harder. I tuck into Aaron's chest again and he holds me against him. When is this going to stop? Why am I hurting so much over such a selfish bastard?

Why am I hurting so much when he's <u>not who I thought</u>?

God, I'm so turned around with wanting him and wanting to pummel him, that I hardly know what to do with myself.

"Emma, you're better off without him," Pierce says firmly. For the past hour, he's been clenching various muscles and grunting as often as he speaks. I wouldn't put it past him to go find Rayce and start throwing his weight around.

I nod into Aaron's chest. "I know."

"Do you?"

I peek over at Pierce, who's watching me closely. He's angry, but I know he's not angry at me. He's just protective of me, like Rayce was.

Or like I thought Rayce was.

And at that thought, the aching hole deep in my chest throws up a fresh batch of tears. I blot at them furiously. "God, I'm a mess."

I feel Aaron laugh and Pierce offers a sad smile. "Yeah, you are."

I blow my nose and sit up, determined to get myself together. "I know it's better that I found out. I just…I don't know he just…" I look from one friend's concerned face to the next. My throat gets tight again. "He made it feel so real."

Aaron rubs my back.

I sink back against the couch again. "And I was so, so happy."

"Emma," Pierce says firmly, holding my eyes. "Some guys are master manipulators."

I get a sinking feeling in my stomach at that phrase, <u>master manipulator.</u>

"Do you hear me?" He's still holding my eyes.

I nod slowly. I hear him. It just sucks.

"You would be best off assuming anything he's ever said to you was a lie."

Everything a lie.

That's exactly what makes this hurt so much. I keep replaying all the amazing moments we had together. To think he was just coldly feeding me whatever lines he thought would get him what he wanted…

It kills me.

I've heard about guys like this, but... even now my heart is in stubborn, foolish denial. I so want to believe I meant something to him, too. How could he do this to me?

"God, I'm *right* back where I started. I don't know who I hate more, Rayce or myself."

Pierce doesn't miss a beat. "I hate Rayce."

Aaron pats my shoulder. "Hey," he says gently. "Don't hate yourself. At least you're out of it now."

Here's yet another *I told you so* opportunity they're allowing to pass by. All they've ever done is look after my best interests. Why didn't I listen better before?

Because you were already caught in his web.

His beautiful, beautiful web.

"Uuuugggggghhhhh," I groan, sliding down in my seat until I'm practically lying down.

"Let yourself cry it out," Aaron says. "But then you just have to pick yourself up and move on."

"I can't cry *too* long. I'm back to job hunting." God, I'm such a loser. Yet again, I'm left with rent to pay and no job and no references. "Maybe I shouldn't have quit, but—"

"No." Aaron's lack of hesitation is reassuring. "You did the right thing."

Finally.

Pierce reaches over and nudges Aaron's knee. "Hey, tell her about that job."

Aaron shakes his head sharply, like he didn't want Pierce to bring it up. "Later."

I sit up and look at Aaron, wiping my cheeks. "Is there a job?"

"I'd rather talk to you about it later, when you're more calm."

Pierce looks annoyed, like he'd really rather tell me.

"Please. If it'll give me any hope at all, I want to hear about it now." I need *something* good to hang on to.

"I really don't think you're in the right frame of mind."

"Why? What is it?"

But Aaron doesn't answer, clearly determined not to change his mind.

"Oh for fuck's sake," Pierce says, looking at me directly. "It's teaching ballet at an arts academy for high school kids. It's good money and the job's in the bag if you want it. It wouldn't start until second semester when their current teacher moves back to Maryland or whatever the fuck, but I think you should suck it up and take it. No one's going to expect you to be a rail when you're teaching a bunch of high school kids."

I blink at him.

My body is calm and still. In fact, this is the most calm I've felt all night. "Okay."

They glance at one another in disbelief. "Okay what?" Pierce asks.

"If they want to hire me, I'll take it."

He straightens and raises his eyebrows. Aaron turns to gape at me. Well, what do they want? They're right, and besides, I'm in no position to be picky.

Not to mention that one itty, bity thing I will never confess, given the circumstances. Ever since I danced for Rayce, all the resistance I've had toward dancing professionally is gone.

Just... gone.

That deep core of my soul woke up that night. That night when I opened my deepest heart for him to see. That night when I really looked at myself for the first time since leaving dance and felt no fear of what such scrutiny might make me do.

It was the same night we both said we loved each other and I thought it was real.

I *do* think I could handle a teaching job— hell, it even sounds appealing—and that never would've happened without that night.

The unfortunate truth is this: if I'm able to go back to dance, I'll have Rayce to thank for it.

"That lying bastard," I say, popping off the couch and storming toward the bathroom.

"Where are you going?" Aaron asks.

"Taking a shower." I manage not to slam the door but now that I'm alone I want to throw or smash everything in sight. Good. I fucking hate the crying stage. I'd rather rage so I can move through whatever the fuck all the grief stages are and get on with my life.

I grip the edge of the sink and stare down my own reflection.

My hair's a mess. It looks like it hasn't seen a brush all day and there's a big clump sticking up in the back. My eyes are bloodshot and I have puffy bags under my eyes.

"You are <u>done</u> crying over that man." I hold my own gaze a minute longer, because I need to mean it.

It's long past time I get my shit together.

# Chapter 44

## Rayce

Since she stormed out of my office yesterday, I've sent Emma enough texts and tried to call her enough times that if I do it any more it's bordering on harassment. I need to come up with some other plan, but I'm too tired to figure out what because I'm running on so little sleep.

I came into work on time, even though I was too tired to be effective. I pretty much stayed in my office anyway. I'm not interested in subjecting myself to the questioning looks and speculative glances of my employees. I'm keeping my head high and saying little about it until we hear back from Taylor's lawyer. At least, that's what George Hollister told me to do.

We both agreed I should try to keep things looking normal for the sake of the staff, but by two I'd had enough and told Lizzy I was leaving early. She's being cordial, if a little cool, but at least she's speaking to me. When I asked if she was ready to talk about things she said, "Not yet," and I didn't push. I'm not ready yet either. All I can think about is Emma anyway.

As I'm driving through my neighborhood, heading home, the gloomy clouds that have been darkening the sky all day still can't seem to make up their minds about things. Little pinpricks of rain are tentatively dotting the windshield of my car.

As I get closer to the house, my pulse starts to race because there's a car pulling into my driveway. A light blue Acura; the car I bought for Emma. And yes. Sure enough. That's her behind the wheel.

"Thank god."

But when I pull in behind her, she spots me in the rearview mirror and appears to curse.

Okay. Maybe she wasn't coming to see me after all. Then like an idiot, I realize exactly what she's doing.

We get out of our respective vehicles at the same time, and I walk toward her. She pushes the button on the key ring and the car lets out a soft honk, indicating it's locked.

"Emma, we need to talk." The rain is coming. Cool drops hit the top of my head and forehead, and start to dot the white concrete of the drive.

"I'm not interested in talking." She drops the keys in my hand. "Here's your car back. Thank you for letting me borrow it."

Then she circles around me, heading for the street. I'm right behind her. "Where are you going?"

"Home."

"If you won't come inside, at least let me give you a ride."

"Not necessary. I'll get an Uber." Yeah, because she needs that kind of expense when she's out of a job again. Which is completely my fault.

"I can take you home," I say, gesturing to my car as we walk right by it.

"Don't bother."

The rain starts coming down harder. I blink against a drop that hits my lashes. Neither one of us slows. "It's not a bother, Emma. I want to talk to you."

"I know you do."

I've had enough.

I stop walking. "Emma," I say in a stern voice.

She stops automatically, and hovers there for a moment. She slowly looks over her shoulder at me. The rain is coming down in sporadic, fat drops, working itself up to something bigger. "That's not going to work."

But she stays where she's at.

Her eyes reflect that familiar mix of longing and restraint I saw so often before we finally got together, but this time there's something else in those eyes, too: a deep well of pain.

She's trying to guard herself, I see that. I can't blame her for being angry or hurt or distrusting. This is all my fault. I should've told her long before now. And she definitely should've heard it from me.

"Emma," I say softer, approaching her gently so she doesn't bolt again. I know her default panic mode is to run.

She watches me warily as I go around until I'm standing in front of her. Her floral scent mixes with the heavy scent of an approaching storm. I thought she was beautiful the first moment I saw her, but that was before I knew the beauty of her heart or the magnificence of her love. I am overwhelmed by this woman's soul.

I want to reach out and caress her soft cheek, embrace her lips with a sweet kiss until the hurt I see in her eyes disappears. Instead, I keep just enough distance to show I understand that she needs it.

"It's my fault this is fucked up. That's not on you. But if we meant anything at all to you, at least listen to my side of the story before you decide what it means about us."

Her expression softens for a moment, and my heart pinches with desperate hope. Then her eyes darken and her mouth hardens into a frown. A veil drops over her, like she's closing herself off to me and has no intention of coming back.

But I refuse to accept that this is over.

"One conversation," I say.

She doesn't answer.

Praying she follows me, I walk around to the passenger door and pull it open. I look back at her, two steps from the street. She's folded her arms, but she's watching me. The rain is clacking on the roof of the car.

Arms still folded, she shrugs and starts coming over. "Fine." Thank *god*. "I'll let you say what you need to say." She comes up right in front of me and gives me a firm look. "But then we're done."

Then she slides into the car and closes the door herself.

# Chapter 45

## Emma

If someone looked up the word "fool" in the dictionary, they'd see my name right next to it. Because all I have to do is look at his face and hear his voice and I want to give in. I've been hurting without him every minute since I stormed out of his office. It doesn't matter that he's just another asshole player. My chest aches with longing for him all the time.

That's why I cannot budge an inch. Because if I do, he will reel me in all over again and I'll become one of those women other people shake their heads about.

I can't keep making the same mistake over and over again. I can't. I have to put my life back together, and for real this time. I have to remember that womanizing men are just what Pierce says they are: master manipulators.

Never mind that my heart *wants* to be manipulated by him. Never mind that I *long* to believe the beautiful lie that is Mr. Rayce Rivers.

I'm shutting all that down. He wants to talk and feed me some bullshit story? Fine. I'll let him. But I won't listen.

I'm throwing up a wall, because that's the only way to protect myself from this man.

And my own foolishness.

# Chapter 46

## Rayce

By the time I get into the driver's seat, she's buckled herself up. Her gaze is locked forward, and she's hugging her crossed arms tightly to her body in that universal, "I don't want to talk to you or listen to a word that comes out of your mouth" gesture.

Now that I finally have her attention, such as it is, I don't know how to approach it. I start the car, turn on the windshield wipers, and back out of the drive, trying to gather my thoughts. This isn't how I thought things would be when I finally told her. It's so much worse.

"Emma, I'm really sorry this is how you found out about those affairs. I really was going to tell you."

"Yeah, since you're getting sued."

"No. She'd sent a few weird emails so I knew something could be up, but I didn't think she was going to sue and didn't know anything about it until I saw the column." I explain how things went down in Guido's but it seems she doesn't believe a word of it. Who can blame her?

"Right. The paper knew about it before you did." She doesn't say this like she's mad, or even invested at all. She says this with as much passion as a person would have reading the ingredients label on a cereal box.

"Maybe Taylor tipped her off. I don't know. I don't really care about Taylor right now."

"Or ever, probably," she says flatly.

I exhale, pressing my fingertips to my temple. I don't think there's a thing she could say to get me mad at her. I deserve whatever she wants to throw at me. But the blood is pumping so hard in my head I feel like I'm going to bust a vein. How am I going to explain this to her?

There's probably no good way to do it, so I just dive in. I tell her who they were, when they were, how long they went on.

The whole time, she just sits there with her arms folded, eyes forward, as if she couldn't care less about any of it. This distance is more disturbing than her anger was. Am I already too late? Have I already lost her?

"So," she says, like nothing I say will matter and she's just entertaining the conversation until she can get out of the car, "did you wisk them away on your little out-of-town getaways, too? Hole up in your house for days so you could have your fun without anyone knowing?"

"Hell, no." A getaway with Taylor Norrell? I damn near cringe at the thought. "Jesus. I don't do getaways, and I certainly wasn't going to do that with any of them. Or have them in my house. We weren't even dating it was just..."

I stop. I do not want to say what it was.

"Cheap, meaningless sex?" Emma offers flatly.

"Yes."

She doesn't answer. The sound of the pounding rain and the thumping of the windshield wipers fills the space between us until it feels like a mile.

"I'm not proud of this, Emma. I don't see anything wrong with casual dating or one-night stands if everyone involved is on board, but that's not what these were and I think you know that. No, I didn't coerce anyone. Yes, it was mutual. But it was dark and toxic because that's exactly what I needed it to be."

Out of the corner of my eye, I see her slowly look at me for the first time since getting in the car. I look over and hold her eyes for a moment, my chest aching with the desperate hope that she might be willing to listen to my side. She pulls her gaze away.

I merge onto Hill Avenue, the street busy and wet.

"I just needed to feel something other than pain and guilt. It was either that or drink myself into oblivion every night, which was really fucking tempting, if I'm putting it all out there. It was out of control and a big, fucking mess, but it was the only distraction powerful enough to push away everything I was trying to avoid."

She looks out the window, a thoughtful expression on her face. <u>Please God, let me finally be reaching her.</u>

"I'm sorry I didn't tell you sooner. I should've. I wish to hell I would've. And I'm not trying to excuse what happened. I only want you to understand it so you can see that's not what's happening with us."

Still looking away, she frowns. She's still, like she's afraid to move or concede anything.

"I was afraid I'd lose you. What I told you before was the truth, Emma. You *are* different. This *is* different than what happened with your old boss, and it's different than what happened with me. There was nothing cheap or meaningless about us. Not for me."

I've been watching her face, and I can't read it. Her arms are still crossed, she still won't look at me, but her jaw seems to have softened.

She swallows thickly, then says quietly. "How do I know you're not just saying what you think I want to hear? How am I supposed to trust any of this?"

I sigh, watching the road and waiting for a good answer to that. Fuck. What can I say? I lean my elbow on the windowsill. Have I broken our trust beyond all repair? What am I supposed to do about that? I can't make her trust me if she doesn't.

Rubbing my forehead with my fingers, I say, "I don't know, Emma. I don't know how I can prove it to you and I can't blame you for doubting me either. I guess all you can do is… trust your own heart."

Her eyes fly to mine.

"Trust my heart?" she repeats quietly, like she's saying it to herself and the very idea of trusting herself is a revelation. But I don't really know what she's thinking because her expression is a carefully constructed mask designed to keep me out.

My phone starts to ring, the tone echoing through the car. I don't register it at first. I'm just looking between the road and her, trying to decipher what I see on her face and wondering how I can get her to let me in again.

Give me another chance. Please.

Then I realize.

My phone's ringing.

I look at the Caller ID on the screen: <u>Connor.</u> I look back at Emma. The wipers swipe across the windshield and the rain pelts the car even harder.

I don't want to take this call. I want Emma to tell me what she's thinking. But my blood pressure rises as it goes from the second ring to the third.

My little brother is calling.

I glance between her and the screen, not knowing what to do.

Her face softens. "Just take it," she says, without malice.

"I'll be just a second."

She nods but goes back to looking out the window, her expression giving me no clues to what she's thinking.

I answer, ready to get Connor off the phone quickly. Only it isn't Connor. It's Whitney. "Rayce?"

Only a few times in my life have I heard this sort of heightened panic in a person's voice. My heart jumps into my throat, my entire body pounding. "Whitney?"

There's all kinds of noise in the background. I can barely hear her. "Whitney?"

Nothing but noise and shit reception. Emma and I exchange glances, the wall between us momentarily gone. She's as worried as I am.

"They're rock climbing today."

Her face morphs into dread.

I call again. "Whitney!"

"Rayce? Can you hear me?"

"Yes. What's wrong?"

"It's Connor," she says and her voice breaks.

No.

I clutch the steering wheel so hard I could rip it off. I've identified the sounds in the background of the call. "Are you in a helicopter?"

She continues in a trembling voice thick with fear. "There was an accident. They had to lift us out. We're on our way to the hospital."

My blood turns to ice and the edges of my vision darken. Emma's hands fly to her mouth.

"You need to come," Whitney says.

Not to say goodbye. Don't you dare tell me I need to come say goodbye.

"What kind of accident?" I manage to say steadily. I'm not even sure how I'm staying on the road. "What happened?"

"We were climbing a ridge and this big boulder came loose above us and..." her voice breaks again. "And it hit him and his line broke and he fell."

My body is surging with adrenaline. No. This can't happen again. Not to Connor. No, please no.

The hospital's in the other direction. I make three rapid lane changes, then spot an opening just big enough to maneuver us through a tight U-turn.

Emma grabs my thigh. "Rayce," she says in a warning tone.

But my senses are laser focused on both the conditions of the road and my call with Whitney. She tells us that he fell approximately twenty-five feet, with the boulder landing partly on top of him, tearing up the left side of his torso. He's losing blood, has a collapsed lung, and whether or not he broke his back is unknown. He's not conscious, and I don't know if that's good or bad, given the amount of pain he'd probably be in if he were awake.

Whitney describes how she repelled down to him with 911 on the phone, and followed their instructions to try to contain the bleeding and stabilize him until they got there. If I'm understanding her correctly, it sounds like he would've bled out right there without her. Thank God she kept her cool.

Through it all, Emma's hand is on my thigh, an anchor of comfort in the midst of yet another tragic family storm.

I just barely make it through a light before it turns red, and take a left down Alameda Boulevard, the fastest route to the hospital.

"Rayce," Emma says, her hand still on my thigh. "Let me drive."

"No, I'm fine. Wait, Whitney, which hospital? Swan Pointe Medical Center?" I hope to God he doesn't need emergency care somewhere else. That would not be a good sign.

"I... What?..." It sounds like she's talking to somebody else, probably one of the medics. "Rayce, do you know Connor's blood type?"

I press the accelerator harder. "A positive. Swan Pointe Medical Center, right?"

"Yes."

Thank God.

"I have to go," Whitney says. "We're here."

We can't lose him.

"Have you called anyone else?" I ask her.

"No. I called you first."

"I'll take care of it. We'll be there soon."

Hang in there, Connor. Fight.

"Okay." She sounds on the verge of tears again.

"Whitney," I say firmly. "Stay strong."

"Okay." Then she's gone and the car echoes with the rain pelting the ceiling and the glass. Emma's hand is still on my thigh, thank God. I need her. I need her now and forever, but especially now.

I hit the button to call Lizzy, wishing I could spare her this. I was the one to call her when Mom and Dad went missing. I was the one to tell her when they found the bodies. I

496

was the one to tell Connor what happened when we finally tracked him down days later.

By the time this evening is over, am I going to have to tell her she's lost a brother, too?

Emma squeezes my thigh. "He'll be okay."

She doesn't know any better than I do, but it's reassuring to hear her say it anyway.

After I've placed calls to both Lizzy and Corrine, who are both closer to the hospital than we are and may just beat us there, there's nothing to do but drive. It seems every car on the road is nothing but an obstacle. I wish everyone would just get the hell out of the way.

We finally pull up to the hospital only to see at a glance that the parking lot's packed. I growl in frustration.

"Go to the front," Emma says. "I'll park for you."

God bless her.

"Thank you." I pull up to the emergency room doors, throw the car into park, grip her hand, and turn to her. I don't want to leave her, but have to get in there. "Come find me."

Please.

She nods. "I will."

# Chapter 47

## Emma

I'm not even thinking at this point, I'm just acting. I know it's not the same as what Rayce has to be feeling, but I'm worried about his brother, too. And Whitney, and Rayce, and all of them.

I end up getting a spot nearby—someone else was pulling out—so I'm not far behind Rayce. I go through the sliding doors to find him on the far side of the ER waiting room approaching a sizeable group of people who are still standing and seem to have recently gathered together themselves.

I know Ms. Elizabeth Rivers from the resort, of course, but I know everyone else in attendance too, because Rayce has shown me pictures and told me all about them. Lizzy's fiancé, Brett, is there, as well as their slender, dark-haired cousin Corrine, and her brick wall of a boyfriend, Mason. He is a giant next to her, but has his hand placed protectively on the small of her back.

The last person in the group is Whitney. Even if I hadn't seen pictures of her, I would've known who she was simply because she's wearing outdoor gear that's clearly spent the day in the great outdoors, and because her face carries more fear and worry than any of them.

No one has spotted me, but they've spotted Rayce. Lizzy's face instantly changes as she rushes toward him and clings to him, burying her face in his neck. My steps slow, unwilling to interrupt this moving, big brother moment. I'm an outsider here in general, and not sure if I should go over there or hang back and wait for him to notice me and take charge from there.

As I'm hesitating, he seems to be saying something comforting in his sister's ear, because she nods against his neck, then pulls back and wipes her eyes determinedly.

That's when she spots me. Her gaze sharpens and he turns.

"Emma."

He comes toward me and I start moving toward him again. "You're just outside the door," I say, gesturing toward the side of the entrance where his car is parked.

"Thank you," he says, but before I can give him his keys and leave him to his family, he grabs my hand and pulls me over to them. This is less the light, affectionate handhold of a date, and more the strength-gathering handhold of someone in crisis.

I respond instinctively, holding him firmly back.

"Whitney, this is Emma," he says, beginning a round of quick introductions that's peppered with curious glances between Rayce and I. But there's hardly any time for their curiosity to turn into awkwardness. He tells me, "Connor's in surgery," and the group is immediately back to the more pressing matter at hand.

Rayce asks Whitney a question that gets her explaining what the medics did for his brother in transit and what else they said about his condition, but before things can go any further, we hear an authoritative female voice call, "Whitney Rivers?"

We all turn to find a nurse in yellow scrubs with tiny stethoscopes all over them coming this way. The group moves forward as one to meet her.

"I'll take you back to surgical waiting," she says.

"Is he out?" Rayce asks.

"No, sir. I don't have any information. I was just told to bring the family back."

When she tells them to follow her, I'm prepared to give Rayce his keys and tell him I'll be praying for his brother, but instead he tugs my hand and brings me with them.

I don't even know if he realizes he's done it. He's talking to the nurse, asking questions, the clear authority and patriarch of this family. He is strong and focused and... gripping my hand like his life depends on it.

I think back on what he told me in the car, turning it over in my mind. If he really was manipulating me with that story about why he was with those other employees, he truly is a master. I find it totally believable that he would fall apart like that at the loss of his parents. His deep devotion to his family has been obvious from the start and is even more clear now.

I can just imagine myself telling Pierce what Rayce said, and Pierce giving me the 'men like that know how to put women under a spell' speech all over again. I can just hear him reminding me not to fall for it and to assume anything Rayce says is a lie. 'Because there's *words*, and there's <u>evidence</u>,' Pierce has said. 'Anyone can spit out words.'

Maybe he's right about the kind of man Rayce is, and the kind of woman I am, because with or without words, all Rayce has to do is be near me and I want to be under his spell.

My damned foolish heart doesn't even care that he's a rascal, it just wants him no matter what. But even in the midst of all this worry over Connor and dismay at my own emotional weakness, at least my brain has the sense to remind my heart that the answer is still *no*.

We find our seats in the surgery waiting area, away from the only other two people here, huddled together on the other side of the room. That's when I realize just how watchful of his family Rayce is. The other men are offering comfort to their women, too, but he seems to be keeping an eye out to make sure there is not even the slightest unmet need.

Brett is too busy speaking words of comfort to his fiancée to notice she needs a tissue, so Rayce quietly hands her the box. Corrine rubs Whitney's back and offers to get her some coffee, so Rayce gives an unspoken signal to Mason, who willingly says, "Stay here, honey. I'll get it. Does anybody else need anything?"

But the person this family's protector is watching the closest is Whitney. Her husband isn't here to comfort her, and she seems quietly numb to everyone else's efforts. She's probably in shock.

But what can anybody do?

It's not until everyone's settled and the true waiting begins that he seems to realize he's been gripping my hand this entire time.

He blinks at it, then looks at me apologetically.

He leans slightly closer and I lean in slightly, too. My pulse kicks up a notch, and I catch a soft whiff of his cologne.

"I didn't even ask if you wanted to stay," he whispers.

"It's okay," I whisper back. "I'll wait with you." I don't care what else is going on. I'm not leaving him at a time like this.

He squeezes my hand tightly and holds my eyes like he has so much to say, but between the sorrow of this situation and the mess between us, he can't.

"I'll wait," I say again.

"Thank you." Then he does something to make me want to crawl right into his lap and beg him to change his womanizing ways just for me: he puts a gentle, almost tentative kiss on the back of my hand.

I catch Lizzy watching him do this. Her eyebrows raise slightly, then she looks at me in surprise. She looks at Rayce with a kind of wonder. Is she not used to seeing that kind of tender affection from her sturdy, older brother? Or is she surprised he should be so ballsy to be this openly affectionate with the employee with whom he was having an illicit affair?

Is he being surprisingly sweet or shockingly cocky?

The RN comes around the corner from the nurse's station and everyone straightens, hopeful, but she heads for the couple on the far side of the room. We all settle back in, resigned to more waiting. But I am watching Rayce, and Rayce is watching Whitney, and Whitney is staring pale-faced at a spot on the floor.

# Chapter 48

## Rayce

We've been waiting an hour, and still no word. The couple who had been in the waiting room with us initially has since gone, and later been replaced by an older gentleman. The same nurse who brought us here comes in again, but this time for the old man.

This not knowing is maddening for my own selfish reasons, but is only made worse watching Whitney get more and more agitated.

The nurse leaves the room.

Whitney drops her elbows on her knees and presses her fingers against her eyes. Noticing this, Corrine rubs her back. But Whitney doesn't need more back rubs. She needs information. We all do.

I stand, Emma's hand still in mine. "Come on." I gesture to Whitney and she rises immediately.

I lead her around the corner to the nurse's desk and draw our nurse over with the crook of my finger. "What can you tell us about Connor's condition?"

"I'm sorry," she says in a practiced, professional voice. "We just have to wait for the doctor to get out of surgery."

"Anything you can go back and find out for us would be appreciated."

"I'm sorry but—"

"She needs *something,*" I say firmly, putting my hand on Whitney shoulder.

The nurse looks between us then nods. "Yes, all right. I'll see what I can do."

As the nurse shuffles off, Whitney turns to me. "Thank you," she says softly, still looking so pale.

"Of course," I say, turning toward the waiting area and wishing I could do more.

"Wait," she says.

I face her. She's looking uncertainly between me and Emma. For a second I think she's going to ask Emma to leave, because she clearly has something she wants to say, but then she goes ahead with it. "There's a part I didn't tell you."

I don't even have the chance to ask what when she says, "The boulder."

"The boulder?"

"It wouldn't have hit him except…" Her eyes well up with tears. "…He… he pushed me out of the way." Her expression crumples and she covers her face with her hands.

"Hey, now." I let go of Emma's hand for the first time and bring Whitney into my arms. She falls against my chest, crying into her hands. I tighten my hold on her, trying to help her settle. This won't do. She has enough to worry about without adding to her own burdens. "It was an accident."

"But if I'd reacted quicker he wouldn't have had to."

"He would rather it be him than you, I promise you that." I let her cry a bit longer, but not too long. She has to stay strong. She can't fall apart.

Not yet.

I pull her back and hold her firmly by the shoulders. I give her a resolute look. Following my lead, she forces her crying back down, blinking up at me.

"Whitney, listen to me. You did everything right."

She's looking at me like she wants to believe me, really <u>needs</u> to believe me, but is afraid I'm wrong.

I'm not wrong. Connor's sweet wife does not need to start spiraling downward into a pit of self-blame.

"This was not your fault. There's not a person here who would fault you for anything. It was an accident. That's all."

"Okay," she says quietly.

"Do you hear me?"

She nods, her eyes holding mine as she grows more resolute.

"You kept your cool today, and soon Connor will be thanking you for it."

Please don't let me be wrong about that.

She gives me a slight smile, and though the worry is still there, I can see a portion of her burden has been lifted. "Thank you."

There's that strength I knew she had.

I've always liked Whitney. She's been good for Connor, and he's been good for her. I just pray to God I'm not now looking at my brother's widow.

I give her shoulders a final squeeze, and let go.

# Chapter 49

## Rayce

An hour later, Connor is finally out of surgery but still in critical condition. The doctor gives us a thorough report, thankfully being patient about answering our many questions. Connor's back and neck aren't broken, which is nothing short of a miracle, but we're not out of the woods yet as it's unclear whether his body will recover from the onslaught of injuries and repairs. There's a long list of places they had to stitch him up, inside and out. The next twelve to twenty-four hours will be critical.

The truth is, we could still lose him.

The surgeon encourages us to go home and get some rest, as it's a waiting game now. When Whitney asks if she can see him, he tries to tell us it's past visiting hours for the

ICU. I convince him otherwise. Whitney and I are allowed to go back first.

I don't know why the hell I didn't insist Emma come with us. Seeing Connor lying there unconscious, in that state, with his tearful wife telling him to fight for them while she kisses him over and over was almost more than I could stand. And still the question of <u>will he make it or won't he</u> continues to go unanswered.

When we head back to the waiting room to give Lizzy and Corrine the next turn, Lizzy, Brett, and Mason are there, but both Emma and Corrine are nowhere to be seen.

A flight of panic catches in my chest. "Where's Emma?"

"She went to the restroom," Lizzy answers, getting to her feet. I exhale, relieved. "How is he?"

"Sleeping. Sprouting tubes. You and Corrine can go in now. Where is she?"

"In the chapel. I'll get her."

The chapel's in the other direction. "No, you go ahead. I'll get her."

Whitney plops down next to Brett, who pats her on the knee, and I go to fetch Corrine.

The hospital's little chapel is a denomination-neutral round room with soft benches around the edges, a few side tables with artificial floral arrangements, and strategically placed boxes of Kleenex. The lighting is soft and muted, and a stained glass mural of a tree and lilies serves as the focal point of the room.

Corrine is sitting across the room, her forehead resting on her hands, which are clutched together in prayer.

I'm halfway to her when she realizes I'm there. She hops up, the fear of bad news in her eyes.

"There's nothing new," I say, and she takes a breath. "Do you want to go see him?"

"Is it getting too late? Will they let me?"

"They should. Come get me if they don't."

"All right."

She comes in for a hug, and I hold her firmly. "Not used to being on the other side of the hospital bed, are you?"

She lets out a little laugh, still hanging on to me. "Damn right. This sucks."

"He's a fighter. He'll be okay."

Please let him be okay.

She nods, "Yeah." She lets me go and leaves the room, the door closing with a soft whoosh.

In the silence that follows, I simply stand here.

Right in the middle of the room.

This is the first I've been completely alone since I got the call.

I drift to the bench where Corrine had just been sitting, my legs a little unsteady, and slowly sink onto it.

The door opens and there's Emma. My throat tightens at the sight of her. I need her. I need her so much.

She slowly comes toward me and something in me starts to unravel.

She draws near and I reach for her waist, pull her to me, press my cheek to her stomach, and hold on.

Her arms wrap around my shoulders and head and I just squeeze and squeeze her. The whole world is rocking and bucking, threatening to turn everything upside down again.

This entire evening, all I could think about was, 'What will this do to Whitney? What will this do to Lizzy?'

But not until this moment have I allowed myself to ask, 'What will this do to me?'

"I can't lose him. I can't do this again."

Her hold on me tightens. "You don't know that you're going to lose him. He's in good hands."

"What if he doesn't make it? We're barely put back together from the first time." I look up at her. "We can't lose him too, Emma. We can't."

She slides onto my lap, holding my cheeks, and making me look at her. Her presence surrounds me, grounding me. "Don't get ahead of yourself. Take this one step at a time. You don't know what's going to happen. You just have to wait and see how he does."

She's right. We just have to wait.

But what if he doesn't come through? What if my baby brother is dying?

Sensing my despair, she holds my eyes and strokes my hair, somehow managing to soothe me even in a time like this. "You don't have to deal with all the tomorrows right now. You don't even know what they're going to be. You just have to deal with this minute. And then the next. And then the next. Right?"

"Yes," I say quietly. Because I know she's right. I also know I can't live without this woman in my life.

"You're strong. Whatever comes, you'll be able to handle it, and you'll be able to help your family. Just remember, they'll be there for you, too."

*They'll* be here for me. Not *she'll* be here for me. They.

I cup my hand on her cheek and she softens slightly, though it seems she doesn't want to. Am I losing her? What can I do to make this up to her? What can I do to help her know how special and precious she is to me?

"Emma…"

She shakes her head and says sadly, "Don't."

"Will *you* be here for me?"

"We're not talking about this tonight."

Why not? Is it because she doesn't want to break my heart while my brother is somewhere in this hospital fighting for his life? Does she plan on doing it later?

Maybe she's right. Because if that's what she's going to do, I don't want to know.

I slowly soften my hold on her, and she does the same. I release her and she lifts off my lap. I ache over the empty space she's left behind, but I get to my feet and we exit the room in silence.

She doesn't offer me her hand. And I don't reach for it.

# Chapter 50

## Emma

My heart is just bleeding.

Will I always be a fool where Rayce is concerned?

But I wanted to comfort him like I saw him comforting everyone else. And yes, I wanted to believe him and forgive him and pretend like none of it had ever happened. But I feared I was just getting caught in that intoxicating web again, and knew I had to get out of the power of his presence.

So that's what I did.

I was right about Aaron and Pierce. They still think he's full of crap, but hate him even more now for stooping so low as to use his parents' deaths to get himself out of trouble. They think he's extra motivated to control the situation because the lawsuit means he has so much at stake.

I just wonder what is wrong with me that I struggle so much to see what they seem to think is obvious.

When I first found out about all those other employees, everything we'd experienced together was a confused, muddled mess in my mind. Every memory was colored with the black realization that it apparently wasn't what I thought... he didn't love me but was only manipulating me.

The loss of those good memories was almost as sharp and painful as the loss of Rayce himself.

But ever since I heard Rayce's side of the story, I can't put that dark veil over those memories even if I try. I relive them as I did the first time. Like they were magic.

I say nothing of this to Pierce and Aaron—I'm already embarrassed by what they must think of me for screwing myself over like this twice, right in a row—but maybe they sense it.

They keep telling me to stay strong and repeating the same words. <u>Womanizer.</u> <u>Manipulator. Liar.</u>

But were his actions at the hospital the actions of a manipulator? Do Pierce and Aaron really have the full picture of him, given that I had been telling them almost nothing about our relationship and therefore know so little about all the things that made him wonderful?

But maybe I really am being manipulated to feel like this. Because even the paper is confirming the one truth Rayce himself didn't deny: there have been a string of employees he crossed the line with. I can see why Aaron and Pierce think I'm just another. And are they wrong?

Something Rayce said keeps coming back to me: <u>trust your own heart.</u>

But how can I trust my heart when in the past it's been so terribly wrong?

# Chapter 51

## Rayce

The next several days right every wrong but one.

Lizzy and I finally talked, that night in the hospital after Emma went home in an Uber. As worn out as we both were, neither one of us were in a hurry to leave Connor, and she was ready for answers. So I gave them to her.

It was a different conversation than the one with Emma. Lizzy listened, sympathized, and forgave. I guess that's what blood does for you. But still, I couldn't leave the conversation with her thinking I somehow wasn't at fault for my own actions.

"I remember what you were like back then," she said. "It wasn't you."

"It was. I have to own it. But it wasn't the best version of me."

She sighed and put her head on my shoulder. "I know. But it doesn't change things. You're still our rock. You always have been."

I kissed the top of her head, wondering how I got so lucky to have a sister like her. "I'm sorry I let you down."

"Well. No one can be perfect, I guess. Even you."

"That's for damned sure."

She sat up then, and gave me a probing look. "And what about this Emma? What happens with her?"

"I don't know," I said, feeling as hopeless and fearful about her as I was about Connor at the time. "I may have fucked it up for good."

She looked thoughtful, but didn't reply, and hasn't brought it up since.

Connor has come out of it, thank God, and been moved out of the ICU. He's doing well enough that we've all been teasing him that he's never allowed to do anything risky again (at least, I think Whitney and Lizzy are teasing) and he teases back that he'll limit himself to skydiving and bungee jumping.

That kid is never going to change, that's for sure. But the first time we had a moment alone, I told him if he ever scares me like that again, I'll knock him into the next world myself.

He just smiled and said, "I love you, too, brother."

Then there's the little matter of a lawsuit.

Thanks to the thorough paper trail of Taylor's poor work performance, our lawyer convinced hers to get her to drop all charges. That hasn't stopped Rita Becker from squeezing everything she can out of the story anyway. A former friend of Taylor Norrell's gave an exclusive interview for her column, which was three times as long as it usually is so she had plenty of space for every titillating detail.

In the interview, the woman spends quite a bit of time describing Taylor's unstable behavior (she once posted a Facebook Live drunken rant about hens and chicks that she deleted once she sobered up, but apparently there's a link floating around on the internet somewhere). Rita delighted in speculating what character defects I might have, to be interested in such a person.

But the silver lining was this. Taylor's friend frequently got the blow by blow, as it were, of most of Taylor's sexual exploits, including those with me. "They may have been doing it, but she certainly had no objections."

So the threat of this turning into a sexual harassment suit seems to be off the table, at least according to our lawyer who had a raw, off-the-record conversation with her lawyer. Apparently everyone involved thinks Taylor's a little crazy.

Another former employee has come forward to confirm that she'd slept with me, too, right on property. In fact, only ever on property. She also makes it clear the interaction was mutual, which is why she decided to contact Rita about it.

But I don't come off looking good: "A relationship? No. It wasn't a relationship. All he cared about was sex. The only reason I didn't cut things off sooner is because he was so good at it. But I learned something from the experience. It was exciting at first, but I need more from a guy than a good time. Even a guy like him. I don't think he cared that I ended it. He just moved on to someone else."

While I'm grateful my name is being cleared as a sexual predator, damage has still been done. Worst of all, I fear all these articles are doing is reinforcing in Emma's mind that she was just one more woman in a long line of women, and kept hidden away for all the wrong reasons.

I should've just brought her into the light right away. Why the fuck did I care about my reputation more than her? Any awkwardness or questions we would've faced from the outside world would've been better than what's happening now.

Because her name made it into the column, too.

Just as "unconfirmed" speculation, but still. I guess one doesn't storm out of the boss's office and quit like that without people putting two and two together.

That damned Rita Becker has to be orgasming over this entire shit storm.

Any time I've tried calling Emma, she doesn't answer or return my calls. I texted her to let her know Connor would be okay, and she texted back: *I'm glad to hear it.*

But she wouldn't respond to my texts after that.

What am I supposed to do if she won't even talk to me? Even if she did, what more can I say that hasn't already been said? Either she believes me or she doesn't. And it's clear she doesn't. Or if she does, it's not enough.

And now I'm supposed to just go on with my life as if Emma hadn't ever been in it?

Corrine and I are at the hospital, visiting Connor. He's sitting up now, and the tube's been removed from his lungs. He definitely looks like he's been tossed around and beaten up a bit, but he's steadily improving and his spirits are good. The doctors expect a full recovery. He'll even be out in plenty of time for Lizzy's wedding, though he has

527

several months of follow-ups and physical therapy to look forward to.

We're playing three-man gin and Corrine just laid down a winning hand, not surprisingly.

"Have pity on me." Connor says. "I let you win when *you* were in the hospital."

"You did not! I always won fair and square."

Connor and I exchange amused looks. Corrine is not exactly a gracious loser, though she's been better since Mason came along to put her in her place.

Lizzy comes into the room and plops her purse on the counter by the little sink. "Hey," Connor says, surprised. "I thought your shift wasn't until tonight."

We've coordinated visits so he has plenty of company, but he wasn't supposed to know. Guess he figured it out.

"They're not shifts," Lizzy says, bending down and kissing him on the cheek. "Can't I come see my brother whenever I want?"

"Are you staying?" Corrine asks as she and I both stand to take turns giving Lizzy hugs.

"For a bit," she answers, hugging both of us and then pulling up a seat. "I'll still come back tonight. I found a cool article I'll bring for you," she says to Connor.

"Nice."

"Actually," she turns to me, crossing her long legs and giving me an expression I can't read. "I was just over at the Fairstreet Apartments checking on the new landscaping."

When we had the Big Talk hashing out this whole employee affair thing, I told her that the reason I wanted her to buy and remodel those apartments was so Emma would have a decent place to live. The former owners were drowning in maintenance expenses and looking for a way out anyway.

It cost a little more to push the deal through more quickly, not to mention rushing renovations on the third floor. Lizzy knows enough about business to know it wasn't the smartest way to acquire a real estate investment, though she'll make it back in the long run and turned down my offer to front the investment capital for it. At the time, I'd only told her I needed it as a favor and she did it, almost no questions asked.

That's the kind of trust she had in me.

But now, she's giving me a shrewd look. I have no idea why. All I can think about is Emma over there and torn to bits that I can't have her. "Yeah? How's it look?"

"Just fine," she says without interest. "Afterward, I stopped at a café just up the street for some coffee and guess who I saw working there?"

My blood starts to pound in my throat. I know without her even saying. "Emma?"

She nods.

"Did you talk to her?"

"Just for a minute. She asked about Connor. She wouldn't talk about you."

No, of course not. Because she's obviously over me. I sink lower in my chair. "Well, at least she has a job."

I wonder what they're paying her. I wonder if she has health insurance. I wonder if she has enough money for a car yet. I still haven't figured out how to get her into a car without her knowing I'm the one behind it.

It kills me that I can't do one damned thing to take care of her.

Or talk to her. Or hold her. Or smell her sweet scent.

I notice Connor staring at me with this dumbfounded expression.

"What?" I almost growl.

"I have never seen you like this."

"Like what?"

"Like a love-sick puppy. Look at you. You're a mess."

We've already talked about Emma. This should not be news to him.

"You should've seen the way he looks at her," Corrine tells him.

"And the way she looks at him," Lizzy adds.

"And how he kissed the back of her hand." Corrine puts her hand on her chest and makes that swoony sigh girls make.

Connor sits up, wincing a little. "You kissed the back of her hand? In front of people or were you guys spying on him?" He directs this last part to Lizzy and Corrine.

"No!" Corrine protests. "He did it in the waiting room with all of us right there."

Connor raises his brows.

"I've never seen him like that either," Lizzy says to Connor. "He has it bad."

"All right, that's enough," I say. "Is this supposed to be helping or are you just getting your revenge?"

Connor gives a half grin. "Hey, we're entitled to a little light-hearted revenge. Like, for a <u>while</u>, man. But, are you sure it's over?"

"Positive."

"Why don't you go over there and talk to her?" Lizzy suggests.

"No."

I'm not going to just show up at her work.

"She's there until six."

"Oh my god. No. She's made it clear she doesn't want to talk to me. I'm not going to turn into the crazy ex who stalks her."

"Well, you don't have to be a creepy ass about it," Connor says. "But if the problem is that she's doubting your sincerity, maybe there's still a chance to help her believe you."

"What am I going to do? Go over there and beg her to take me back? I don't think so. If I'm going to do anything… I don't know. I would need a better plan."

"You don't have to plan *everything*, you know," Corrine says. "Why don't you just go over there and figure it out? What's the worst that could happen?"

"She could stomp all over my heart again, only this time, in front of the whole world to see."

But this protest sounds hollow. That's *not* the worst thing that could happen. The worst thing is I end up right back where I am now: without her.

They're all looking at me, but all I can think about is Emma. Am I really going to just let this go? Or is the woman of my dreams worth fighting for, no matter what?

"Is <u>that</u> really the thing you care about?" Connor asks seriously.

"No." I get to my feet and head to the door. "That's not what I care about at all."

# Chapter 52

## Emma

"Don't forget to use the new tip log," my new boss tells me, for the hundredth time. He's a big, round man in a white, stained t-shirt, manning the grill and making a hobby of barking orders at us waitresses. He can whip up burgers and fries like nobody's business, I'll give him that. But he knows jack shit about managing people. Thank god this is only temporary money until the teaching job starts in January.

"Yes, I remember," I say, as respectfully as I can. I try to keep my you're-an-asshole thoughts to myself.

"Well, make sure Noelle remembers, too. I don't need to spend an hour after closing fixing everyone else's fuckups."

See? Classy.

We can't ever do anything right by this guy.

"And stay in your zone."

"Okay, Mac," I say, grabbing a plate of greasy chicken fried steak and heading for table three. Mac is also an unreasonable asshole about "zones." This guy loves his zones. No matter if my zone is so full I can barely keep up and the next waitress is filling salt shakers for lack of something to do. No, no. He has a plan and we're not allowed to go outside of our stupid zones.

As usual, my zone has twice the customers hers does. It's not so many that I can't keep up, but Noelle is a good girl and sneaks over to help when Mac isn't looking. But he's in a mood tonight and keeps barking at her to stay in her place.

Three and a half more months. I can suck it up and do this for three and a half more months.

It makes me feel no better. But I have rent to pay, so there it is.

And underneath all this aggravation? A lingering sadness with Rayce's name all over it.

Seeing his sister earlier did not help. I have to admit, she was so nice it took a lot of effort not to let her tear down my walls.

Stay strong, Pierce keeps telling me. That advice no doubt extends to Rayce's sister, too. I found out enough to know their brother is going to be okay, thank God, but I shut things down fast after that. She didn't stick around, which was probably for the best.

Right?

I'm pretending the whole thing didn't make my heart ache so much for her brother (the elder) that it hasn't let up one ounce since she left over an hour ago.

The diner is long and narrow, with a door at each end. The bell over the east door rings and I look over to see who it is. I smile at Pierce as he comes in. I walk over as he sidles up to the counter.

"What are you doing on this side of town?"

"I had that installation. She's just up the hill."

"Oh, right. How'd she like it?"

"She loved it. She's thinking about another commission for their office."

"Nice. You just come in to say 'hi' or are you looking for food?"

"I need to grab some dinner but I'll get it to go. I have to get back to the easel. That show's in two weeks."

"You got it." I slide a menu in front of him.

"We miss your cooking," he says, giving the menu a cursory glance.

"Yeah, I'll bet you do."

Neither one of them knows how to do more than brown some ground beef and spice it up with a boxed dinner.

"What do you recommend?"

I lean in and lower my voice. "Here? Stick with the burgers. Everything else just reeks of grease."

"Throw some bacon on it and we'll call it done. How are the fries?"

"Go for the waffle fries."

"Done."

"All right, I'll be right back."

It's nice to have a friendly face in here. As eager as I was to get into a place of my own, I miss seeing those two every day.

I put in his order and dart around from one table to the next, clearing off plates, topping off drinks, and laying down checks.

As I'm taking orders at table nine, Mac calls out "Order up" and places Pierce's Styrofoam to-go box on the stainless steel shelf of the pass through window. At the same time, I hear the little bell that indicates someone's come in the west door. I hope whoever it is goes to Noelle's zone. Poor girl is bored to death. She only has three tables over there.

When I finish up taking table nine's orders, I check to see where the new person decided to land and my heart jumps into my throat.

There's Rayce, settling into table seven— my zone, naturally—and watching me expectantly.

He both does, and does not, look good. He's as handsome as ever, in a casual, navy button-down rolled up to reveal his forearms and sexy, black jeans. This man is a god no matter what he's wearing. He has a bit of scruff, like he decided not to shave for the weekend, but still kept it trim, and those deep blue eyes of his gets my heart beating thick, like they always have.

But he has bags under his eyes, like he hasn't been sleeping well, and he doesn't have the same suave composure he usually has.

Rather, he's looking at me with an imploring expression that says, <u>For the love of god, just come talk to me.</u>

I want to, but instead I head over and grab Pierce's order off the shelf, the aroma of beef and bacon thick in the air. When I drop it in front of him, he's glancing over his shoulder at Rayce, his eyes like steel. "Is that who I think it is?"

"Yes."

"He just won't let it go."

Shouldn't that mean something good, I think, but don't say it.

"Want me to beat the shit out of him?"

"Of course not."

He grunts. "Are you going to tell him to scram?"

"I can't do that. Mac would kill me." Not that it even occurred to me to tell him to scram.

"Want me to tell him to scram?"

"No. I can handle it."

I'm fussing with my order book and pen, pointlessly rearranging them in my pocket because I don't want to see the look he's giving me. Pierce is all about actions versus words, and my actions have shown I'm not too good at handling Mr. Rayce Rivers.

"Promise me you won't let him draw you in."

"I said I can handle it."

"Stay professional. Don't get into a conversation. That's how they try to get you."

By 'they' he means 'every womanizing asshole on the planet, especially him.'

I nod. "I know."

"Stay strong."

My new mantra. "I know."

"And remember, whatever he says, it's just words. All words. And words are easy." He leans in, takes my hand between both of his, and both his expression and his tone of voice changes. "You're the only woman for me." Wow. That sounded kind of sincere! "I will love you until the day I die."

I yank my hand back. "Knock it off. You're freaking me out."

He points at me and says in a stern voice. "You remember that. Now go tell that asshole to go home."

I nod, trying not to look in Rayce's direction. It's so unfair that my foolish heart still reaches for him.

"Don't let him suck you in. If he tries to draw you into a conversation, just tell him to go home. If he keeps trying, just say it again. <u>Go home.</u> That's all you have to say, all right? <u>Go home.</u>"

"Okay."

# Chapter 53

## Emma

I leave the counter and approach Rayce, my apprehension growing with each step. His presence is a tangible thing, and the closer I get, the more I'm enveloped inside of it.

Rayce watches me approach, his blue eyes seeming to drink me in.

I stop just at the far edge of his table, and he says in that intimate voice I know so well, "Hi, Emma."

I raise my pad and pen, as if I'm going to take his order. But I don't ask him what he wants. "Did your sister tell you I was here?" I ask quietly.

The tables near us are unoccupied, so there's little chance of being overheard. By all appearances we're doing nothing out of the ordinary, but we're both keeping the volume down anyway.

He nods. "I'd like to talk to you."

"Yes, I know." <u>And I'm working hard to keep up some sort of shield to protect me against your magic powers</u>. I glance back over my shoulder. Pierce is sitting at the counter, his boxed up order untouched, covertly watching the whole thing. He gives me a firm look that means, <u>stay strong.</u>

I turn back to Rayce. He's not looking at Pierce, or seeming to be frustrated or angry the way Pierce is. He's giving me that same intimate look he's given me any time we've talked alone, like there's nothing else in the world that matters except for that. He says, without any hint of resentment, "Are they telling you to stay away from me?"

I sigh. Could you please stop seeming so amazing? "I'm the one staying away."

"Are you?" he asks gently. "Or are you running again?"

I bristle, my shield falling away. In fact all of it falls away: Pierce, my boss, the restaurant. I take a step closer, gripping my pen as it hovers over the order pad. My breath is tightening in my chest. "Hey!" my voice is still low, but charged now. "I'm not running. And even if I am, can you blame me?"

"No."

"What would you do if you were in my shoes?"

"I'd be suspicious. But I'd think I'd listen, and I'd take into consideration everything I know about you and give you some credit for it. At least, that's what I did before."

I startle. My hand with the pen drops as I clutch the pad to my chest. I take another step closer and lean in slightly. He's close to me. So close. I'm torn between wanting to throttle him and wanting to kiss the fuck out of him. It's tearing me in two.

"At least I told you my dirty, little secret," I say quietly, being as careful as I can to not draw any attention to us. "You didn't tell me anything. I found out from this gossipy little bitch I can't stand—" My voice breaks as pain cracks through my anger. His eyes soften with sympathy. I lower my voice to a trembling whisper. "And the *whole town* found out with me. So I don't think it's the same."

"No," he says softly, "it's not the same. And I'm so fucking sorry. I *didn't* tell you like I should have and you have every right to be put out about it."

I don't even know what to say to that. I'm worn out. I'm so worn out from this whole thing. The bell dings and Mac calls out the table number… in my section. "What do you want from me, Rayce?"

Keeping his eyes on me, he scoots to the end of his seat. "I want you to give me a chance to prove you can trust me."

"I…" My heart pinches at the expression on his face. He seems so goddamned sincere. Pierce's voice comes to me. *Words. Just words.* But I don't *want* them to be just words. I don't know that they *are* just words.

Trust your own heart, Emma.

But I don't know if I should or even if I can.

"Emma, I've done nothing but chase after you for days. Does that tell you nothing?"

My heart thump, thump, thumps against my chest. Doesn't it? Doesn't it tell me something? Or am I just too stupid to know when I'm being played?

The bell dings again and Mac barks, "Order up!" God. I truly hate this stupid job and my stupid boss and the stupid stench of week-old grease. And I hate the fact that my brain and my heart can't seem to agree on what the hell I'm supposed to do.

After standing here so long, I really shouldn't leave the table without an order, because all Mac's going to do is grill me about it, but I need to get that stupid order from the pass-through window before he gets on me about that instead.

More than anything, I need to take a breath and get my thoughts together about the seemingly heartfelt man in front of me before I lose my ever-loving mind.

I turn away in frustration, but apparently Rayce thinks I'm leaving for good because he speaks my name in a sort of panic. He reaches for me, wraps his arms around my waist, and clings to me like I'm the only thing in the world he needs. Just like he did in the privacy of the chapel.

But this time, we're not alone.

Stunned, I can only stare at him.

His eyes search mine in desperation. "Emma," he says again, drawing my name out in a low, painful breath of longing. "Look at what you *do* to me."

I gape at him, my mind spinning. What's happening? What does this mean?

Somewhere to my left is the artificial shutter sound of someone's smartphone taking a picture. I glance around at the other customers in the diner, still stunned by Rayce Rivers making such a display. In public.

People are definitely watching, or noticeably trying not to. A red-headed woman in the corner wearing a deep green scarf is staring at us unabashedly.

I look back at Rayce. He's still hanging on to me, unashamed and seemingly unaware of any of them.

"Rayce," I whisper. "People are looking."

"I don't care," he says firmly, holding me with those strong, blue eyes.

I blink at him. Far, far behind me, Mac's voice cuts through the fog, "Order up, Emma!" But I don't move. I can't look away from Rayce's face.

This is not just words.

He shakes his head and says it again. "I don't care what they think. I only care what *you* think. Please, Emma, please. I beg you. Don't leave. Don't do this to us."

"For God's sake." I startle at the sound of Pierce's voice right next to me. He's come up and I stumble a bit as he pulls me out of Rayce's grasp. "Are you trying to cost her another job?" He throws a massive arm protectively around my shoulders. "She said no. Leave her alone."

Then he turns me and leads me away.

I follow numbly, almost unaware that I'm walking. I don't have the spare brainpower to be aware of it. I'm too stunned by a series of revelations, one right after another, like a string of firecrackers. Pop, pop, pop.

One. Actually, I *haven't* said 'no'. I haven't said 'no' once since I heard Rayce's side of things. This is because, as usual, my heart won't let that word cross my lips when it knows the real thing I want to say to him is *yes*.

Two. This isn't just words. He has shown me, with tangible actions, that he means exactly what he says. He *has* done nothing but chase me for days. He kept me hard and fast by his side in the middle of a family crisis and he <u>wouldn't</u> leverage his family just so he could manipulate someone. He cares far, far too much about them.

And there are two other things I know about Rayce: he does care about his reputation and he does not beg. But he just begged right in front of everyone who cared to look because I <u>have</u> done something to him.

I <u>am</u> different.

If I'd really wanted to let myself see it, I would've seen it long before now. The only reason I haven't been able to trust the thing that is so fucking obvious is because of revelation number three.

It isn't Rayce I can't trust. It's me.

It's always, always been me.

I've been wondering how to trust my heart, and now I know.

I choose it. That's all.

If it turns out to be a mistake, I'll own it, but right now I think the biggest mistake I've made is trying to ignore what my very core knows to be true.

As Pierce marches us away, I look at his angry profile, and my heart softens at the love and concern he has for me.

I know he only wants what's best for me. I know he's only trying to protect me because he thinks I've done such a poor job of protecting myself. I know he has all of his reasons for thinking Rayce is nothing but a piece of scum trying to get whatever dastardly thing he wants from me.

But that's the thing. Of the two of us, he's not the one who knows Rayce best.

I am.

"No." I stop suddenly and come out of his arms. Turns out I can say that word after all.

He looks back at me, stunned. Then his expression changes from stunned, to wary. My intentions must be all over my face. "Don't, Emma."

I shake my head and take a step back. "You don't get to decide this."

"Don't. Think about what you're doing. You're going to regret it."

But I take another step back. "No. The only thing I'm going to regret is not trusting my own heart."

I spin around, the internal war inside of me won at last, but Rayce's booth is empty.

He's walking away, almost to the door, his normally erect posture slightly rounded.

"Rayce!"

He turns and I start toward him. He faces me fully, takes a step toward me, his expression pained and desperately hopeful. "Emma?"

Walking isn't enough. I need him right now. I pick up the pace, then run the last several steps as he hurries toward me and scoops me into his arms.

He clutches me to him and I tuck my forehead into his neck, hanging on as my entire body goes limp with the relief of being held by him again. The security of his strong arms, the reassurance of his solid chest, the intoxicating comfort of his scent, the safety of his heart.

This. This is what's true. I trust him, and I trust myself enough to know that I can.

"Emma," he chokes out, sounding in pain.

I'm hanging on, too, still tucked under his chin. "I don't care what people think, either."

He pulls back enough to cup my face in his hands, but keeps me close. There's nothing but me and him. "I'm so sorry."

"I'm sorry, too."

"You haven't done anything wrong."

"I don't know that I've done anything right."

Still holding my eyes and my face, he caresses my cheeks with his thumbs. "Are we okay now?"

"We're okay."

"I'm so sorry, sweetheart."

"Don't." My voice thickens with the lump forming at the base of my throat. I don't want him to hurt. I only want him to feel loved. By me. "That's not what I need."

"What do you need? Do you need to hear how much I love you? Or how much I cherish and adore you? Should I tell you how I will never be the same again, all because you came into my life? I will tell you every, single day, my love. I will show you every minute. I will give you so much love you will never have cause again to doubt how precious you are to me." He rests his forehead on mine, his voice deepening tenderly. "Tell me what you need, Emma. My love. My life. I will give you anything."

My throat tightens, and I wish we really were alone so I could wrap myself around him and hold on so tight. All I can do is whisper through my tears. "Just take me home."

"Emma, come pick up these goddamned orders!"

We both startle at Mac's abrupt interruption. Rayce scowls over my shoulder at my ridiculous excuse for a boss. Noelle hustles to the counter, grabs the order and delivers it herself. She's giving me the eye-roll we reserve for Mac.

Rayce looks back at me. "Emma, do you even want this job?"

"No. I have another one!" I'm suddenly excited to tell him. I want to tell him all the things he's missed, and hear everything I've missed from him. I want to fill in the gaps with all the forgiveness and love and trust that should've been there all along. "I'll be teaching ballet at the New Arts Academy this fall!"

His eyes light up. "Really?"

"I've been dying to tell you."

He cups my face and kisses me over and over again. "That's wonderful. I'm so proud of you."

"This job here is just to help me pay rent through summer."

He pinches his eyes shut briefly, then gives me that man-in-charge look. "Or you can tell that asshole to shove it and let me take care of you between now and then. For the love of all that's holy."

I chuckle a bit and soften in his arms, a sense of safety and security sinking deep into my bones. It's not the kind of safety I felt when Aaron and Pierce rescued me from L.A. It's not even the safety I feel from bringing home my own paycheck. It goes far deeper than that, and has nothing to do with money.

It has everything to do with knowing someone has your back, no matter what, and knowing you have theirs as well.

Rayce continues, "I know you can take care of yourself, Emma. But I don't want this dive job for you and I don't think you do either. Will you trust me to get you from here to there?"

"Yes, I trust you," I say, cupping his face, his five o'clock stubble tickling my palms. "I trust everything."

# Chapter 54

## Rayce

### *Six months later*

The grand ballroom has been transformed with draped gold fabric dotted with twinkle lights, and a crowd draped in excitable murmurs. On one end of the ballroom is an artificial stage that has a Renaissance city backdrop that Emma convinced the local theater company to lend for the cause, a professional twenty-piece orchestra off to one side, and an elegant-looking platform and podium on the other. Facing it all are rows and rows of chairs, filled with people waiting for the evening's most anticipated event.

The inaugural Grand Gala Annual Fundraiser for the Grant and Sharon Rivers

Foundation, spearheaded by Whitney Rivers, has already been a smashing success. Aside from the grandeur of the evening—most of Swan Pointe's finest are here in their tuxes and gowns—the primary aim of the event has already been met. All the monies raised haven't been completely tallied just yet, but ticket prices and the silent auction alone put us well over goal.

Thanks to Whitney's hard work, there will soon be a new addition to the local women's shelter, enabling them to more than double their current capacity. Our parents would have been proud.

I'm in the front row, along with my siblings and their spouses, and Corrine and Mason. Pierce has a place of honor, too. It took a while for him to trust me, but once we made it past that particular hurdle, we were both surprised to discover how well we get along.

The seat next to Connor—who has fully recovered from his rock climbing accident—is empty since Whitney is currently at the podium introducing the next event.

She leaves the podium and joins her husband. The lights dim, except for the spotlights directed at the stage. The music starts.

My heart catches and releases in anticipation of her.

Emma wouldn't let me watch her practice. She wanted me to see her return to the stage when she was in costume so I could get the full effect. I told her that nothing could top watching her dance for the first time, wearing only my button-down shirt.

She gave me a wry look and told me that after all the practice she's been doing, this had damn well better top it. But she had that glittering spark in her eyes and I could see she was pleased.

She and Aaron enter the stage from the left and begin to dance, but I have eyes only for her. She's wearing a luxurious costume that is made all the more beautiful by the woman wearing it. The burgundy velvet bodice is trimmed with elaborate gold embroidery and the white tulle ballerina skirt is trimmed with hand-sewn burgundy accents. Skin-toned ballerina tights conceal her lovely tattoo, but I fully intend to see her in this costume without them. Later. In our bedroom.

It's become clear that tattoo or no, my Emma could dance anywhere she chose. Her act of rebellion was not enough for anyone with any sense to turn her down. When the LA Ballet Troupe heard she was doing this performance, they called her up and offered her a position. I can see why. Aaron was right; even among primas, Emma is a rare talent.

She turned the offer down, though. Instead, she's starting her own dance company and will be doing things her way. Aaron was the first person she hired.

When she and Aaron conclude the first segment, she segues smoothly into her pas seul, or solo. It's an out of body experience, watching her leap and soar, in command not only of every inch of the stage, but of every soul in the room. It's breathtaking. I barely hear the music. All I see is her, and all I hear is my heartbeat.

She is an angel sent to me to make me the man I always should've been. And all I want is to walk through life with her by my side.

At the conclusion of the performance, the audience erupts in applause, but I'm the first one on my feet. Her eyes find me immediately, and we beam at one another.

My heart is pounding in agitation, and not just because of what we just witnessed.

But because of what comes next.

# Chapter 55

## Emma

I am awash with the charged energy of a standing ovation. I extend my arm toward Aaron, who's been waiting in the wings, and he joins me on stage to a fresh swell of applause. We're both beaming at the crowd. God, I forgot how amazing this moment feels, even more so now that I stand here with a kind of confidence in myself and my body I didn't have before.

Rayce was right. I didn't leave the ballet. I just took a needed break from the stage so I could come back a better person than I was. He's smiling up at me, chest puffed out with pride, and I swear I can hear his clapping above all the others. I blow him a kiss and the audience twitters with sighs and sounds of approval.

We end up taking several more bows before the applause finally settles down and the audience takes their seats. Whitney is back to the podium and thanks the "spectacularly talented Aaron Eastham and Emma Swanson", before excusing Aaron, who elegantly kisses the back of my hand and exits the stage.

A flutter of panic ripples through my stomach. Have I forgotten something important? Earlier in the evening, I helped Lizzy present the Sharon Rivers Good Heart Award, which is their new foundation's way of recognizing volunteers who go above and beyond the call of duty. Was there something else I was supposed to do?

"You'll notice that your program indicates we'll be adjourning to the Starlight Room for the cocktail mixer," Whitney says, addressing the audience. "But before we do…" She tosses a curious grin in my direction. "We'd like to invite Mr. Rayce Rivers back onto the stage."

He rises, looking terribly dashing in his fine black tux, and gives me a tender, tentative smile as he climbs the steps. Now

I'm really confused. I'm trying to figure out what part of the program I'm forgetting. He already gave a heartfelt, impressive speech before my performance, thanking everyone in attendance for their generosity. What's left for him to do?

As he climbs the steps, Whitney reaches into a cabinet below the podium and pulls out a huge bouquet of white roses. How sweet. He's going to present me with flowers. I just want to kiss this man.

I smile at him as he takes the flowers from Whitney and walks up to me, all dashing and Rayce-like. My love for him swells and flutters against my chest.

"You were amazing," he says in a quiet voice, keeping his praise intimate and special. He places the bouquet in my arm. "I'm so proud of you, sweetheart." He gives me a kiss on the cheek and I beam up at him.

"Emma," he says, now in his normal, steady voice.

The audience is so still and quiet as they watch us that I know his words are carrying throughout the room.

Holding my eyes, he continues. "I have long felt that I will never be worthy of you and all the love you give me. But," he starts to sink to one knee, "I would like to spend the rest of my life trying."

The sound of gasps from the audience fills the beautiful room and my shaking fingertips fly to my lips as he pulls a black velvet ring box out of his pocket. He opens it to reveal a stunning diamond ring fit for an American queen, glittering in the stage lights.

I look at him and whisper, "Oh my god."

He smiles and his eyes soften, overflowing with love for me. "From the first moment I saw you, you captured my heart. Your grace, integrity, intelligence, and goodness shines through in everything you say and everything you do. I'm so lucky to have you in my life, and want to spend the rest of my days striving to give you the kind of happiness you deserve. Emma Swanson, will you please do me the honor of becoming my wife?"

I'm already nodding my head and offering my hand to him. "Yes, yes!"

He slides the sparkling ring on my finger and I bend over and cup his face in my hand, giving him an eager kiss.

My future husband.

Holding our kiss, he slowly rises until he's the one leaning over me, wrapping his arms around my waist and pulling me close to him. The sound of the cheering audience fades away and I'm lost in the embrace of the man my heart has been saying *yes* to all along.

# Epilogue

From The Voice

Renowned Resort Owner to Wed Swan Pointe Darling

by Rita Becker

The whole town is buzzing about the upcoming nuptials of Mr. Rayce Rivers and his beautiful fiancée, Emma Swanson. Their love story has enchanted the entire city; it seems there's no one who doesn't adore the fascinating woman who tamed Swan Pointe's most sought-after bachelor.

Since her sudden splash on the Swan Pointe scene, Ms. Swanson has proven herself a valuable member of the community. A former prima for the distinguished LA Ballet Troupe, Ms. Swanson has spoken to local high school students about positive body image while donning trendy outfits that

566

showcase part of her infamous symbolic tattoo, stood by Mr. Rayce Rivers' side while he delivered the toast at the resort's traditional New Year's Eve Gala, and most-recently graced the stage of the Swan Pointe Civic Center in a stunning solo performance benefiting the Swan Pointe Battered Women and Children's Shelter. These efforts to strengthen the community have been accented by the many endearing sightings of her and Mr. Rivers around town.

[Click here for photos of the adorable lovebirds.]

In spite of a public persona that has sometimes come across as impersonal and that was occasionally marred by rumors and scandals, Mr. Rivers' popularity has reached new heights. His announcement to expand the Rivers Paradise Resort brand to locations in Hawaii and Florida reportedly has investors abuzz, but that isn't the only thing contributing to his recent meteoric rise.

It is this reporter's opinion that his future bride is no small part of Mr. Rivers' public transformation. It is his clear devotion to her that's had such a strong effect on his standing within the community. A source close to the couple confirms Ms. Emma Swanson has brought out a softer side of the elder Mr. Rivers. "She's her own woman," a source close to the family reports, "and he completely adores her."

## The End

# About the Author

Jordyn White writes steamy romances featuring smart, sexy women and the swoon-worthy men who adore them. Her sexy love stories are full of passion but don't skimp on the tenderness. She's addicted to trendy coffee houses, poolside lounging, and HEAs. When not tapping blissfully away on her laptop, she takes time to enjoy life with her husband and their children.

**JordynWhiteBooks.com**

Printed in April 2022
by Rotomail Italia S.p.A., Vignate (MI) - Italy